PRAISE FOR *KITTY'S MIX-TAPE*

"Comfort food for the urban fantasy soul. Carrie Vaughn never disappoints. It was so nice to see my friends again! If you've loved Kitty's adventures, you have been waiting for this book!"
—Seanan McGuire, author of *Come Tumbling Down* and *Every Heart a Doorway*

"A Carrie Vaughn story is a guarantee of quality entertainment and a night of no sleep as I stay up late to devour it!"
—Patricia Briggs, bestselling author of the Mercy Thompson series

"Vaughn offers readers one last trip into the world of Kitty Norville, the werewolf talk radio host last seen in 2015's *Kitty Saves the World*, in this nostalgic collection of 15 urban fantasy shorts, which splits focus between the delightful Kitty and other fan favorite characters who've been caught up in her adventures over the years. Vaughn offers star turns to Kitty's lawyer husband Ben ('What Happened to Ben in Vegas'), ancient vampire Rick ('It's Still the Same Old Story'), and bounty hunter Cormac ('Kitty and Cormac's Excellent Adventure'). Kitty's own jaunts—which see her attending her high school reunion ('Kitty Walks on by, Calls Your Name'), dealing with bureaucracy ('Kitty Busts the Feds') and investigating a werewolf boxer ('Kitty Learns the Ropes')— are suffused with humor and pop culture references. A genuine sense of playfulness abounds, especially in several cute flash fiction pieces about the effects of different lunar events on Kitty's lycanthropy. Though the uninitiated won't want to start with this, the insights into Kitty's supporting cast and illumination of previously unseen moments from the series will delight longtime readers. For those devoted fans, this will be a delicious final taste of Kitty's complicated life."
—*Publishers Weekly*

"Like the rest of the Kitty Norville series, these stories are wise, kind, and always entertaining. I loved returning to Kitty's world and enjoying these new adventures."
—Kevin Hearne, author of The Iron Druid Chronicles

"For many, reading in the time of COVID-19 is a challenge, making comfort books a good fallback. This collection of paranormal stories of various lengths is a delightful read for those who have enjoyed Vaughn's novels featuring Kitty Norville, the late-night talk show DJ who was bitten by and turned into a werewolf, including *Kitty Rocks the House* (2013)."
—*Booklist*

PRAISE FOR CARRIE VAUGHN

On the Kitty Norville series

"Enough excitement, astonishment, pathos, and victory to satisfy any reader."
—Charlaine Harris, author of *Dead After Dark*

"[Vaughn] manages to combine outright thrills with an offbeat sense of humor and then mesh it with Kitty's dogged determination. The result—entertainment exemplified!"
—*Romantic Times*

"Fresh, hip, fantastic—a real treat!"
—L. A. Banks, author of *Minion*

"Readers of Kim Harrison's 'Hollows' series and Jim Butcher's 'Dresden Files' will appreciate Kitty's sarcastic wit, ingenuity, and independence."
—*Library Journal*

Other Books By Carrie Vaughn

Kitty Norville Novels
Kitty and The Midnight Hour (2005)
Kitty Goes to Washington (2006)
Kitty Takes a Holiday (2007)
Kitty and the Silver Bullet (2008)
Kitty and the Dead Man's Hand (2009)
Kitty Raises Hell (2009)
Kitty's House of Horrors (2010)
Kitty Goes to War (2010)
Kitty's Big Trouble (2011)
Kitty Steals the Show (2012)
Kitty Rocks the House (2013)
Kitty in the Underworld (2013)
Low Midnight (2014)
Kitty Saves the World (2015)

Collections
Kitty's Greatest Hits (2011)
Straying from the Path (2011)
Amaryllis and Other Stories (2016)

The Golden Age Saga
After the Golden Age (2011)
Dreams of the Golden Age (2014)

The Bannerless Saga
Bannerless (2017)
The Wild Dead (2018)

Other Novels
Voices of Dragons (2010)
Discord's Apple (2010)
Steel (2011)
Martians Abroad (2017)

Novellas
The Immortal Conquistador (2020)

Kitty's Mix Tape
Copyright © 2020 by Carrie Vaughn, LLC

Introduction: "Kitty and the Missed Opportunity" copyright © 2020 by Emma Bull

Interior and cover design by Elizabeth Story

Tachyon Publications LLC
1459 18th Street #139
San Francisco, CA 94107
415.285.5615
www.tachyonpublications.com
tachyon@tachyonpublications.com

Series Editor: Jacob Weisman
Project Editor: James DeMaiolo

Print ISBN 13: 978-1-61696-325-5
Digital ISBN: 978-1-61696-326-2

Printed in the United States by Versa Press, Inc.

First Edition: 2020
9   8   7   6   5   4   3   2   1

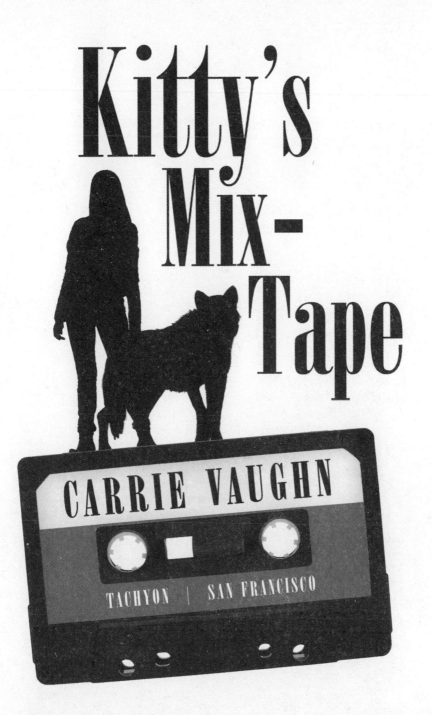

Kitty's Mix-Tape

CARRIE VAUGHN

TACHYON | SAN FRANCISCO

TABLE OF CONTENTS

KITTY AND THE MISSED OPPORTUNITY

INTRODUCTION BY EMMA BULL

Here's how I remember it: I had the chance to provide a cover quote for *Kitty and the Midnight Hour*, and I didn't.

Now I should warn you, I'm not the most reliable narrator. Writers love a good story more than almost anything, and when you ask them about their memories, you should expect narrative structure, not strict adherence to fact. Maybe I did provide a quote. But what's stuck in my head is that I didn't realize at the time how much I liked and admired that introduction to Kitty Norville, late-night DJ and talk-show host, determined pursuer of truth, and reluctant celebrity werewolf.

I'd been a DJ at my college radio station. Kitty's late-night life in front of a microphone, solitary but connected to a host of people she can't see, felt familiar. That familiarity vouched for the story; if that part was right, it suggested the rest of Kitty's world was authentic, too. Even the werewolves.

And what werewolves! They were convincingly both human and lupine, with the instincts of each species, and a mixed social structure that made sense for people who had to live with ordinary humans but keep their difference secret.

If that makes you think of metaphoric possibilities, I'm not going to warn you off. But you should understand that writers don't always know when we're crafting metaphors. Sometimes we discover them as readers do: when we read the finished work and see the subtext, the supporting mesh, of the story we've told. Even if we've intended a deeper, parallel meaning in a work of fiction, readers may find a different metaphor in the tale, one that hits closer to their lives and experience.

Fantasy is one of the best mediums for telling two stories (if not more!) at once. They layer on one another: reality and make-believe, life and myth, perception and fact. "Unternehmen Werwolf," on its face, is the story of a young soldier in World War II tasked with a mission we can't sympathize with. But the story asks: Can we look past the mission to see the man? "Kitty Learns the Ropes" puts Kitty in a tough place between her two communities, human and werewolf. But underneath the action, it asks a question just as tough: Is it ever right to "out" someone, to take away their control of what the world knows of them?

Speaking of communities, the characters in these stories (I think of them as Kitty and the friends she hasn't met yet) don't move through life alone —like wolves, they need their pack to survive, whether they know it or not. Each story is as much about a community as about individuals, and characters succeed because of the connections they make and the bonds they form with others. The lone hero who triumphs on solo strength, knowledge, and determination? That character may be a regular in adventure fiction, but in the world where we live, that's more commonly the person whose neighbors are quoted as saying, "They were quiet. Kept to themselves. We had no idea all those bodies were in the basement." That focus on connection and community is another thing that makes these stories feel real, as if they're happening right around the corner.

After I finished *Kitty and the Midnight Hour*, I found myself telling people, "There's this book about a woman who's a DJ on nighttime radio, and she's secretly a werewolf, and there are more werewolves, and some vampires, but they're not *those* sorts of werewolves and vampires — Anyway, you should read it."

An audio version of a cover quote, maybe? Definitely an act of community-building.

The kind folks at Tachyon have allowed me to remedy my original lapse. But now it takes a whole introduction to recommend Carrie Vaughn's work, because after a series of novels and this delicious collection of short stories, there's so much more to say. If you aren't already part of the community —the *family* —that knows and loves Vaughn's real and fantastic universe, think of this volume as its Welcome Wagon, arrived on your doorstep with a plate of brownies and an intriguing air of mystery. Go ahead. Invite it in.

Emma Bull
March 2020

KITTY WALKS ON BY, CALLS YOUR NAME

BEN PARKED, and we sat in the car for what seemed like a very long time, not saying anything, staring grimly ahead as if we were about to go into battle.

"It's not too late to back out of this," he said finally. "There's nothing in the universe that says you have to go to your high school class reunion."

Ten years. With everything that had happened to me over the last ten years, it seemed like a century ought to have passed. On the other hand, I could still remember what it felt like to walk down those stinky school halls and worry about grades and graduation and the rest of it. Ben was right, I didn't need to do this, I didn't need to be here, and I certainly didn't need to drag him along.

He was wearing a suit and tie, his courtroom best, a fresh shave and brushed hair, all the polish and not his meeting-clients-at-the-county-jail-at-two-in-the-morning scruff, which meant he was taking this seriously. I was in a very mature cocktail dress, black with a red belt, in a style that showed off my figure. My blond hair was up, and I'd put on makeup. Retro elegance. Looking in the mirror before we'd left home made me think I ought to dress up more often.

Did I really want to do this? We could start the car back up and turn around right now.

I wouldn't even have known the reunion was happening except Sadie Martinez sent me an email. She'd reached out and practically begged me—she didn't want to be here alone. Sadie and I had been best friends, study partners, double dating to prom, all of it. And I hadn't talked to her since junior year of college because I hadn't talked to anyone since junior year of college. The year I'd been attacked by a werewolf and transformed into something that didn't normally think much about high school class reunions.

My life fell into two halves: before I was turned into a werewolf and after. High school was before. It had happened to someone else. Now, I'd walk through those hotel ballroom doors and wouldn't know anyone, and the ones I did know would be angry that I'd stopped talking to them. If they didn't run screaming because I was a monster. Because I wasn't just a werewolf. I hosted a talk-radio advice show on the supernatural and had been caught shape-shifting on national television. I was a *famous* werewolf.

Part of why we wanted to turn around was the off chance someone might have brought a gun with silver bullets, thinking they'd be doing the world a favor. But I felt like I owed it to Sadie, after all the years I'd dropped out of sight.

"Did you go to your high school reunion?" I asked. Ben was enough older than me that his ten-year reunion had happened before I met him a few years ago.

"Oh hell no," he said. "I couldn't get out of there fast enough."

"You weren't even a little bit curious about what happened to people?"

"Nope." He grinned. "My dad was in prison by then, I had no interest in explaining all that to that crowd."

I was suddenly daunted. I was going to have to explain the werewolf thing over and over again. "Maybe I don't want to do this," I murmured.

"Okay," Ben said. "Just to get it out in the open, why are we doing this?"

"Because I'm super curious and this is the kind of thing that only happens once, and if I miss it I'll always wonder."

"All good reasons. Right. Let's go. We can always ditch if things go sidewise."

"But they're not going to go sidewise. It's a high school reunion, what could possibly go wrong?"

He gave me a scowling look. Don't ever ask what could go wrong, I knew that lesson.

We left the warm, late-evening June air and entered the excessive air-conditioning of the hotel ballroom lobby. A few people, also in suits and cocktail hour finery, mingled, talking in groups. There was nervous laughter. I didn't recognize anyone, not right away. I looked for Sadie with a sudden spike of fear that I wouldn't recognize her either.

Ben guided me toward a table where a couple of unassuming soccer-mom types were standing guard over rows of name-tag stickers. They seemed familiar—one was brunette, average build, and might have been a cheerleader. The other tanned, dark-haired. Also a cheerleader? Maybe we'd had algebra together?

We found our stickers, and the women's smiles remained relentlessly cheerful—maybe they didn't recognize me either. This had been a pretty big high school. So, now what? Just keep wandering around until I recognized someone?

This wasn't how high school reunions looked in the movies, where the bitchy popular girls came back as stuck-up suburban housewives, the jocks were out-of-shape used car salesman, the oppressed nerds were billionaire tech geniuses, and the people who were most unhappy had found their way while the people who were bullies got their comeuppance. High school reunion: a chance to right old wrongs and take revenge on the cool kids.

But that wasn't how this looked at all. Everyone was scanning faces, walking past each other like we were at some kind of statue gallery, searching for signs of the people we had been years ago. Searching for familiarity. So many of the men—I had to shave twenty pounds off them before they looked familiar, and it wasn't that they had gotten fat, but that they filled out. They weren't scrawny boys anymore. Names hovered on the tip of my tongue. I should have looked in the yearbook for a refresher before coming here. We were like deer in the headlights, amazed that any of us had survived at all. Because enough time had passed to make us realize that nobody in high school thought they were cool, they just acted out on their worst insecurities and struggled to get through in one piece.

High school felt *so big* while we were living it, but the percentage of our lives those years represented got smaller and smaller as time went on. What was an entire quarter of our lives ten years ago was now, what, fourteen percent? And in ten more years it would be ten percent. And the beat goes on.

"You look like you're about to start crying," Ben said.

"I think I'm sad," I said.

"Let's go find you a glass of wine—"

"Kitty!" I turned to the call, coming from down the foyer. A woman rushed toward me. She had honey-brown hair in a bob, and was stout and confident, in a cute black dress and loud earrings. Sadie hadn't changed a bit. Except neither one of us had the confidence and poise for slinky cocktail dresses back in high school. Now look at us, like we were grown-ups or something.

She ran up to me. In wolf language, this—a fellow predator coming at me with arms outstretched—was an attack. But I was a civilized werewolf and she was a friend, and I was just so happy that I recognized her, and she knew me. And this right here made me glad I came. I reached for and accepted the enthusiastic hug. A little of the tension I'd been feeling slipped away.

"I've missed you!" she said into my hair, holding tight.

"I'm sorry I lost touch," I murmured. "You look really good!"

"So do you." We separated and beamed at each other in admiration.

"How are you? What have you been doing?"

"We have so much to talk about!" She glanced appraisingly at Ben. "And you are . . ."

"Sadie, this is Ben." I presented them to each other.

"Nice to meet you," Ben said neutrally.

"Hm," she purred.

"Do you want to go get a glass of wine or something?"

"Oh God yes." We hooked arms and stalked into the ballroom. Ben followed, amused.

After acquiring wine and staking out territory at one of the white-cloth-draped tables, we caught up. Sadie had gone to school at Northwestern, then law school, returned to Denver to work for the legal department of an environmental non-profit, which was exactly the kind of thing she always said she'd do, if maybe not exactly the way she thought. She'd had dreams of riding Greenpeace Zodiacs to save whales, which I was just as glad she never did. This was safer. She and Ben instantly bonded over law-school anecdotes and seemed relieved that their areas of expertise were so far apart they'd never had to meet professionally.

As for me . . . I didn't have to explain much because Sadie said she listened to my show sometimes. As soon as I'd gotten a website with a contact form she'd thought about sending me a note. The reunion finally prompted her to do it.

I couldn't explain why I hadn't ever reached out to her. "I . . . had a rough couple of years there. And then I figured you'd be too angry to want to hear from me." It sounded stupid now, and her frown of reprimand told me that yes, it was stupid.

"So," she said, idly running a purple-painted nail around the base of her wineglass. "You talk to Jesse at all?"

Jesse Kramer. Another set of memories crashed over me. Part of the old life, again. I shook my head. "I haven't talked to him since graduation."

"Ah," she said suggestively.

Ben caught the tone. "And who is Jesse?"

"Just a guy," I said, pretty sure I was blushing. I didn't want to talk about this. Ben arced a brow.

"Her boyfriend senior year."

5

"Oh really?" Ben's brows went up. "Any chance I'll get to meet this guy?"

"I doubt it," I said quickly. "He moved away right after graduation."

Sadie leaned in. "They broke up right in the middle of prom, it was amazing."

"You've never told me *any* of this," Ben said admiringly.

Honestly, I hadn't thought much about it until now. It hadn't been very relevant to the post-werewolf life.

"He won't come to this," I said, almost pleading with Sadie to agree with me. She shrugged expansively.

"So, Sadie, you have any embarrassing pictures of Kitty I should know about?" Ben asked.

I blanched. "We don't really need to go looking—"

She grinned. "They've got some old yearbooks at the front table if we want to go check."

The place filled up, and I recognized more and more people, and somehow we all looked completely different than we had, and we hadn't changed a bit, both at the same time.

"Hi, Kitty?" An upbeat woman with her dark hair in a ponytail, wearing a silky pantsuit, came up to me. "I don't know if you remember me—"

"Amanda, we worked on yearbook together," I said and accepted a quick hug. We did the one-minute update of the last ten years of our lives, and I repeated the same exchange with a dozen other people. Wolf slowly settled; these weren't strangers, we weren't in danger, even though this definitely didn't feel like our territory. It helped that Ben was looking out for us. He patiently let himself be introduced over and over. *This is my husband, Ben. And what do you do, Ben? Lawyer, criminal defense.* Yeah, that got a couple of stares. And a raised eyebrow when one of the old marching band crowd asked him for a business card.

"You were on yearbook?" Ben asked, incredulous.

"Yup."

"I had no idea. I'm learning all kinds of things about you. I suppose you were all over spirit week and went to all the football games?"

"I was practically normal, back in the day."

"Before," he said.

"Yeah, before."

He squeezed my hand and kissed my cheek.

"Sadie?" A tough-looking guy with an expensive-looking haircut and dark jacket came up to our table, and Sadie's eyes widened. "*Trevor?*"

Trevor Ames? *He'd* changed. He hadn't just put on that filling-out weight that everyone else had, he'd put on muscle, and moved with a practiced efficiency. He was a fighter. Back in school he'd been one of our crowd, Sadie and Jesse and me and the rest of us who weren't cool enough to be in the cool crowd but weren't goth or jocks or nerds enough to be in any other clique so we just made our own. He'd joined the army right after graduation, and was another one I'd completely lost track of when I lost track of everybody.

"He's got a gun under that jacket," Ben whispered in my ear.

I looked sharply at him. "Silver bullets?"

"Can't tell."

He smiled wryly as Sadie insisted on hugging him. They separated, then he looked right at me, a challenging stare, and his smile thinned.

"Kitty. You really are a werewolf."

"You saw the YouTube video, just like everyone else," I said drily.

He looked me up and down. "I could just tell." He looked Ben up and down the same way, meaning he'd spotted both of us. We usually didn't tell people about Ben being a werewolf too.

You could spot a werewolf just by looking, if you knew what to look for. This meant Trevor knew what to look for. And *how*, exactly?

"That a problem?" I asked.

"No," he said. "No, it isn't."

I wondered . . . what would make it a problem?

"This is making me so happy," Sadie said, beaming. "All of us together again—"

"Do you know if Jesse's coming?" Trevor asked me.

"I don't," I said. "I kind of lost touch with everybody."

"I figured if anyone knew . . ." He trailed off and shrugged.

Ben said brightly, "I really want to meet Jesse. I hope he shows up."

"He's not going to show up," I said.

The guy who'd been class president went to a podium at the front of the room and tapped on the microphone, which was indeed on and screeched in disapproval. I winced—what had that poor mic ever done to him? He gave a speech about how happy he was, how great it was to see everyone, and how happy he was again, and so on. Then he announced that there were prizes. Prizes? Shouldn't we all get a prize just for being here?

Former class president went down the list. Who had traveled the farthest to be here? Someone had come from Amsterdam, and why would anyone leave Amsterdam to come back to freaking Aurora, Colorado? Who had the most kids—four. Well, someone had been busy. The prizes were gift certificates to local restaurants for the most part, which was kind of ironic for the guy who'd come from Amsterdam. A few more categories followed, and I started to tune them out.

"And who has the most interesting job?" the guy asked. "The winner is . . . Kitty Norville!"

What? Who had decided this? I had a suspicion that Trevor's job was way more interesting than mine, which hardly seemed like a job most of the time. Maybe I should have brought my own mic and recorder and done an episode of the show from here. People were clapping. Everyone was looking at me. I had to get up. Probably a good thing I hadn't had a second glass of wine yet.

I managed to get to the podium, collected my gift certificate, and murmured a polite thank you into the microphone before fleeing. They might have expected more, considering my job involved talking into a microphone. But no one was paying me for this, and nobody stared at me in radio. One of the other members of the reunion committee cornered me before I could get back to my territory. I didn't remember ever knowing her.

"It really was no contest about the job thing," she said. "You seem to meet so many interesting people on your show!"

"I suppose I do." She wasn't wrong, I did meet some interesting people. And that was only what I could be public about. Just last winter I'd consulted for the army, trying to help werewolf veterans returning from Afghanistan. Maybe I deserved that fifty dollars for Mario's Italian Bistro.

I tried to escape. She kept talking at me. "So what's it like, being a werewolf?"

I honestly didn't know how to answer that. It was strange. It was personal. It was too big. "It's hard to explain."

Thoughtfully, she put a finger on her chin and her gaze went unfocused. "I suppose a condition like that, it must be a little like fibromyalgia," she said.

I stared. "It's nothing like—yeah, sure, it's a little like that." Because that was easier than trying to explain. "If you're really curious you could tune into the show sometime."

"Oh, of course, I'll be sure to do that!"

She was never going to listen to my show.

Back at our table, Ben offered me a fresh glass of wine and I gratefully drank it down.

"What'd you get, what'd you get?" Ben asked.

"Food."

"Hm, the night almost pays for itself." He cheered my wine with his glass of water.

With the speeches over, the dancing began. The DJ started the first set with Smash Mouth's "All Star." So, it was going to be like that, was it?

"So," Ben asked. "Why'd you break up with this Jesse guy?"

I narrowed my gaze. "Is this going to be a problem, you being jealous of a guy I dated ten years ago?"

"Just curious."

"He was going away to Boston for college. He made noises about trying to stay together, but . . . it was just noise. We'd have been setting ourselves up to fail."

"It might have worked out."

"And if it had, we wouldn't be here," I said.

If Jesse and I had managed to stick together and make it work . . . my life would be so completely different I had trouble fathoming it. For one thing, I wouldn't be a werewolf. Which sounded good until I also realized it meant I wouldn't have my radio show, and I wouldn't have Ben.

I tried to avoid regretting pretty much anything. Regret had no boundaries once it started.

Trevor was standing a little apart from the table, watching the crowd, noting every face, turning to the doorways every time someone entered or left.

"You look like a hunter on the prowl," I said.

He chuckled. "Yeah, I suppose you'd know all about that."

"What's your story? You joined the army, and then . . ."

He shrugged. "Here and there, this and that. It's not that interesting."

"Not like me," I said, waving the envelope I'd won for having the most interesting job. Trevor laughed.

Next up on the set list: "Tubthumping." That got a couple of people out on the dance floor for some half-hearted bouncing.

Ben said preemptively, "I'm not dancing, that's my line in the sand."

"I will not ask you to dance, I promise," I said.

Suddenly, his chin tipped up, his nose flaring. His brow furrowed, and a tension tightened his shoulders. An intrusive smell caught his attention. I took a breath to find the scent he'd spotted. A body moving into the ballroom. Chilled, corpse-like but not rotting, cold with death but still alive. A vampire.

We both turned to the man who had just entered the ballroom. Svelte, wearing a dark shirt and gray slacks, casual and stylish, his hair slicked back. Everyone was eyeing him. He looked *good*. Of course he did, it was how vampires attracted prey. I gasped and slapped my hand over my mouth, astonished, because it finally clicked and I recognized him.

Jesse Kramer, my high-school sweetheart, broke-up-at-prom-drama ex-boyfriend, was a vampire.

Across the room, he met my gaze. And I let him, and I think Sarah McLachlan came up on the set list right that moment. For just a moment, he looked into my eyes with his vampiric, mesmerizing stare, and I was frozen—

"Oh my God, he's actually here," Sadie exclaimed.

I shut my eyes and shook my head to clear it. Had Jesse actually tried his vampiric hypnotism on me? The bastard . . .

"There he is," Trevor murmured and stalked toward him. Jesse spotted him. His eyes widened, and he turned and walked out.

"Wait a minute—" I ran after Trevor.

"What—" Sadie ran after me. I assumed Ben followed as well.

In a foot race between a vampire and a mortal human, I'd put money on the vampire every time. Trevor must have known he couldn't win a straight-up race, so in the ballroom lobby he veered to a side door while Jesse charged out the front. I kept after Jesse.

"Jesse, get back here, you jerk!" I shouted.

This was almost exactly what had happened at senior prom, which made me even more furious. You cannot escape the past, you can only repeat it. I pounded out the doors to the lighted nighttime parking lot and caught him just about to round the corner of the building. Wolf loved this. This was a chase. We had him in our sights. Next was the pounce, the grabbing him by the throat, the ripping—

No. I just wanted to talk.

"Jesse!" I yelled, and it must have come out partly like a growl, because he pulled up short. Slowly, he turned around.

Jesse couldn't have been a vampire for more than a couple of years—he looked to be in his mid-twenties. Now, if this had been the twentieth reunion, there'd have been questions about how well preserved he appeared.

Still, I had *a lot* of questions.

"Hey, Kitty." He scuffed his foot, tried to smile.

I had to take a moment to slow my breathing down so I didn't, like, freak out and sprout fur. A reunion to remember.

"What . . . what is this?" I gestured vaguely at him, his condition, unable to formulate a concise question to take it all in. "Although this is pretty much the first time I've met a vampire and known exactly how old he is."

"Good to see you, too," he said, chuckling.

That moment, Trevor came around from the other side of the building, aiming a handheld crossbow loaded with a wooden bolt. Without thinking, I sprang, getting between Trevor and his target. I ended up pushing my ex-boyfriend into the wall, covering him with my body. A wooden stake would barely scratch me.

"Kitty, get out of the way!" Trevor ordered.

That was the moment Ben jogged up with Sadie and saw me and Jesse locked together.

"This must be the famous Jesse," Ben said evenly.

Great. Just great. "Trevor, put that thing down!" I said. He didn't. I bared my teeth. "Trevor!"

He lowered the crossbow. Jesse relaxed, just a bit.

"Put it on the ground, now!" I said. He did. I stepped away from the wall, straightened my dress. I was blushing. I resisted an urge to pour out apologies to Ben. *This isn't what it looks like . . .* I trusted he knew that.

"What the hell is going on?" Sadie demanded, her voice edging into panic.

I looked back and forth between the two men, the vampire and the apparently professional vampire hunter. "What are the odds, really?" I muttered. "Trevor. Why are you trying to kill Jesse? I mean, is this something you make a habit of, killing vampires? And Jesse . . . why the hell are you a vampire!"

"You're a vampire?" Sadie said, taking a step back.

"Who is that?" Jesse said, pointing at Ben. "I don't remember you."

"We've never met. Hi, I'm Ben, I'm Kitty's husband." He stepped forward, offered his hand and, a slave to social conventions, Jesse shook it. Ben appeared to squeeze extra hard.

"Husband?" Jesse said. "Oh. And you're a werewolf too. I guess that makes sense."

Sadie stared at Ben. "You are?"

"We don't make a thing of it," Ben said.

I pointed at Jesse and Trevor. "I need you two to answer my questions."

"You first," Trevor said.

"No," Jesse stated. So I glared back at Trevor.

Trevor said, "It isn't personal. Jesse crossed some bad people. I took the contract on the off chance he might be here. And I was right."

"You can't murder people at the class reunion!" I yelled.

"Is it murder if it isn't human?" Trevor said, leering.

"Oh my God, are we really going to have that conversation?"

Jesse backed away. "Kitty, this is between the two of us, you should probably get out of here—"

"You have silver bullets in that gun?" I asked Trevor.

"Oh my God, you have a *gun*?" Sadie demanded.

Ben was at Sadie's side. "Sadie, you'd probably better get back inside—"

"No! These are my friends. At least I thought they were."

And didn't that break my heart just a little. Meanwhile, Ben had his phone out and was talking to someone, walking just far enough off that I couldn't hear.

"Well, Trev?" I asked.

"Um."

"So that's yes, you do have silver bullets." Along with the visceral jolt of panic, I was offended and furious. "Were you planning on killing me too?"

"Only if you try to stop me."

"Here I was thinking how this isn't at all like class reunions in the movies and you have to go pull some *Grosse Pointe Blank* shit!"

"I wasn't *trying* to pull some *Grosse Pointe Blank* shit, it just happened," Trevor said.

"Shit like this doesn't *just happen*," I muttered.

Sadie said, "Maybe if we all went back inside and had a drink—"

"I don't think you want that," Jesse said, grinning.

I covered my face with my hands. This was too much.

"So. Um," Jesse said, sticking his hands in his pockets and losing all his vampire suave. "It's good to see you guys. Really."

"I didn't think you'd actually be here," Trevor said.

"So, if you hadn't been trying to kill Jesse, you wouldn't be here?" I asked.

"No," he admitted.

I turned to Jesse. "Then why did you come?"

He looked at each of us. Not with the vampire hypnotism. Just a nervous glance, which dropped to his feet.

"I'm here because it's my last chance," Jesse said. "My last chance to hang out with people my own age and look like I belong. Twenty years, they tell me. Twenty years after being turned is when it hits that you won't get older and you stop fitting in. I . . . I wanted to feel like I fit in, one more time."

He didn't seem so much sad as resigned. This was his life now. His unlife. He was saying goodbye to the old.

This was getting too maudlin even for me. I sighed and glared at him. "Jesse, you never fit in. I mean, did any of us? We certainly don't now."

"Kitty, this is exactly like one of your shows but in real life!" Sadie said.

"I don't listen to your show," Trevor said. "Sorry."

"Neither do I." Jesse winced.

"Well, maybe you should, you might learn something! Thank you, Sadie, for listening to my show, I don't think I said that yet but thank you."

"You're welcome."

"Christ, Kitty, couldn't you have at least changed your name if you were going to become a werewolf?" Trevor said, exasperated.

"Seriously," Jesse agreed, and they glanced at each other. "I mean, if we'd voted for who was least likely to become a werewolf it would have been you. What happened?"

"I don't like to talk about it. I was attacked, it was bad, let's leave it there. It changed every single thing about my life, I wasn't going to let it take my name, too."

That killed the conversation.

"I wanted the power," Jesse said finally. "I know that's a cliché. But I didn't have the money or the social connections or anything else to get anywhere. But this?" He shrugged. "You don't like the game, you break the rules."

"You just traded out for a different set of rules," I said.

"But I get to live forever."

"Unless some ex-military bounty hunter yahoo sets his sights on you!" I glared at Trevor. His turn now. "Would you really have done it? Come back here and killed your old friend for a few bucks?"

"A few? Try a quarter mil."

Even I whistled low at that. Jesse had the gall to look pleased. "Wow, I didn't know I was that dangerous."

"You just really know how to piss people off," Trevor countered.

"I can't believe you people," Sadie muttered.

Ben rejoined us, slipping his phone back in his pocket. He pointed at Trevor. "This guy works for the Master of Boston." Then he pointed at Jesse. "And I'm guessing you were part of a recent attempt to overthrow that Master."

"You called Cormac," I said, smiling. Cormac, Ben's cousin, and a supernatural bounty hunter himself. He had contacts. He knew the gossip.

"Cormac Bennett?" Trevor said. "How do you know Cormac Bennett?"

"He's family. Oh, I also put a call in to Rick. Master of Denver. He wants to know if he needs to come over and help sort things out."

Jesse stared. "You can just call the Master of Denver and have him come over?"

I made a play of casually studying my fingernails. "We're pretty tight."

"I won't go back to Boston," Jesse stated. "I'll keep out of sight. Just drop the contract."

"A quarter million dollars, Jesse," Trevor pleaded, as if Jesse was just supposed to sacrifice himself.

Sadie's eyes were bugging out of her head. "It would make me really happy if my friends didn't kill each other!"

Trevor looked at her. "You're not, like, a secret witch or magician or something supernatural that we should know about?"

"No, I'm a lawyer."

"I thought you were going to go live in Antarctica and rescue penguins," Trevor said.

"Yeah, well, sometimes dreams die hard. Turns out I like takeout and hot running water too much."

"So, nobody's killing anybody," Ben said. "That's from Rick."

"Fine. Contract's off," Trevor said.

"You won't get in trouble for dropping the contract?" Jesse asked.

"Nice of you to care, but no. I may even be able to throw the client off. Convince them you were never part of the conspiracy and were too stupid to realize what was happening."

"Gee, thanks."

"And stay out of Boston."

"You'll never see me again," Jesse said.

I sank to the concrete and sighed. "And that's what reunions are for, realizing you have so little in common anymore with your high school friends that you'll probably never see each other again."

That was when the police cars pulled up, three of them, red and blue lights flashing. No sirens, at least. So probably no one was dying.

"Did you call the police, too?" Trevor pointed accusingly at Ben.

"Hell no," he said, looking on with interest.

A trio of cops got out and entered the lobby.

"What did we miss?" I said.

Sadie touched my arm. "I'll go find out." She ran off, back to the ballroom.

After not too much longer, the cops returned, dragging two men in handcuffs with them. The men were clearly drunk, belligerent, shouting curses at each other, seemingly oblivious to the fact they were in the process of being arrested. One of them had a bleeding cut over his eye, the other a split lip. A pair of women, likely wives, trailed after them, crying, also yelling curses—at their husbands.

"If you'll excuse me for just a minute," Ben said, drawing business cards out of his pocket. He made a beeline for the women.

"Oh man, he isn't just a lawyer, he's an ambulance-chasing lawyer! I didn't know that about him!" I exclaimed. I might have wiped a proud little tear from my eye.

"He take good care of you?" Jesse nodded after Ben.

This sounded more like the Jesse I remembered. He'd been kind and fun and . . . directionless, back then. He'd just wanted to get away. I'd gotten mad at him for not being satisfied with being here, with me. I wondered if he'd ever be satisfied with anything.

"Yes," I said. "He takes good care of me."

"Good." He smiled.

Sadie ran up then, eyes wide and full of glee. "Drunken brawl! Chris Hancock and Pete Kirkland, hitting on each others' wives. This is why you don't marry someone else's high school sweetheart, amiright? Talk about your Tubthumping."

"Well, I have to admit, I'm glad I came after all," Trevor said. "Just to see what it's like."

"And now we never have to do it again," Jesse said.

Ben returned to join us after distributing business cards, and we all ended up sitting on the sidewalk, leaning against the wall, watching the proceedings. A crowd, the entire reunion it looked like, had spilled onto the sidewalk to gawk. We had a pretty good view.

So, that was the class reunion, one for the books, disintegrating into chaos and it wasn't even any of our faults.

Ben looked the row of us over and scowled. "This is so John Hughes I kind of want to gag."

Five of us, all lined up. Looking thoughtful, disheveled, and disaffected. Yeah, even a little John Hughes. "Which one are you, honey?" I asked.

"The brain, clearly."

"And that would make me the basket case."

He reached out, and I snuggled under his arm as he pulled me close and kissed the top of my head.

Sadie said, "Would you guys do me a favor and keep in touch this time? Like even a Christmas card or something. Or a text message every six months. And don't kill each other?"

"Monthly coffee date?" I suggested.

"You're on."

"I do miss coffee," Jesse sighed. "The trick is finding someone who's just had a double venti latte, then drink their blood—"

I looked at him. "I didn't need to know that."

Trevor laughed.

I could almost hear music coming from the ballroom, over the chatter of the crowd. With so few people left inside, the sound echoed and carried. "That poor DJ isn't still trying to keep things going, is he?" I said.

"'My Heart Will Go On' was on when I ducked in," Sadie said.

And wasn't that just terrible? "What's playing now?"

We all got quiet, trying to make out the hint of a chorus. Jesse, who probably had the best hearing of any of us, leaned forward, head tilted. Then, he laughed.

"Oh, it isn't," I said. Then we all heard it.

Don't you forget about me . . .

It's Still the Same Old Story

Rick awoke at sunset and found a phone message from an old friend waiting for him. Helen sounded unhappy, but she didn't give details. She wouldn't even say that she was afraid and needed help, but the hushed tone of her voice made her sound like she was looking over her shoulder. He grabbed his coat, went upstairs to the back of the shop where he parked his silver BMW, and drove to see her.

The summer night was still, ordinary. Downtown Denver blazed. To his eyes, the skyscrapers seemed like glowing mushrooms; they'd sprung up so quickly, overwhelming everything that had come before. Only in the last forty years or so had Denver begun to shed its cow town image to become another typical metropolis. He sometimes missed the cow town, though he could still catch glimpses of it. Union Station still stood, the State Capitol of course, and the Victorian mansions in the surrounding neighborhoods. If he squinted, he could remember them in their glory days. Some of the fire from the mining boom era remained. That was why Rick stayed.

Helen lived a few miles south along the grid of streets around the University of Denver, in a house not quite as old or large as those Victorian mansions, but still an antique in the context of the rest of the city. She'd lived there since the 1950s, when Rick bought her the place. Even then, Denver had been booming. The city was an ever-shifting collage, its landmarks rising and falling, the points around which he navigated subtly changing over the decades.

Points like Helen.

He parked on the street in front of her house, a single-story square cottage, pale blue with white trim, shutters framing the windows, with a front porch and hanging planters filled with multicolored petunias. The lights were off.

For a moment, he stood on the concrete walkway in front and let his more-than-human senses press outward: sight, sound, and taste. The street, the lawn, the house itself were undisturbed. The neighbors were watching television. A block away, an older man walked a large dog. It was all very normal, except that the house in front of him was silent. No one living was inside—he'd have smelled the blood, heard the heartbeat.

When he and Helen became friends, he'd known this day would come. This day always came. But the circumstances here were unnatural. He walked up the stairs to the front door, which was unlocked. Carefully, he pushed inside, stepping around the places on the hardwood floor that creaked, reaching the area rug in the living room. Nothing—furniture, photographs, bookcase, small upright piano in the corner—was out of place. The modernist coffee table, a cone-shaped lamp by a blocky armchair, silk lilies in a cut-crystal vase. They were the decorations of an old woman—out of place, out of time, seemingly preserved. But to Rick it was just Helen, the way she'd always been.

His steps muffled on the rug, he progressed to the kitchen in back. He found her there, lying on the linoleum floor. Long dead—he could tell by her cold skin and the smell of dried blood on the floor.

Standing in the doorway, he could work out what had happened. She'd been sitting at the Formica table, sipping a cup of tea. The cup and saucer were there, undisturbed, along with a bowl of sugar cubes. She must have set the cup down before she fell. When she did fall, it had been violently, knocking the chair over. She had crawled a few feet—not far. She might have broken a hip or leg in the fall—expected, at her age. Flecks of blood streaked the back of her blue silk dress, fanning out from a dark, dime-sized hole. When he took a deep breath, he could smell the fire of gunpowder. She'd been shot in the back, and she had died.

After such a life, to die like this.

So that was that. A more-than-sixty-year acquaintance ended. Time to say goodbye, mourn, and move on. He'd done it before—often, even. He could be philosophical about it. The natural course of events, and all that. But this was different, and he wouldn't abandon her, even now when it didn't matter. He'd do the right thing—the human thing.

He drew his cell phone from his coat pocket and dialed 911.

"Hello. I need to report a murder."

She walked through the doorway, and every man in the place looked at her: the painted red smile, the blue skirt swishing around perfect legs. She didn't seem to notice, walked right up to the bar, and pulled herself onto a stool.

"I'll have a scotch, double, on ice," she said.

Rick set aside the rag he'd been using to wipe down the surface and leaned in front of her. "You look like you're celebrating something."

"That's right. You going to help me out or just keep leering?"

Smiling, he found a tumbler and poured her a double and extra.

"I have to ask," Rick said, returning to the bar in front of her, enjoying the way every other man in Murray's looked at him with envy. "What's the celebration?"

"You do have to ask, don't you? I'm just not sure I should tell you."

"It's not often I see a lady come in here all alone in a mood to celebrate."

Murray's was a working-class place, a dive by the standards of East Colfax; the neighborhood was going downhill as businesses and residents fled downtown, leaving behind everyone who didn't have anyplace to go. Rick had seen this sort of thing happen enough; he recognized the signs. Murray wasn't losing money, but he didn't have anything extra to put into the place. The varnish on the hardwood floor was scuffed off, the furniture was a decade old. Cheap beer and liquor were the norm, and he still had war bond posters up a year and a half after V-J Day. Or maybe he liked the Betty Grable pinups he'd stuck on top of some of them too much to take any of it down.

Blushing, the woman ducked her gaze, which told him something about her. The shrug she gave him was a lot shyer than the brash way she'd walked in here.

"I got a job," she said.

"Congratulations."

"You're not going to tell me that a nice girl like me should find herself a good man, get married, and settle down and make my mother proud?"

"Nope."

"Good." She smiled and bit her lip.

A newcomer in a clean suit came up to the bar, set down his hat, and tossed a couple of bills on the polished wood. Rick nodded at the woman and went to take the order. Business was steady after that, and Rick served second and third rounds to men who'd come in after work and stuck around. New patrons arrived for after-dinner nightcaps. Rick worked through it all, drawing beers and pouring liquor, smiling politely when the older men called him "son" and "kid."

He didn't need the job. He just liked being around people now and then. He'd worked at bars before—bars, saloons, taverns—here and there, for almost two hundred years.

He expected the woman to finish quickly and march right out again, but she sipped the drink as if savoring the moment, wanting to spend time with the crowd. Avoiding solitude. Rick understood.

When a thin, flushed man who'd had maybe one drink too many sidled up to the bar and crept toward her like a cat on the prowl, Rick wasn't surprised. He waited, watching for her signals. She might have been here to celebrate, but she might have been looking for more, and he wouldn't interfere. But the man spoke—asking to buy her another drink—and the woman shook her head. When he pleaded, she tilted her body, turning her back to him. Then he put a hand on her shoulder and another under the bar, on her leg. She shoved.

Rick stood before them both. They hesitated midaction, blinking back at him.

"Sir, you really need to be going, don't you?" Rick said.

"This isn't any of your business," the drunk said.

"If the lady wants to be left alone, you should leave her alone." He caught the man's gaze and twisted, just a bit. Put the warning in his voice, used a certain subtle tone, so that there was power in the words. If the man's gaze clouded over, most onlookers would attribute it to the liquor.

The man pointed and opened his mouth as if to speak, but Rick put a little more focus in his gaze and the drunk blinked, confused.

"Go on, now," Rick said.

The man nodded weakly, crushed his hat on his head, and stumbled to the door.

The woman watched him go, then turned back to Rick, her smile wondering. "That was amazing. How'd you do that?"

"You work behind the bar long enough, you develop a way with people."

"You've been bartending a long time, then."

Rick just smiled.

"Thanks for looking out for me," she said.

"Not a problem."

"I really didn't come here looking for a date. I really did just want the drink."

"I know."

"But I wouldn't say no. To a date. Just dinner or a picture or something. If the right guy asked."

So, Rick asked. Her name was Helen.

Rick answered the responding officer's questions, then sat in the armchair in the living room to wait for the detective to arrive. It took about forty-five minutes. In the meantime, officers and investigators passed in and out of the house, which seemed less and less Helen's by the moment.

When the detective walked in, he stood to greet her. The woman was average height and build, and busy, always looking, taking in the scene. Her dark hair was tied in a short ponytail; she wore a dark suit and white shirt, nondescript. She dressed to blend in, but her air of authority made her stand out.

She saw him and frowned. "Oh hell. It's you."

"Detective Hardin," he answered, amused at how unhappy she was to see him.

Jessi Hardin pointed at him. "Wait here."

He sat back down and watched her continue on to the kitchen.

Half an hour later, coroners brought in a gurney, and Hardin returned to the living room. She pulled over a high-backed chair and set it across from him.

"I expected to see bite marks on her neck."

"I wouldn't have called it in if I'd done it," he said.

"But you discovered the body?"

"Yes."

"And what were you doing here?" She pulled a small notebook and pen from her coat pocket, just like on TV.

"Helen and I were old friends."

The pen paused over the page. "What's that even mean?"

He'd been thinking it would be a nice change, not having to avoid the issue, not having to come up with a reasonable explanation for why he knew what he knew, dancing around the truth that he'd known Helen almost her entire life, even though he looked only thirty years old. Hardin knew what he was. But those half-truths he'd always used to explain himself were harder to abandon than he expected.

With any other detective, he'd have said that Helen was a friend of his grandfather's whom he checked in on from time to time and helped with repairs around the house. But Detective Hardin wouldn't believe that.

"We met in 1947 and stayed friends."

Hardin narrowed a thoughtful gaze. "Just so that I'm clear on this, in 1947 she was what, twenty? Twenty-five? And you were—exactly as you are now?"

"Yes."

"And you stayed friends with her all this time."

"You say it like you think that's strange."

"It's just not what I expect from the stories."

She was no doubt building a picture in her mind: Rick and a twenty-five-year-old Helen would have made a striking couple. But Rick and the ninety-year-old Helen?

"Maybe you should stick to the standard questions," Rick said.

"All right. Tell me what you found when you got here. About what time was it?"

He told her, explaining how the lights were out and the place seemed abandoned. How he'd known right away that something was wrong, and so wasn't surprised to find her in the kitchen.

"She called me earlier today. I wasn't available but she left a message. She sounded worried but wouldn't say why. I came over as soon as I could."

"She knew something was wrong, then. She expected something to happen."

"I think so."

"Do you have any idea why someone would want to kill an old woman like this?"

"Yes," he said. "I do."

One night she came into the bar late during his shift. They hadn't set up a date so he was surprised, and then he was worried. Gasping for breath, her eyes pink, she ran up to him, crashing into the bar, hanging on to it as if she might fall over without the support. She'd been crying.

He took up her hands and squeezed. "What's wrong?"

"Oh, Rick! I'm in so much trouble. He's going to kill me, I'm dead, I'm—"

"Helen! Calm down. Take a breath—what's the matter?"

She gulped down a couple of breaths, steadying herself. Straightening, squeezing Rick's hands in return, she was able to speak. "I need someplace to hide. I need to get out of sight for a little while."

She could have been in any kind of trouble. Some small-town relative come to track her down and bring home the runaway. Or she could have been something far different from the fresh-faced city girl she presented herself as. He'd known from the moment he met her that she was hiding something—she never talked about her past.

"What's happened?" he asked.

"I'll tell you everything, just please help me hide."

He came out from behind the bar, put his arm around her, and guided her into the back room. There was a storage closet filled with wooden crates, some empty and waiting to be carried out, some filled with bottles of beer and liquor. Only Rick and Murray came back here when the place was open. He found a sturdy, empty crate, tipped it upside down, dusted it off, and guided her to sit on it.

"I can close up in half an hour, then you can tell me what's wrong. All right?"

Nodding, she rubbed at her nose with a handkerchief.

"Can I get you anything?" he asked. "Bottle of soda? Shot of whiskey?"

"No, no. I'm fine, for now. Thank you."

Back out front, he let his senses expand, touching on every little noise, every scent, every source of light and the way it played around every shadow. Every heartbeat, a dozen of them, rattled in his awareness, a cacophony, like rocks tumbling in a tin can. It woke a hunger in him—a lurking knowledge that he could destroy everyone here, feed on them, sate himself on their blood before they knew what had happened.

He'd already fed this evening—he always fed before coming to work, it was the only way he could get by. It made the heartbeats that composed the background static of the world irrelevant.

No one here was anxious, worried, searching, behaving in any other manner than he would expect from people sitting in a bar half an hour before closing. Most were smiling, some were drunk, all were calm.

That changed ten minutes later when a heavyset man wearing a nondescript suit and weathered fedora came through the door and searched every face. Rick ignored him and waited. Sure enough, the man came up to the bar. His heart beat fast, and sweat dampened his armpits and hairline.

"What can I get for you?" Rick asked.

"You see a girl come in here, about this tall, brown hair, wearing a blue dress?" the man said. He was carrying a pistol in a holster under his suit jacket.

Some of the patrons had turned to watch. Rick was sure they'd all seen Helen enter. They were waiting to see how he'd answer.

"No," he said. "Haven't seen her. She the kind of girl who'd come into a place like this by herself?"

"Yeah. I think she is."

"We're past last call. I doubt she'll come in this late. But you're welcome to wait."

"I'll do that."

"Can I get you something?"

"Tonic water."

Rick poured the drink and accepted his coins. The guy didn't tip.

Patrons drifted out as closing time approached, and the heavyset man continued watching the door. He kept his right hand free and his jacket open, giving ready access to the holster. And if he did see Helen walk through the door, would he shoot her then and there? Was he that crazy?

Rick wondered what Helen had done.

When they were the only two left in the bar, Rick said, "I have to close up now, sir. I'm sorry your girl isn't here."

"She's not my girl."

"Well. Whoever she is, she isn't here. You'll have to go."

The man looked at him. "What were you in the war, kid?"

"4-F," Rick said.

He was used to the look the guy gave him. 4-F—medical deferment. Rick appeared to be a fit and able-bodied man in the prime of his life. People assumed he must have pulled a fast one on the draft board to get out of the service, and that made him a cheat as well as a coward. He let the assumptions pass by; he'd outlive them all.

"If you don't mind me asking . . . ," the guy prompted.

"I'm allergic to sunlight." It was the excuse he'd given throughout the war.

"Huh. Whoever heard of such a thing?"

Rick shrugged in response.

"You know what I was? Infantry. In Italy. I got shot twice, kid. But I gave more than I got. I'm a hell of a lot tougher than I look."

"I don't doubt it, sir."

The guy wasn't drunk—he smelled of sweat, unlaundered clothes, and aftershave, not alcohol. But he might have been a little bit crazy. He looked like he was waiting for Rick to start a fight.

"If I see this girl, you want me to tell her you're looking for her?" Rick said.

"No. I'm sure she hasn't been anywhere near here." He slid off the stool and tugged his hat more firmly on his head. "You take care, kid."

"You too, sir."

Finally, he left, and Rick locked the door.

He wouldn't have been surprised if he'd returned to the storeroom and found Helen gone—fled, for whatever reason. But she was still there, sitting on the crate in the corner, her knees pulled up to her chest, hugging herself.

"Someone was here looking for you," Rick said.

She jerked, startled—he'd entered too quietly. Even so, she looked like someone who had a man with a gun looking for her.

"Who was he? What'd he look like?" she asked, and Rick described him. Her gaze grew anguished, despairing. "It's Blake. I don't know what to do." She sniffed, wiping her nose as she started crying again. "He'll kill me if he finds me, he'll kill me."

"If you don't mind your coffee bitter, we can finish off what's in the pot and you can tell me all about it." He put persuasion into his voice, to set her at her ease. "I can't help if I don't know what's wrong."

"I don't want to get you involved, Rick."

"Then why did you come here?"

She didn't have an answer for that.

He poured a cup of coffee for her, pressed it into her hands, and waited for her to start.

"I got this job, right? It's a good job, good pay. But sometimes . . . well. I make deliveries. I'm not supposed to ask what's in the packages, I just go where they tell me to go and I don't ask any questions."

"You told me you got a job in a typing pool."

"What was I supposed to do, tell you the truth?"

"No, you're right. It wasn't any of my business. Go on."

"There's a garage out east on Champa—"

"Rough neighborhood."

"I've never had any trouble. Usually, I just walk in, set the bag on the shelf, and walk right back out. Today I heard gunshots. I turned around and there's Blake, he'd just shot Mikey—the guy from the garage who picks up the drops—and two other guys with him. He's holding this gun, it's still smoking. He shot them. I didn't know what else to do; there's a back door, so I ran for it, and he saw me, I know he saw me—"

He crouched beside her, took the coffee cup away, and pressed her hands together; they were icy. He didn't have much of his own heat to help warm her with.

"Now he wants to tie off the loose ends," Rick said.

"Of all the stupid timing; if I'd been five minutes earlier I'd have been fine, I wouldn't have seen anything."

Rick might argue that—she'd still be working as a runner for some kind of crime syndicate.

"Have you thought about going to the police? They could probably protect you. If they can lock Blake up, you won't have anything to worry about."

"You think it really works like that? I can't go to the cops. They'd arrest me just as fast as they'd arrest him."

"So leave town," Rick said.

"And go where? Do what? With what money?"

"I can give you money," Rick said.

"On a bartender's salary? That'll get me to where, Colorado Springs? No, Rick, I'm not going to ask you for money."

He ducked to hide a smile. Poor kid, thinking she was the only one with big secrets. "But you'll ask me for a place to hide."

"I'm sorry. It's just I didn't know where to go, I don't have any other friends here. And now I've dragged you into it and if Blake finds out he'll go after you, too."

"Helen, don't worry. We'll figure it out." He squeezed her hands, trying to impart some calm. She didn't have any other friends here—that he believed.

"You probably hate me now."

He shrugged. "Not much point to that."

She tilted her head, a gesture of curiosity. "You're different, you know that?"

"Yeah. I do. Look, I know a place where Blake absolutely won't find you. You can stay there for a couple of days. Maybe this'll blow over. Maybe they'll catch Blake. In the meantime, you can make plans. How does that sound?"

"Thanks, Rick. Thanks."

"It's no trouble at all."

One of the uniformed officers came in to the living room to hand Hardin a paper cup of coffee. Rick declined the offer of a cup for him.

"So she had a criminal background," Hardin said. "Did she do any time?"

"No," Rick said. "She was a runner, a messenger. Never anything more serious than that."

"Prostitution?"

"No, I don't think so." He was pretty sure he would have known if she had. But he couldn't honestly say what she'd done before he met her. "I know she saw a lot that she probably wasn't supposed to see. She testified in a murder trial."

"You said that was over sixty years ago. Surely anybody who wanted to get rid of a witness is long gone," the detective said.

"You only asked if I knew why someone would want to kill her. That's all I can think of. She didn't have much property, and no family to leave it to even if she did. But I do know that sixty years ago, a few people did have a reason to want her dead."

"Only a vampire would think it reasonable to look into sixty-year-old motives for murder."

He hadn't really thought of it like that, but she was right.

"Do you have any other questions, Detective?"

"What did she do since then? I take it she wasn't still working as a runner."

"She went straight. Worked retail. Retired fifteen years ago or so. She led a very quiet life."

"And you said she doesn't have any family? She never married, had kids?"

"No, she didn't. I think her will has me listed as executor. I can start making arrangements."

She rested her pen again. "Do you think she was lonely?"

"I don't know, Detective. She never told me." He thought she probably was, at least some of the time.

"Well, I'll dig up what I can in the police records, but I'm not sure we even have anything going that far back. When was that murder trial she testified in?"

"1947," he said. "The man she testified against was Charles Blake. He got a life sentence."

She shook her head. "That still blows my mind. And I suppose you'll tell me you remember it like it was yesterday?"

Rick shook his head. "No. Even I know that was a long time ago."

In fact, he had to think a moment to remember what the Helen of that time had looked like—young, frivolous, hair in curls, dresses hugging her frame. When he thought of Helen, he saw the old woman she had become. He didn't even have any strong feelings about the change—it was just what happened. His mortal friends grew old and died. He preferred that to when they died young.

Many of his kind didn't bother, but Rick still liked being in the world, moving as part of it. Meeting people like Helen. Even if it meant saying goodbye more often.

Hardin's gaze turned thoughtful. "If I were immortal, I'd go see the world. I'd finally learn French."

Rick chuckled; he'd never learned French. "And yet vampires tend to stay in one place. Watch the world change around them."

"So you've been here for five hundred years?"

"Not here in Denver, but here in the west? Yes. And I've seen some amazing things."

"A lot of murders?" she asked.

"A few," he said.

She considered him a long time, pondering more questions, no doubt. In the end, she just shook her head. "I'll call you if I need any more information."

"Of course you will."

She smirked at that.

The police were in the process of sealing the house as a crime scene. Yellow evidence tags were going up, marking spots in the kitchen—the teacup, the table, spots on the floor, the counter. Yellow tape, fluttering in a light breeze, decorated the front porch. Time for Rick to leave, then. Now and forever. He paused for a last look around the living room. Then he was done.

He drove, at first aimlessly, just wanting to think. Then he headed toward the old neighborhoods, the bar on Colfax and the garage on Champa. The shadows of the way they'd been were visible—the outline of a façade, painted over a dozen times in the succeeding years. Half a century's worth of skyscrapers, office complexes, and high-end lofts had risen and fallen around them. The streets had widened, the pavement had improved, the signs had changed. The cars had changed, the clothing people wore had changed, though at this hour he only saw a few young men smoking cigarettes outside a club. None of them wore hats.

If Charles Blake was even alive, he'd still be in prison. Did he have relatives? An accomplice he'd hatched a plan of revenge with? Rick could call the Department of Corrections, talk them into releasing any information about Blake. Just to tie off that loose end and finish Helen's story in his own mind.

Or he could let Detective Hardin do her job. Hardin was right, and Helen's sixty-year-old criminal life probably had nothing to do with her death. It might have been an accidental shooting. Some gang misfiring on a drive-by. Anything was possible, absolutely anything. Hardin didn't need his help to find out what.

Time to let Helen go.

He brought her to Arturo's.

Arturo was the Master vampire of Denver, which meant he made the rules, and any vampire who wanted to live in his territory had to live by those rules. And Rick did, mostly. What he didn't agree to was living under Arturo's roof as one of his dozen or so minions. Instead, Rick kept to himself, lived how he wanted, didn't draw attention, and didn't challenge Arturo's authority outright, so Arturo let him have his autonomy. A lot of the other vampires thought Rick was eccentric—even for a vampire—and he was all right with that. In the meantime, Arturo's was the one place in the city Blake would never find Helen.

Arturo owned the squat brick building east of downtown. The ground floor housed a furniture dealer who did sporadic business, but his real work was deflecting attention from the basement. Underground, away from windows and sunlight, the city's vampires lived and ran their little empire.

He walked Helen the dozen blocks from Murray's bar to the furniture store, his arm protectively across her shoulder. She huddled against his body, glancing outward fearfully. Blake would never find them, not the way he moved, casting shadows, pulling her into his influence. But she didn't know that.

In the back of the furniture shop, a concrete staircase led down, below the street level, to a nondescript door. Rick knocked.

"Blake won't find you here," he said.

"I trust you," she said. She was still looking up the stairs, as if she expected Blake to appear, gun in hand.

What he really ought to do was put her on a train back to whatever town she came from. Tell her to find a good husband and settle down. Instead, he was bringing her here, and she trusted him.

The door opened, and Rick faced the current gatekeeper, a young woman in a straight silk dress ten years out of date—not that she would notice. Estelle hadn't been above ground during most of that time.

Helen stared. To her, Estelle would look like a girl dressing up in her mother's cast-off clothes, the skirt too long and the neckline too high.

"Hello, Estelle. I just need a room for a couple of nights."

"Is Arturo expecting you?" she said, looking Helen up and down, probably drawing conclusions.

"No. But I don't think he'll mind. Do you?"

Pouting, she opened the door and let them in.

The hallway within was carpeted and dimly lit with a pair of shaded bulbs.

"Is he in his usual spot?" Rick asked over his shoulder.

"Sure. He's even in a good mood."

Helen looked to him for an explanation. He just guided her on, through the doorway at the end of the corridor and into a wide room.

The place had the atmosphere of a turn-of-the-century lounge, close and warm, dense with subdued colors and rich fabrics, Persian rugs and velvet wall hangings. One of Arturo's dozen minions, Angelo, a young hothead, was smoking, purposefully drawing breath into his lungs and blowing it out again—breathing for no other reason than to smoke. It wasn't as if the tobacco had any effect on him. Maybe he liked watching the smoke. Or maybe it was just habit. He was only a century old.

Most of Arturo's vampires were young to Rick's eyes. Then again, just about everyone was.

Sated with the human blood that kept them alive, they'd most likely been discussing the evening's exploits. Their latest mode of hunting involved finding a dinner party, inviting themselves over, mesmerizing the whole group, and then having a taste of everyone. They didn't kill or turn anyone, which would draw too much attention, and the group would wake up in the morning thinking they'd had a marvelous—if strange—evening. Rick sometimes suggested to Arturo that he should open a restaurant or club and let the party come to him.

Arturo—by all accounts dashing, with golden hair swept back from a square face—lay in a wingback armchair, legs draped over one of its arms. He looked at Rick and raised his brows in surprise. "What have you brought for us, Ricardo?"

The dozen vampires, men and women, straightened, perking up to look at Helen like a pack of wolves.

"She needs a place to stay," Rick said. "She's under my protection."

"Ricardo?" Helen whispered to him, and he hushed her.

"I'd just like to use the spare room for a couple of nights, if that's all right."

The young man—he looked to be in his midtwenties, a little younger than Rick appeared—considered, tapping a finger against a chin. "Certainly. Why not?"

"Thanks."

His arm still around her shoulders, he turned Helen back to the hallway, where he opened the first door on the right and guided her inside.

"Rick? What is this place, some kind of boardinghouse?"

"Sort of."

"Who are all those people?"

The room was absolutely dark. Helen gasped when he closed the door behind her. "Rick?"

He didn't need to see to find the floor lamp in the corner and turn it on.

The room had a double bed with a mass of pillows and a quilted satin comforter, an oak dresser, the lamp, and not much else. The place was for sleeping out the day and storing clothing. A rug on the hardwood floor muffled footsteps.

Helen stared. "It's a brothel. You've brought me to a brothel."

If he argued with her, he'd have to explain, which he wanted to avoid.

"Do you mind?" he said. "I could find somewhere else."

She hesitated before shaking her head and saying, "No. It's okay. As long as it isn't one of Blake's."

"It's not."

She squared her shoulders a little more firmly, as if steeling herself. "I think maybe I'm ready for that drink you offered earlier."

"I'll have to go back to the parlor for it. You mind waiting here?"

"I'll be fine," she said, wearing a brave smile.

He left the room, and Arturo was waiting in the hallway, leaning against the wall, his arms crossed.

"Ricardo."

"Arturo," he answered.

"You brought her here because you want to hide her. Why?"

"She's in trouble."

"What kind of trouble?"

"The straightforward kind. In over her head with the wrong people."

"Small-town girl trying to make it in the city?"

"Something like that."

"Hmm. Quaint. Well, I'm always happy to do a good deed for a pretty girl. But you owe me a favor now, yes?"

Rick ducked his gaze to hide a smile. He handled Arturo by letting him think he was in charge. "That's how it usually works, yes."

"Excellent."

"I assume the alcohol cabinet is included in the favor?"

"What? You're having to get your girls drunk first now?" Arturo said in mock astonishment.

"Thank you, Arturo." Rick slipped around him and into the parlor.

He returned to the room with a tumbler of ice and a bottle of whiskey. Helen was on the bed. Her jacket was off and lying on the dresser, her shoes were tossed in a corner, and she was peeling off her stockings. Rick started to apologize and back out of the room again, when she called him over.

"I'm sorry, I just wanted to get comfortable since I'm going to be here a while," she said.

He set the tumbler on the dresser and poured a finger.

"Ricardo, is it?" she said. "Are you Mexican? Because you don't look Mexican."

"Spanish," he said. "At least, if you go back far enough."

"Spanish, hm? That's romantic."

He handed her the whiskey, which she sipped, smiling at him over the glass. "You only brought one glass. Don't you want any?"

"I'm fine," he said.

"Will you sit here with me?"

This was a turning point. He'd been in enough situations like it to recognize it. "Helen, I didn't bring you here to take advantage."

"Despite the bed and this being a brothel?" Her smile turned wry.

"You really will be safe here," he said, though his protestations were starting to sound weak. Truth be told, he wanted to sit by her, and his lips grew flush from wanting to press against her skin.

She'd touched up her lipstick while he was gone. The top button of her blouse was undone, the hem of her skirt lay around her knees, and her legs were bare. She thought she was seducing him. But as soon as he sat on that bed, she wouldn't be in control of the situation. She didn't know that. And if he played it right, she never would know. So. What was the right thing to do, really?

She drained the whiskey and patted the bed next to her—right next to her—and he sat. He laid his arm across the headboard behind her, and she pressed herself against him.

"I don't meet a lot of nice guys, working the way I do. You're a nice guy, Rick."

"If you say so."

"Yeah, I do."

Pressing her hand to his cheek, she drew him close and kissed him on the mouth. She was eager, insistent. Who was he to deny her? She tasted of whiskey and heat, alive and lovely. He drew the tumbler from her hand and set it on the floor, then returned to kissing her, wrapping his arms around her, trapping her. She scratched at the buttons on his shirt.

The fire that rose up in him in response wasn't sexual. It was hunger. A visceral, primal, gnawing hunger, as if he hadn't eaten in centuries. His only nourishment, his only possible release, lay under her skin. If he let that monster go, he would tear into her, spilling her over the bed, swimming in her innards to better feed on her blood.

There was a better way.

He worked slowly, carefully, kissing across her mouth and jaw, sucking at her ear as she gasped, then moving down her neck, tracing a collarbone, unfastening her blouse button by button, pulling aside her brassiere to gain access to a perfect handful of breast. She wriggled, reaching back to unfasten the whole contraption. When he'd first encountered the modern brassiere, he'd thought it was so much easier than a corset. But the undergarment had its own idiosyncrasies. And like undoing corsets always did, it gave them both a chance to giggle.

She sat up enough to yank at his shirt, and he let her pull it off and throw it aside. Then, once again, he pressed her to the bed and took control, peeling away her clothing—the girdle and garters were more pieces of modern clothing he was still coming to terms with—and running his cool hands over every burning inch of her, kissing as he went. Only after she came for him did he take what he needed, from a small and careful bite at her throat.

Her blood was ecstasy.

Her heart, aroused and racing, pumped a strong flow for him. He could have drained her in moments, but took in only a few mouthfuls. Not enough to completely satisfy, but enough to keep him alive for a couple more days. Vampires had learned this long ago—how much more efficient to keep them alive and producing. And how much richer to coax it from them, instead of spilling it.

He licked the wound, encouraging the blood to clot. She'd gone limp, and her breathing had settled. Propping himself over her, he turned her face so that he was looking straight down at her. Her eyes were wide, pupils dilated. Her brow was furrowed, her expression both amazed and confused. Maybe even hurt. Holding her gaze, he focused on her, *into* her, and spoke softly.

"You won't remember this. You'll remember the bliss and nothing else. I'm just a man, just a lover, and you won't remember anything else. Isn't that right?" Slowly, she nodded. Her worried expression, the wrinkles around her eyes, faded. "Good, Helen. Remember the good, let the rest go. Now, sleep. Sleep until I wake you up again."

Her eyes closed, and she let out a sigh.

Dawn had nearly arrived. The room had no windows, but he could feel it. The warm and sated glow that came after feeding joined with the lethargy of daylight. He was safe and calm, so he let the morning pull him under until he fell unconscious, still holding her hand.

The next night, Rick had a message from Detective Hardin waiting for him. He called back immediately.

"Hello, Rick?" she said. "Do you even have a last name?"

"Have you found something, Detective?" he said.

"Yeah. Charles Blake? I looked him up. Not only is he still alive, he got out on parole four months ago."

The air seemed to go still for a moment, and sounds faded as he pulled his awareness to a tiny space around him—the phone, what Hardin had just told him, how that made him feel. Cold, tight, hands clenching, a predator's snarl tugging at his lips.

He drew a couple of calm breaths to steady himself, and to be able to speak to the detective. "You think he killed her?"

"I think he hired someone to do it for him. He might have collected favors in prison and called them in when he got out. Guy was a real peach, from what I gather. I can't go into too many details, but the crime scene is pretty slim on evidence, which speaks to someone with experience. The back door was unlocked. We think he might have come to see her earlier in the day. That must have been when she called you."

How small, how petty, to carry a grudge over such a length of time. How like a vampire. And yet, how human as well. That grudge might very well have kept Blake alive all this time.

"How are you doing?" she asked. "This must come as a shock to you."

It sounded like something she said to any victim's family. He smiled to think she'd next offer to refer him to grief counseling. "I'm all right, Detective. It wasn't a shock. I've been expecting this for sixty years. About Blake—do you know where he is? Have you arrested him?"

"I'm afraid I can't discuss an ongoing investigation any further. I just thought you'd want to know about Blake."

"Thank you. I appreciate it."

They both hung up, and he considered. He could find Blake. He'd be an old man now, ancient. Not much to live for, after spending most of his life in prison. He'd exacted his revenge, and Rick didn't think he'd spend a lot of time trying to get out of town or hide. And this was Rick's city, now.

Detective Hardin hadn't arrested Blake yet because she was building her case, searching for evidence, obtaining warrants. Rick had every confidence that she'd do her job to the utmost of her ability and that through her, justice would be served.

In this case, he wasn't interested in waiting.

After killing Arturo and replacing him as Master of Denver, Rick had transformed the lair. The parlor was now an office, with functional sofas and a coffee table, and a desk and bookshelves for work. He paced around the desk and considered. Blake would have a parole officer who would know where he was. The man might even be living in some kind of halfway house for ex-cons. After so long in prison, it was doubtful he had any family or friends left. He had no place else to go. And if he was right about Blake's state of mind, the man wouldn't even be hiding.

He flipped through a ledger and found a name, recently entered. A woman who'd run a prostitution ring in the seventies—with blackmail on the side. She'd served her time, she knew the system, and she owed him a favor.

"Hello, Carol. It's Rick. I need to know who the parole officer is for a recently released felon."

Night fell, and Rick woke.

Helen had turned over on her side and curled up, pressing against him, her hands on his arm. She looked sweet and vulnerable.

He leaned over and breathed against her ear. "Wake up, Helen."

Her eyes opened. Pulling away from him, she sat up, looking dazed, as if trying to remember where she was and how she'd gotten here. Her clothes were hanging off her, loose, and her hair was in tangles.

"You all right?" he asked.

She glared. "Did you put something in my drink?"

"No."

She looked herself over, retrieving her clothes, fastening buttons, and running fingers through her hair. Wryly, she said, "You never even took your trousers off, did you?"

He answered her smile. "Never mind. As long as you're all right."

"Yeah, I'm fine. More than fine. You're something else, Rick, you know that?"

"There's a washroom across the hall."

"What time is it?"

"Nightfall," he said. "I'm about to head to Murray's to see if Blake shows up. You should stay here."

She closed up at the mention of Blake, slouching and hugging herself. He smoothed her hair back and left a gentle kiss on her forehead.

"I'll be safe here?" she asked.

"Yes. I promise."

"What happens if Blake does show up? What can you possibly do? Rick, if he hurts you because of me—"

"It'll be fine, Helen."

He washed up, found a clean shirt, ran a comb through his hair, and left the lair.

Blake did, in fact, show up at the bar that night. Rick kept his place behind the taps and watched him scan the room before choosing a seat near the bar.

"Bourbon," he muttered. Rick poured and pushed the tumbler over.

Scowling, Blake drained the liquor in one go. After some time, when it was clear Helen wasn't going to appear, he set his stare on Rick, who didn't have any trouble pretending not to notice. Leaning on his elbow, Blake pushed back his jacket to show off his gun in its shoulder holster.

"So. Did she ever show up?" the man said.

"Who? The girl?"

"You know who I'm talking about."

"Can I ask why you're looking for her?"

"I just want to talk to her. We can work something out. You know where she's hiding, don't you?"

"Sir, I really can't help you."

Blake narrowed his gaze, looking him up and down—sizing him up, and Rick knew what he was thinking. He was thinking he was looking at a wimp, a coward, a young guy who'd sat out the war, who'd be easy to take down in a fight. Blake was thinking all he'd have to do was wave the gun around, break his nose, and he'd take him right to Helen because no broad was worth sticking up for like that.

Rick smiled, knowing it would make him crazy. Blake scowled and walked out.

Rick had the rest of the night mapped out. He knew what would happen next, how it would all play, a bit of urban theater, predictable yet somehow satisfying. Last call came and went; he offered to close up. After locking the doors, he set chairs upside down on tables, gave the floor a quick sweeping and the bar a wipe-down, turned off all the lights, and went out the back, where Blake was waiting for him.

Blake lunged from the shadows with a right hook, obviously intending to take Rick out in a second and keep him from gaining his bearings.

Rick sidestepped out of the way. Blake stumbled, and Rick pivoted, grabbing Blake's shirt, yanking him further off balance, then swinging him headfirst into the wall. The man slid to the ground, limbs flailing for purchase, scrabbling at Rick, the wall, anything. The sequence took less than a second—Blake wouldn't have had a chance to realize his right hook had missed. He must have thought the world turned upside down.

Wrenching Blake's arm back, Rick dragged him a dozen feet along the pavement in the back alley. The shoulder joint popped; Blake hollered. With a flick of the same injured arm, Rick flipped Blake faceup—bloody scrapes covered his cheek and jaw. Jumping on him, Rick pinned him, holding him with strength rather than weight—Blake was the larger man. He brought his face close to smell the rich, sweet fluid leaking from him. Rick could drain the man dead.

A floodlight filled the alley, blinding even Rick, who shaded his eyes with a raised arm. Squinting, he needed a moment to make out the scene: a police car had pulled into the alley.

"You two! Break it up!" a man shouted from the driver's-side window.

Climbing to his feet, Rick held up his hands. Next to him, Blake was still scrambling to recover, scratching at the cut on his face, shaking his head like a cave creature emerging into the open.

The cop had a partner, who stormed out of the passenger side and came at them, nightstick in hand. He shoved Rick face first to the brick wall and patted him down. "What's this? A couple of drunks duking it out?"

Rick didn't speak and didn't react. He could have fought free, stunned the officer, and disappeared into the shadows. But he waited, curious.

"What have you got there?" the driver asked.

"A couple of drunks. Should we bring 'em in?"

"Wait a minute—that guy on the ground. Is that Charles Blake?"

The cop grabbed Blake by the collar and dragged him into the light.

"That's it, bring 'em both in."

Rick rode in the back of the squad car next to Blake, trying to decide if he should be amused or concerned. Dawn was still a few hours away. He had time to watch this play out. Blake was hunched over, breathing wetly, glancing at Rick every now and then to glare at him.

Within the hour, Rick was sitting in a bare, dank interrogation room, talking to a plainclothes detective, a guy named Simpson. He lit a cigarette and offered one to Rick, who declined.

He said, "You were picked up fighting with Charles Blake behind Murray's."

"That's right," Rick answered.

"You want to tell me why?"

Rick leaned back and crossed his arms. "I expected to be thrown in the drunk tank when I got here, but you're interested in Blake. Can I ask why?"

"What do you know about him?"

"He's been bothering a girl I know."

"Your girl?" Rick shrugged, and the detective flicked ashes on the floor. "That's why you were beating on him? I don't suppose I can blame you for that."

"Is Blake dangerous?"

"Do you think he is?"

"Yes," Rick said.

The detective studied him, but Rick didn't give much away. If he needed to, he could catch the man's eye and talk him into letting Rick go. It would certainly come to that if he was still here close to dawn.

Finally, the detective said, "You're right. He's the primary suspect in a murder case. You have anything else about him you want to share?"

This gave Rick an idea. "I might know someone who can help you."

"*If* I let you go—I know how that works."

"I'm the bartender at Murray's—I won't disappear on you."

"And how good is this information of yours?"

"Worth the wait, I think."

"You know what? You're a little too cagey for a bartender. Is that all you do?"

Rick chuckled. "Right now it is."

"I need evidence to lay on Blake if we're going to keep him locked up—and keep him away from your girlfriend. Can you help me out?"

"Stop by Murray's tomorrow night and I'll have an answer."

The detective let him go.

Rick knew he'd be followed—for a time, at least. He returned to Arturo's by a roundabout route and managed to vanish, at least from his tail's point of view.

Helen was waiting for him in the parlor, sitting with Arturo on a burgundy velvet settee. Rick calmed himself a moment and didn't instantly leap forward to put himself between them. She was smiling, and Arturo wasn't doing anything but talking.

"Ricardo! I was hoping you wouldn't return, and that you'd left Helen here with us."

Helen giggled—she held an empty tumbler. They'd probably been at this for hours.

"Thanks for entertaining her for me," Rick said.

"My pleasure. Really."

"Helen, we need to talk," Rick said, gesturing to the doorway.

"Your friend's a charmer, Rick," she said.

"Yes, he is. Let's go."

She pushed herself from the seat. Glancing over her shoulder, she waved fingers at him, and Arturo answered with an indulgent smile. Rick put an arm over her shoulder and guided her into the safe room.

"Don't be angry," she said. "I needed to ask him if there was a phone."

"Who did you need to call?"

"The police," she said, and ducked her gaze. "I didn't want you to get hurt, so I called the police and told them there might be trouble at Murray's."

And there was trouble, and the police had shown up.

"I'd almost taken care of Blake when the police arrived," he said. He didn't say, *You should have trusted me.*

She paled. "What happened?"

"He's in jail now, but he's not going to stay there unless they get some proof that he committed those murders. They know he did it, they just don't have evidence."

She paced back and forth along the foot of the bed. Her shoulders tightened, and she hugged herself.

"I think you should go talk to them, Helen. You can testify, Blake will go to prison, and he won't bother you again. You'll be safe."

"I can't do that, Rick. I can't say anything. He'll kill me, he'll—"

"Not if he's in prison."

"But what if he gets out? The first thing he'll do is come after me."

"I'll kill him first," Rick said.

"Rick, no. I don't want you to get in trouble over me. I don't even know why you're looking out for me, you barely know me—"

"I'm doing it because I can," he said. "But if you go to the police, they'll take care of Blake."

She moved close, pressing herself to him, wrapping her arms around him and resting her head on his chest. This again. She was so close, he could hear blood pouring through her veins, near the surface. She was flushed and so warm. He rubbed his face along her hair, gathering that warmth to him.

"Helen," he said with something like despair.

"What's the matter?" she said.

"I'm not . . . right for you. This is dangerous—"

"Why?" She stepped away. "What's up with you? You're so nice,

47

but you're not afraid of Blake, and you keep talking like I ought to be afraid of you. What aren't you telling me?"

Such a large answer to that question. He shifted her, so that he could see her face, trace the soft skin of her jaw, then drop to trace the pulse on her neck. He should send her to sleep and make her forget all this. He never should have taken her on that first date. And life was too long for that kind of regret. It didn't matter how immortal you were, you still needed friends.

"Have you ever read *Dracula*?" he said.

"What, like Bela Lugosi?"

"Not quite like. But yes."

"Yeah, ages ago. I like the movie better."

"Vampires exist. They're real."

She chuckled. "Sorry?"

He took her hand and placed it on his chest, where his dead heart lay still. "What do you feel?"

Her smile fell. She moved her hand, pressing it flat to his chest, his ribs digging into her palm. She stared at him. "What am I supposed to say? Tell you you're crazy?"

"Lie still," he said.

"What?"

He sat her on the bed, stacked up the pillows, and forced her back so that she reclined against them. He kissed her, and she kissed back, enthusiastic if confused. Taking in her scent, her warmth, and the feel of her blood, he let the appetite grow in him.

Planting a final kiss on her neck, he held her hand and drew her arm straight before him. No hypnotism this time, no shrouding her memory. Let her see what he was. He put his lips to her elbow—more kisses, slow and tender, tracing her veins with his tongue. She let out a moan.

He sucked on her wrist, drawing blood to the surface.

"Rick? What are you doing? Rick?"

"I said lie still." He pushed her back to the pillow and returned his attention to her wrist.

Finally, he bit, and she gasped. But she lay still.

Her blood was not as sweet as it might have been—she was too wary. But it was still sweet, and she didn't panic, and when he licked the wound closed and glanced at her, her gaze was clear. Uncertain, but clear. He was relieved. He folded her arms across her belly, wrapping her in an embrace, her head pillowed on his shoulder. She melted against him.

"I don't understand," she whispered.

"I don't expect you to. But do you trust me to look after you if Blake goes free?"

She nodded. He kissed her hair and waited for her to fall asleep.

Rick brought her to Murray's the next night, and Detective Simpson was waiting for them. Her hands were trembling, but Rick stayed close to her, and she stood tall and spoke clearly. Simpson promised she wouldn't be charged with any of the petty crimes she'd committed, in exchange for her testimony. The case against Blake went to trial, and Helen was the prosecution's star witness. Blake was convicted and sent away for a long, long time. Rick was sure he'd never see the guy again.

He only needed a little digging—a visit to a parole office, some obfuscation and inveigling, a deep look into an informant's eyes—to learn which halfway house Blake was staying at, east of downtown. He drove there with a single-minded intensity. He wasn't often wrong these days, but he'd been wrong about Blake, and he'd failed Helen. Petty revenge wouldn't make that right. But it might help tip the scales back in the right direction.

The house was back from the street, run-down and lit up, and gave no outward sign of what it was. Rick wondered if the neighbors knew. He parked his car on the curb, stuck his hands in his pockets, and headed to the front door.

The house pressed outward against him; his steps slowed. The place was protected—he wasn't sure it would be, given its nature, and the fact that people were always moving in and out. Did that make it a public institution, or a home? But here was his answer—this was a home. He couldn't enter without invitation. By the time he reached the front door, the force was a wall, invisible; he could almost press his hands against it—but not through it.

Well. He'd have to try normal, mundane bluffing, wouldn't he?

He knocked on the door. A shadow passed over the peephole, and a voice called, "Who is it? What do you want?"

"My name is Rick. I'm an old friend of Charles Blake, and I heard he was here. Can I see him?"

"Do you know what time it is?"

"Yes—sorry about that. I just got off work. Bartender."

"Just a minute. I'll get him."

"Mind if I wait inside?"

After a brief, wary moment of waiting, the deadbolt clicked back, and the door opened. A gruff man in his forties stood aside and held the door. "Come on in."

Rick did.

The living room was worn and sad, with threadbare furniture and carpets, stained walls, a musty air. A bulletin board listed rules, notices, want ads, warnings. The atmosphere was institutional, but this might have been the first real home some of these men had known. Halfway house, indeed.

"Stay right here," the man said, and walked to a back hallway.

Rick waited, hands in pockets.

The doorman returned after a long wait, what would have been many beats of his heart, if it still beat. Behind him came a very old man, pulling a small oxygen tank on a cart behind him. Tubes led from it to his nose, and his every breath wheezed. Other than that, he had faded. He was smaller than the last time Rick had seen him, withered and sunken, skin like putty hanging off a stooped frame. Wearing a T-shirt and ratty, faded jeans, he looked sad, beaten. The scowl remained—Rick recognized that part of him.

The old man saw him and stopped. They were two ghosts staring at each other across the room.

"Hello, Blake," Rick said.

"Who are you? You his grandson?"

Rick turned to the middle-aged doorman and stared until he caught the man's gaze. "Would you mind leaving us alone for a minute?" He put quiet force into the suggestion. The man walked back into the hallway.

"Bill—Bill! Come back!" Blake's sandpaper voice broke into coughing.

"I'm not his grandson," Rick said.

"What is this?"

"Tell me about Helen, Blake."

He coughed a laugh, as if he thought this was a joke. Rick just stared at him. He didn't have to put any power in it. His standing there was enough. Blake's jaw trembled.

"What about her? Huh? What about her!"

Rick grabbed the tube hanging at Blake's chest and yanked, pulling it off his face. Blake stumbled back, his mouth open to show badly fitted dentures coming loose. Wrapping both hands in Blake's shirt, Rick marched him into the wall, slamming him, slamming again, listening for the crack of breaking bone.

"You thought no one would know," Rick whispered at him, face to face. "You thought no one would remember." Blake sputtered, flailing weakly, ineffectually.

The front door crashed open. "Stop!"

Rick recognized the footfalls, voices, and the sounds of their breathing. Detective Hardin pounded in, flanked by two uniformed officers. Rick glanced over his shoulder—she was pointing a gun at him. Not that it mattered. He shoved his fists against Blake's throat.

Blake was dying under his grip. Rick wouldn't have to flex a muscle to kill him. He didn't even feel an urge to take the man's blood—it would be cool, sluggish, unappetizing. Rick would spit it back out in the man's face. He could do it all with Hardin watching, because what could the detective really do in the end?

"Rick! Back away from him!"

Hardin fumbled in her jacket pocket and drew out a cross, a simple version, two bars of unadorned silver soldered together. Proof against vampires. Rick smiled.

Blake had to have known he wouldn't get away with murdering Helen. What had he been thinking? What had he wanted, really? Rick looked at him: the wide, yellowing eyes, the sagging face, pockmarked and splashed with broken capillaries. He expected to see a death wish there, a determined fatalism. But Blake was afraid. Rick terrified him. The man, his body failing around him, didn't want to die.

This made Rick want to strangle him even more. To justify the man's terror. But he let Blake go and backed away, leaving him to Hardin's care.

The old man sank to his knees, knocking over the oxygen canister. He held his hands before him, clawed and trembling.

"He's dead! Dead! He has to be dead! He has to be!" He was sobbing.

Maybe leaving him on his knees and crying before the police was revenge enough.

Rick, hands raised, backed out of the line of fire. "I could have saved you some paperwork, Detective."

"You'd just have forced me into a whole other set of paperwork. What the hell did you think you were doing?"

The uniforms had to pick up Blake and practically drag him away. They didn't bother with cuffs. Blake didn't seem to know what was happening. His mouth worked, his breaths wheezed, his legs stumbled.

"I take it you got your evidence," Rick said.

"We found the shooter, and he talked. Blake hired him."

He certainly didn't look like he'd pulled any triggers in a good long time.

"So that's it?"

"What else do you want?"

"I wanted to get here five minutes earlier," he said. Not that any of it really mattered. It all faded from the memories around him.

"I need to ask you to depart the premises," she said. She wasn't aiming the gun at him, but she hadn't put it away. "Don't think I won't arrest you for something, because I will. I'll come up with something."

Rick nodded. "Have a good night, Detective."

He returned to his car and left the scene, marking the end of yet another chapter.

Rick hadn't been able to attend the trial, but he'd met with Helen every night to discuss the proceedings. She came to Murray's, tearing up with relief and rubbing her eyes with her handkerchief, to report the guilty verdict. He quit his shift early and took her back to his place, a basement apartment on Capitol Hill. With Blake locked up, he felt safe bringing her there. He owned the building, rented out the upper portion through an agency, and could block off the windows in the basement without drawing attention. The décor was simple—a bed, an armchair, a chest of drawers, a radio, and a kitchen that went unused.

They lay together on the bed, his arm around her, holding her close, while she nestled against him. They talked about the future, which was always an odd topic for him. Helen had decided to look for an old-fashioned kind of job and aim for a normal life this time.

"But I don't know what to do about you," she said, craning her neck to look up at him.

He'd been here before, lying with a woman he liked, who with a little thought and nudging he could perhaps be in love with, except that what they had would never be entirely mutual, or equitable. And he still didn't know what to say. *I could take from you for the rest of your life, and you'd end with . . . nothing.*

He said, "If you'd like, I can vanish, and you'll never see me again. It might be better that way."

"I don't want that. But I wish . . ." Her face puckered, brow furrowed in thought. "But you're not ever going to take me on a trip, or stay up to watch the sunrise with me, or ask me to marry you, or anything, are you?"

He shook his head. "I've already given you everything I can."

Except for one thing. But he hadn't told her that he could infect her, make her like him, that she too could live forever and never see a sunrise. And he wouldn't.

"It's enough," she said, hugging him. "At least for now, it's enough."

The Island of Beasts

S HE WAS A BUNDLE on the bottom of the skiff, tossed in with her skirt and petticoat tangled around her legs, hands bound behind her with a thin chain that also wrapped around her neck.

She didn't struggle; the silver in the chain burned her skin. The more she moved, the more she burned, so she lay still because the only way to stop this would be to make them kill her. They wanted to kill her. So why didn't they? Why go through the trouble of rowing this wave-rocked skiff out to this hideous island just to throw her to her likely death? To save themselves the taint of murder? To keep themselves clean of whatever small sin her death would engender on their souls? Surely her life was not so large that her death would be such a burden.

"Why? Why not just kill me and be done with it?" she growled.

Her captors—the two rough men on the oars and the gentleman with the tailored frock coat and fine manners who sat at the prow—were wolves, like her. They smelled of musk and wild and moorland, of the beasts that hid inside their flesh. But they were *civilized*. They followed orders and bowed to their betters. Not like her. They also smelled of hearth fires and smugness. She smelled of fury.

The gentleman, Mr. Edgerton, laughed sourly. "You are not worth the cost of the silver ball it would take to kill you."

She was not valuable enough to keep and not dangerous enough to kill. There was a pretty fate. Too dangerous to keep and not valuable enough to bother taming. And so here she was, dumped on the edge of the world, off the coast of Scotland. She could laugh and cry both, but her throat was too locked up with stifled screams. Edgerton would like it if she screamed. He'd tell his master, the Lord of Wolves in London, that she screamed. He'd likely tell the Lord that anyway, but it wouldn't be true, and that would be something. She'd make the fine gentleman a liar.

Edgerton drew out a spyglass and used it to search the island's shore.

"See anything, sir?" one of the oarsmen asked. The men at the oars were servants, lower wolves who bowed and scraped and thus got their meat thrown to them. They wouldn't save her.

"Not a thing. They're hiding from us. Biding their time."

"Maybe they're all dead," said the other. "Maybe they all killed each other."

"Perhaps they did. You'll have the island to yourself," Edgerton said to the woman and grinned. The bottom of the skiff hit sand. "That's enough, no need to go all the way up."

"Sir?"

"Let her walk the rest of the way." He would never say it, but he was afraid.

Her hands jerked; the silver chain seared her neck. Her bonds were suddenly loose, but in the next moment she was rolled over the side of the boat and into the freezing North Atlantic water, wool skirt instantly sodden and pulling her down. She flailed, reached out. Put her feet down on the sand, stood. Was only knee deep in the churning surf, watching the skiff row away, the men laughing. Edgerton held up the silver chain in a gloved hand. It was worth more than she ever was.

"Damn you all! Damn you all for cowards and bastards! You

could have just killed me, but you're cowards, aren't you just!" She screamed after them, and their laughter carried to her in reply. They, all of them who condemned her to this exile, need never think of her again.

She stood with the waves pushing back and forth around her legs, shoving 'round her skirt, freezing water pulling at her. The sand reached from the lapping surf to a stretch of sea grass and crumbling gray rock. The sky was gray, the water was gray, dark slate, pushing up the thick stretch of pale sand. Beyond, the land was green and spare, grass kept short by wind and whatever gnawed at it. Sheep had been here days ago, and oddly the scent of their droppings gave her hope. There was food here, if she could get it.

Past the beach, up a slope, was a craggy outcrop, stones tumbled down from some exposed hillside. Wasn't as good as a fort or a tower, but maybe she could defend the spot. She needed a place. She needed weapons. She needed time. Soaking wet, she wanted a fire. A fury had built up in her heart to the breaking point. She would snap and strip and the wolf would burst through her skin and run wild, and if that happened she was done for, she'd have nothing.

No matter. It was finished. She was here, and she knew that she was not alone on this island.

She got to work.

By the time the cold rain started, she had something resembling shelter. She'd piled driftwood and rushes over a cleft in the jagged rocks and made a little cave for herself. With the rain, well, she had fresh water. Though she was hungry, food could wait until tomorrow. The gray sky was turning dark, the sun setting, the slate ocean turning black, and the rush and crash of the waves went on and on. Survive the night, that was all she had to do. Then the next night, and the next.

God damn them who put her here, but she would live. If for no other reason than to spite them.

Wasn't time for the full moon—breaking clouds revealed a three-quarters waxing moon. Wolves howled anyway. Five, six of them, calling out with high, sharp territory songs. *We know you are here, we sense you, we smell you, we are coming for you.* Curled up in her cave, huddled in her skirts, hugging her knees, she listened to them.

Weapons. She would need to find weapons tomorrow. Build a palisade around her cave and hold them off as long as she could. There would be no silver on the island she could use to kill them. Or herself.

They would be wild. They had been exiled to the island because they could not control themselves, because they were dangerous. Likely, they spent more time in their wolf shapes than as men. Why would they need to walk upright, why would they need hands and voices and manners here? And they would all be men. Wolf women were rare, and she was the only one to ever be exiled to the Island of Beasts. The men, the wolves already here—they would tear her apart.

She would not let them.

Morning, she tried to keep sleeping, curled up tight and shivering. If she slept, this might be a dream, she might wake up in her attic servant's room. She imagined a bushy tail pulled up against her face like a blanket to keep her warm. A whole coat of thick fur, sharp claws and fierce teeth to catch rats and vermin to eat. She was already wild, they said. Was why they exiled her here. She could *be* wild. And lose her clothing, her shelter, her wits, her dignity. The ability to stand with her chin up. As a wolf, she could murder them all.

Come full moon she wouldn't have a choice.

No, she would have a plan by then. She would make a plan, she would survive as her own self and not the beast inside her. She would keep herself, and what was left of her soul. Everything was damp: the rock, the ground she slept on, her clothes, bodice, and petticoats. Her tangled hair she shook out and pinned back up. Brushed out her skirt, stamped feeling back into her booted feet, and went out into the bleak morning.

Along the shore she found a couple of crabs, dug for clams and ate them raw, gnawed on seaweed. She collected more driftwood and thought about how to sharpen pieces without so much as a penknife. Found a stand of heather on the far side of the hill and hauled an armload of it to her little hovel to dry.

Piling up wood and brush, she built what she could of a wall to protect the sheltered room. Dragged some stones up to anchor it, grateful for her wolf's strength. It wouldn't hold against attack, but she had high ground here. She would see whatever approached. She chose a couple of good sturdy lengths of driftwood she could use as clubs, and commenced to shaving another down into a rough spear. Even through the heart, a wooden spear wouldn't kill the wolves. But she could give them pause.

Some distance out from her fort, she squatted and pissed in an attempt to mark some territory. She smelled other piss marks, at least two different wolf men farther out on the field. She didn't piss on them directly—it would be taken as a challenge, and they would come for her even sooner, to meet the challenge. This way she only meant to carve out a little space for herself, to send a message: leave me alone, I am no threat.

Still, it didn't take long for the residents of the Island of Beasts to find her.

She smelled him well in advance of his arrival, had time to climb up one of the craggy rocks to use as a vantage, carrying one of her makeshift, inadequate spears. He was a rangy thing, black fur and golden eyes. He trotted around the hill, down the slope toward the beach and then back again, head low and scenting, tail out like a rudder. Tightened his circle on each lap, coming closer. He was big, more than two hundred pounds. As a man, he would be a solid brute.

"Get away, you! Go on!" she hollered, as if he were just a dog and she were just a woman, a housekeeper protecting a flock of chickens. She threw a stone at him, missed.

He danced away but instantly spun back, mouth open and tongue lolling. Laughing at her. She screamed a howl of warning, not that it would do any good. If he charged, she was done for. If he had friends, she was done for. But she would deliver as much damage as she could before then. The wolf circled again, giving her a good look-over, then turned to the field beyond her hill and ran, loping off without a care. She slumped against the rock, leaning on her spear. She had survived her first encounter with one of the exiled wolf men of the Island.

More wolves came, but these walked on two legs. She awoke next morning with their scent on the air from upwind, like they wanted to be sure she smelled them. Heart racing, she left her little fort to see how they would attack and how she might hold them off.

But it wasn't like that at all. Two of them waited halfway up the hill. One was muscular, bearded, a hard-looking man with a glare like stone. He wore boots, breeches, linen shirt, and the red coat of a soldier, all the worse for wear, but he stood straight, a thumb hitched into his waistband. The other was tall, lean, and clean-shaven. Imagine, keeping a smooth face here in this place. His shirt was well tailored, and he wore a waistcoat that must have been silk, the way it shone and fit so smooth. His breeches and boots were also fine, and he had a smirk of confidence. A bit of lordly swagger. He must have been a gentleman, once upon a time.

They were wolves. Not just wolves—they had a power to them, a certain bearing. The assumption that they would be listened to and obeyed. They led packs. She had been told that the island was chaos. That there were no packs, that the law of beasts ruled, which meant there was no law, only violence and blood, and she would be at their mercy. She had not thought to expect . . . this.

The gentleman held up a stick with what looked like a worn-out cravat tied to it. Though a little grubby now, it had once been white.

A flag of truce, then. Staring, she leaned out from behind her rock, unwilling to reveal herself further.

"Hallo! You there!" the gentleman called. "Might we have a word?"

She didn't have to come out, she could pretend she wasn't here, but they knew she was. They'd crossed the scent she'd marked.

"I promise, we mean you no harm. We wish to speak with you."

She came out far enough to sit on the rock and laid her spear across her lap. This was as far as she would go, let them do with that what they would.

The gentleman nodded in understanding, even as he frowned.

"I am Mr. Brandon and this is Sergeant Cox. First, however trying the circumstances of your arrival to our Island, may I offer welcome and hope that you are settling in as well as can be expected." His speech was very proper, almost laughably so, given the landscape. He ought to be in a fine drawing room with a matched tea set and ancient portraits on the wall. How had he come to be exiled? Did he know Edgerton?

The soldier, Cox, glared at him a moment, then rolled his eyes. Brandon huffed a little. "Yes, well. To explain the rest to you, then . . . each of us commands one of the Island's two packs. We are here to . . . invite you, I think is not too strong a word. That is, we'd each like to make an offer, so that you may choose which of us to ally yourself with."

"You'll be safer with one of us." Cox's accent was rougher, his manner straightforward. Not a gentleman. She caught his scent, studied the hint of gold in his eyes—he was the rangy black wolf who'd visited her yesterday. A scouting mission.

"And so we do you the courtesy of offering a choice, rather than resorting to . . . more direct persuasion." The gentleman showed his teeth, a flash of a smile, and her stomach clenched. As laughably proper as he was, she should not underestimate him. His fine manner disguised a monstrous bearing. Others had likely underestimated him. He likely counted on it.

She could not find words. The beast trapped inside her wanted to howl, her hands clenched on her spear, and she could very nearly feel the claws about to rip through her fingertips, bent on slaughter. She would not choose, she would not, and if she tried to speak, the words would come out all at once in a roar.

They must have taken her for a simpleton. They looked at one another, uncertain.

Cox licked his lips and said, "Full moon's in five days. You'll have to come out then. Then we'll have you."

Her lips curled, a snarl. "You will not. I'll drown myself first."

Brandon smiled. "Ah, she speaks."

She stood and shook the hopeless spear at them. "I won't choose! I won't! That's what got me booted to this bloody place. They told me I must choose, I must be some wolf's mate, but I said no, and I fought, and so they sent me here to be torn apart by brutes. And now you tell me that I must *choose*? No, a thousand times no!"

"It isn't . . . you misunderstand us," Brandon said patiently. "You needn't be anyone's mate. But as the sergeant says, you cannot be alone during the full moon, you must have the protection of one of us. So we—or at least I—propose a more conventional domestic arrangement. More suited to your . . . um." He gestured at her simple clothing, as if that explained everything. This choice actually boded worse than the other. Brandon continued, matter-of-factly. "You see, you are a woman."

She looked skyward and laughed. "And what of that?"

"We have been without women's company for some time. And, well—"

"How dare you, how dare you come here and think you can . . . *use* me so!"

Brandon said, "It isn't that, our motives are entirely upstanding. We've no wish to use you in that manner at all."

The rough-looking man said, "What he means to say is he wants someone to wash his shirts."

"And cook for us. We've had no one to do the mending, either, and—"

She screamed. Clenched fists on either side of her face and gave voice to her fury.

"I take that as a . . . no."

She spoke, snarling. "You've all been here for years, and not one of you ever made a stew or darned a sock?"

"We've done what we can, but a woman's touch—"

She left. Slid down the rock and slipped back into her hovel, pulling her knees up and hugging them hard. So. She had come to the Island of Beasts and found . . . civilization. It was civilization that had put her here in the first place. Looking outside to an overcast sky, threatening more rain, she waited. Her nose flared, searching the air for the men's scent.

At last, Brandon called up the hill. "We'll come back after you've had a bit of time to think things over."

"We've got fire," Cox said. "You want a warm fire and a hot meal, you'll come with one of us."

"Just so," Brandon said.

She put her hands to her ears and squeezed shut her eyes, because she didn't want to listen anymore. They went away.

She carried the spear with her when she went foraging on the strand again. She did not trust that they would let her alone, let her choose. The wolves had managed to get themselves arranged in packs—they would fight over her, sooner or later. Why should she believe that they would let her alone?

She'd never been let alone before.

After gathering more crabs and an armful of seaweed that she thought she might knit into a net to catch fish, she went back to her cave to consider how she might find fire and more weapons. How she might survive the full moon night without being torn apart by the Island's wolf packs.

The gentleman, Brandon, was waiting for her. He stayed the

same polite distance halfway down her hill. When she appeared he glanced at her—and away, and did not try to meet her gaze again. In the language of beasts he was saying that he meant no harm, no challenge. She was unconvinced and kept her own gaze on her hand, around the spear.

He had put a tray on the grass in front of him and knelt before it. The tray held a tin kettle with steam coming out of the spout. A pair of little china tea cups, and how on earth had such delicate things reached the island intact? A clay pot of honey, which smelled of the island's own wildflowers.

"Fancy a cup of tea?" he called to her and drew a strainer out of the kettle. "It's not precisely tea, mind you. But there are patches of mint and lavender growing over on the east side of the island. It can be very soothing, if you'd like to try?"

She sat hard on the grass outside her cave. Of all the laughable, unbearable things Brandon could have offered . . . The funny thing was, her mouth watered. She did want tea. Wanted nothing more than to sit with a hot steaming cup in her hands, breathing in the smell of it. She didn't dare.

They both looked down the hill when a new scent came to them. Sergeant Cox, approaching, carrying his own offering. She squinted, not sure she could trust her eyes. But her nose told her: he carried a bundle of scruffy-looking wildflowers.

"What're you doing here?" Cox said in greeting and stopped on the hill some dozen paces from Brandon.

"Exactly what it looks like. Don't be cross just because I thought of it first. And what did you bring?" Cox held out the bouquet, and Brandon snorted. "Very traditional. Well done."

Except that he let the flowers fall away, and hidden within the bundle was a dagger. The kind of thing a soldier might use to cut a rope or slice a throat on the battlefield. He walked a little ways up the hill, set it on the grass, and retreated.

"I see that you've been putting together weapons. Or trying to, rather. This one's not got any silver in it, but it'll do some damage. If you think it'll help."

Brandon scowled as if he wished he'd thought of it himself. Cox gave him a smug smile and hooked both thumbs in his belt.

It was a valuable gift. Couldn't be that many knives or blades of any sort on the island. He was right, it might not kill, but she could do damage. She could defend herself a little better. She didn't dare take it. She didn't dare choose.

"Oh, I almost forgot. The second half of my gift," Brandon said then, and reached behind him to a small hooded lantern with a candle burning inside. He put it on the grass next to Cox's knife.

Fire. He offered her fire. Warmth, cooked food. And hot tea. She'd only been a few days in the wet and cold, and what they both offered seemed like heaven. Seemed worth whatever price. Her shoulders slumped. She scrubbed her hands across her eyes because she didn't dare let them see her cry. Never mind that they would know, that they would smell the tears on her.

"You're trying to buy me. Both of you," she called to them.

"Let's say bribe, rather," Brandon said, with a wry wink. "So? What say you?"

She couldn't. She simply couldn't. Silently, not sure of her voice, she shook her head and looked at the damp, oppressive sky.

They watched her silently. They didn't cajole, they didn't mock her. They simply waited, their gifts sitting in the grass.

"Will you take a cup, Cox?" the gentleman asked his rival.

"That's very upstanding of you, Brandon. I think I will."

So Brandon poured out two cups of a pungent, acrid liquid that was in fact not very much like tea, and they sipped companionably.

She called to them, "How is it you two are even here and not tearing each other's throats out?"

Brandon chuckled. "Turns out there's nothing on this island worth fighting over. Might as well get along, eh?"

"Except . . . now there's you." Cox grinned.

"I won't let you fight over me. I will not be a prize."

"She's a regular Anne Bonny," Brandon said to Cox. "A Boudica."

"Fierce," Cox agreed. "Can see why the Lord exiled her."

"It's Edgerton himself dumped me out of the boat. You know 'im?"

They both did. Their lips curled, their bodies braced. The fur of their other selves would have been standing on end.

Cox said, "Edgerton is a sniveling, toadying, cowardly piece of shit. I'm sorry he ever laid a hand on you." He settled with a growl burring the back of his throat.

"Just so," Brandon added softly.

She glared. "The Lord and Edgerton and the rest are all right bastards. Why'd they exile any of us? We're none of us a threat. They could have just killed us, executed us for standing up to them. Heads lopped off, no coming back from that. But no, they dump us here. Why? Why go through the trouble? I still don't understand."

Cox stared into the murky water in his cup. "They keep us here in case they need us. An army of chaos. We are here to cultivate our wildness, so that they might come back, capture us, cage us, and let us loose upon the world when they have need of beasts. If Napoleon makes for England, they will send us into his camp at night. Can't say I wouldn't enjoy it myself. But. They could have just asked." He spat the last word.

"So you see," Brandon said. "We resist by being civilized. As much as we can, with no bloody tea to be found." He shrugged and finished off the rest of his cup. Pursed his face and hissed at the taste of it. "Ah well."

"Then can't you be civilized and *leave me alone*?" she pleaded.

"Why would you even want to be alone? It isn't natural," Brandon said with an offended, gentlemanly sniff.

"There are twenty-three wolf men on this island," Cox said. "Our command of the others is vague at best. Some of them won't ask. In the end, we're all beasts, and the full moon is coming. Let one of us look after you."

They would save her from damage, and keep her for their own use.

"Let *me* look after you," Brandon said pointedly.

"You're a fop," Cox spat. "You hardly know which way you're pointed."

The gentleman laughed. "We settled this once before, we can do it again. It won't come to a draw next time, I'll warrant—"

"That's right, it won't—"

"Stop it!" she shouted. "I'll look after myself!"

The two wolves stepped a pace or two apart and had the grace to look abashed.

Brandon gave a quick nod. "My dear, at least tell us your name."

Right now, her name felt like a weapon they would use against her. To *civilize* her. "No," she said, and the growl came through. Her wolf had fought before, she would do again.

"We could just carry her off," Cox said to Brandon.

"The entire point of the exercise was to have the lady's cooperation." The gentleman called back up the hill, "What if we shared you? A month with me, the next with Cox—"

Then she did scream, hands tangled in her hair, and the sound had the edges of a wolf's howl to it. She doubled over as the beast cried out. Wolf would break free and tear them all to pieces, she could do it—

"Girl . . ." Cox said warningly.

"Let's be off, shall we?" Brandon said, brushing grass off his neat trousers. "We'll leave you to it."

The pair of them walked away while she crouched, gasping, struggling to keep hold of herself. At last, after a minute or so of breathing as slow as she could, the beast stilled and she was able to look out with human eyes and take stock.

The men left the knife and candle on the hill for her.

Since taking them would feel like putting herself in their debt, she didn't. The knife stayed unclaimed and the candle burned out.

Five more days passed. She could feel the full moon before it rose, sense the coming light against her eyes, the tug against her gut. The creature within began scratching, pain on the inside of her ribs as if they formed a cage it could break free of. Nothing could stop what was about to happen to her. This was the true punishment. The Lord of Wolves, all the wolf packs, offered protection. That was the pact so many of them made. Submit and be safe. Know your place and keep to it, and those in power will shelter you. She had thrown it all away and hadn't regretted it a whit until this moment.

She wondered which of the wolves on this island would find her first, then rape and kill her.

Refusing the tears that threatened, she carefully undressed, folding and setting aside skirt, petticoat, bodice, shift. She couldn't afford to rip them during her transformation; she had no others. That she would return to wear these clothes again was an article of faith. She must believe it would be so. She was strong, her beast was stronger. Together they would survive. They'd made it this far.

She marked her territory, small as it was, again and again and again.

She and her beast had had nights on the moor that were glorious. Miles of space, no one to answer to, she could run and run and run, as free as she'd ever been, wind in her fur, dew on her tongue. Her first months as the beast were difficult, as her skin ripped apart and her bones broke and reknitted and her own mind felt otherworldly. But the reward had been those nights of freedom.

It hadn't lasted. The Lord of Wolves, his dukes and henchmen, had wanted her. England wasn't big enough for them all to run free, they told her. She must submit to one of them, any of them. Instead she fought, and fought, and fought. And now here was where fighting had got her.

The moon rose, her human body stretched and broke, and her long, despairing howls joined the others on the Island of Beasts, their song reminding her that the other wolves were here, they knew where she was, they could find her. She ought to be silent, she ought to hide—

But her beast was furious and so screamed out, *Come find me if you dare, I am strong, I am monstrous!*

A smuggler of whisky rowed his boat past the island that night, and heard such a cacophony of wailing and moaning that he knew the stories that the ghosts of every sailor and fisherman ever lost at sea had washed up on that desolate rock must be true. He dug into his cargo and threw a bottle of his best into the waves as an offering and didn't stop praying until the shadow of the island was out of sight, and its terrible howling gone quiet.

She awoke naked in her den, tangled in her skirt, and safe. She must have snuggled into the fabric and used it as a bed. It smelled like home. The whole place did, which was why her wolf had come back here. She'd been able to come back here.

She never remembered much from the nights of running as a wolf. Images and feelings. The taste of blood on her tongue—so she'd been able to hunt. Her full belly told her she'd eaten. Her wolf had slept contented. Looking herself over, again and again, disbelieving—she hadn't been damaged. No one had touched her.

After putting on her shift and skirt—she couldn't be bothered to lace up her bodice or even put back her hair—she walked on the beach. Closed her eyes and breathed in the sea air. Smiled for the first time in weeks. She had survived. Somehow, she was still standing, and it felt glorious.

A glint in the surf caught her eye. A glass bottle shoved up on the sand, sliding back on the wave, then rolling up again. Splashing barefoot in the water, she grabbed it up, studied it. It was a full and sealed bottle of whisky. A blessing on her morning. She might not have much, but oh, this was a thing to bargain with.

She hiked back to her den to hide it away until she decided what to do with it. Found Brandon and Cox there at the same place, halfway up the hill. Waiting for her.

They looked like wolf men after the night of a full moon always looked, with shadowed eyes and unkempt beards. Even Brandon hadn't shaved in a couple of days and had scruff on his cheeks. His waistcoat was unbuttoned, his collar open. Cox squinted in the sun, frowning in her direction, if not directly at her, and crossed his arms.

However much she wanted to turn and run, fast as her two legs could carry her—or better, let her wolf loose, she could run so much faster on four legs—she stood her ground. They didn't seem angry. Their gazes turned away. Seemingly bored, Brandon scuffed his shoe in the grass. Cox went barefoot.

Brandon finally smiled. "Good morning, there. Did you have a good run? Can't say you look particularly well rested, but then who can, after such a night?"

She looked frightful, her hair in a tangle down her back, her shift and skirt wrinkled and stained after so many days. And found she didn't care. This was the Island of Beasts. Propriety was a secondary consideration. They regarded her exactly the same as they had before. She was a wolf woman after the night of a full moon, and that was fine.

"I had a . . . a decent night, I think. No better or worse than any other such night, I suppose."

"That's a way of putting it," the soldier said. "No better or worse is a thing to hope for, sometimes. You hunted?"

"Yes. Rabbit, I think."

"We got a sheep," Brandon said smugly. "Was our turn for sheep, this month. They'll get one next month." He nodded to the other fellow.

"You take turns?" she said.

"Well, Christmastime we both get sheep. We have to be careful, not to completely depopulate the island. But you got a rabbit. That's good."

"Yes." She moved closer. She wanted a better look at them. Wanted to know what had happened last night, how she'd managed to have the most peaceful full-moon night she'd had in months, here on the Island of Beasts.

"You have a question," Cox stated, matter-of-fact. Brandon studied his fingernails, picking out a bit of dirt from one.

"You . . . you left me alone," she said. "I was prepared to fight, to defend myself. But none of the wolves came for me."

Brandon finished picking his nails and brushed off his hands. "We convinced our men to leave you be."

"Or we'd rip their throats out. No argument." Cox's smile was mean, toothy. A fierce wolf's grin.

"But why?" she asked.

"That is our bribe," Brandon said. "The one gift you might accept. We leave you alone." He flicked his hand, as if releasing a bird to flight.

"And what do you want in return?"

"Your name?" the gentleman said hopefully.

She thought about it a moment and said, "Lucy. I'm Lucy."

"Glad to make your acquaintance, Miss Lucy," he said.

"Likewise," Cox said, more gruffly. "Three packs on the island, then?"

"Agreed," Brandon said with a brief nod. "But Miss Lucy, I hope you'll understand if we don't allot you your own sheep every month."

She shook her head. "Even my beast couldn't eat a whole sheep on her own."

"Just so."

She didn't know what to think, and felt as if she still swayed with the movement of the boat that brought her here. Her legs gave out and she sat heavily in the grass, cradling the bottle of whisky in her lap. Scrubbed her cheek and swallowed back a tightness in her throat.

"What's that you have there?" Cox asked, pointing.

She held it up. "Found it on the beach."

"Good lord, is that what I think it is?" Brandon's gaze narrowed, amazed.

She studied the label, looked back at them. Relished the feeling of safety she had in that moment. The feeling of peace. It wouldn't last, most like. Couldn't last, on a windswept island wracked by storms and monsters.

Then again, maybe it would, if an island of monsters could choose civility for itself. Unlike the world that sent her here. She cracked the seal on the bottle and pulled the cork. Brandon might have moaned a little. Even from several paces off, his wolf could no doubt smell the heady, oaky aroma rising up. For a moment they simply sat quietly and breathed it in.

"I don't have cups," she said.

"Never mind cups. We're monsters, after all," Cox said. "Just take a swig and pass it 'round."

She did so, turning up the bottle, filling her mouth, letting the liquor burn. Cox reached, and she handed it to him. Taking a chance on him. Trusting.

He drank, let out a laugh. "God that's good. See, it's what this island's needed all along, a woman's touch. Place looks better already." He handed the bottle to Brandon.

"Barbaric," Brandon muttered, but didn't turn down his chance. He took his drink and savored it, eyes closed.

Then he passed the bottle back to Lucy. That was when she knew she would be safe on the Island of Beasts. She stuffed the cork firmly back in the bottle's mouth.

Still wincing from the liquor's sting, Brandon said wistfully, "No offense to present company, but I was meant for better than this." He gazed off at a distant point, maybe at a parlor fire or some fine park in London. Lucy would get his story someday.

"Aye, we all were," Cox said. "They will come for us, you know. The Lords of Wolves and Masters of Blood and all the rest. They will come here expecting to find monsters. Tools they can use in their wars."

The wind blew and smelled of rain. They turned their noses up to it, and Lucy breathed deep the free air.

"We will be ready for them," she said.

THE BEAUX WILDE

I T WAS SAID of Miss Elizabeth Weston that she was a young woman of great fortune and little accomplishment. Since the former went some ways toward making up for the latter, all was well, or should have been. But at twenty-two years of age, Miss Weston remained unmarried.

She played the pianoforte adequately, but would not play before strangers. Her needlework was loose at best, her dancing merely functional. She was pretty, with honey-brown hair, a pert face, and clean skin; but she was shy, and so did not catch the eye as she might have if she smiled more. What she liked best was to read, and while conversations and games of whist might go on around her, she would sit alone with a book of Scott or Radcliffe. She could sometimes be prevailed upon to read aloud, but within a line or two her voice would grow so timid and constricted, she must leave off.

Elizabeth knew what people said about her in whispers, behind their fans and glasses of sherry. Since she could not help what they said or what she was, she withdrew further and avoided the kind of company a highly marriageable young woman in her prime should have sought out. It was a paradox that gave her mother and father some anxiety.

Elizabeth would not have attended the ball at Woodfair at all, but Woodfair was the home of the Brannocks. If Elizabeth had a best friend in all the world, it was Amy Brannock, because what Amy said and the feelings behind her words were just the same. When the invitations went out, Elizabeth accepted, because Amy would not question why she did not wish to dance.

Mr. and Mrs. Brannock greeted the Westons at the door, and Elizabeth immediately looked over their shoulders for her friend, but alas, she was not in view, and Mrs. Brannock had another plan. She and Mrs. Weston exchanged a wink that meant they had been conspiring.

"Miss Weston, it is my great pleasure to present to you Mr. Richard Forester. He is a cousin on my mother's side, and expressed a great interest in meeting you after hearing of your many charms!" Mrs. Brannock offered up the handsome young man as if he were wrapped with ribbon.

Blushing enough to make her head ache, Elizabeth curtseyed, and Mr. Forester grinned as he bowed. Her great charms—her fortune, was what he was thinking. Why was that the first thing anyone learned about her?

"Miss Weston," he said, as he was expected to, as this situation was contrived to arrange. "Would you do me the honor of dancing this next set with me?" Music was playing in the adjoining room. Of course the dancing had already begun, and Elizabeth could not have delayed just a half an hour more to miss it. She looked pleadingly at her mother, but Mrs. Weston seemed so happy, Elizabeth could not argue.

"Of course," she said, and held out her hand. He led her to the ballroom, where couples lined up for the next dance.

His touch was cold. Not physically—she was wearing gloves and could not feel his skin. But something in his eyes, a stiffness in his carriage, held a chill all the same.

"If I may be so bold, Miss Weston, you are the brightest ornament at this gathering. My gaze was drawn to you the moment you stepped through the doorway."

The movements of the dance carried her away from him; when next he took her hand, he said, "You are grace itself."

"I thank you, sir," she said, little more than a whisper.

She heard his words, but another meaning entirely lay behind them, some feeling that came off him like the scent of soap used to launder his shirts, rude and unkind thoughts. His true motivation, his true feelings: she was a silly girl, but someone ought to have her money, so why shouldn't it be him? She wasn't even a prize to be won, but an obstacle to be overcome.

The dances here were like hunts, gentlemen and ladies chasing after one another.

Her foot missed a beat and she stumbled. One of the other ladies, the kind Miss Allison, took her elbow and steadied her. Elizabeth caught more than the kind look in her eyes; there was also the belief, the certainty, that Elizabeth was a talentless creature who ought to be pitied. While Elizabeth might not hear the words, the feelings directed toward her were plain, sharp as the screaming edge of knives.

Much speculation went on among her parents and their friends about what could make a girl like Elizabeth so quiet and withdrawn. Mrs. Weston had decided that her dear girl by some accident of birth was simply too sensitive to withstand the rigors of society and the world. Likewise, Mr. Weston declared that the fineness of her disposition made her superior, but also vulnerable. Those outside the immediate family were sure that the girl had obviously been too coddled, too sheltered, and so would always be weak and sniveling. A gentleman who aspired to marrying her fortune would first have to persuade Miss Weston that she was strong enough to accept a firm proposal. But the more forceful a suitor appeared, the more timid Miss Weston became. Another paradox.

These speculations never happened within earshot of Elizabeth. She knew of them, just the same.

In truth, Mrs. Weston nearly had the right of it: Elizabeth felt everything. The thousand petty dramas of the typical gathering were as shouting in her ear. She felt the prides and hurts of others as pains in her own heart. She knew what she shouldn't: which young gentlemen carried on affairs with their mother's maids, which young ladies were so desperate to escape indifferent families they were prepared to throw themselves into unsuitable marriages. Men who worried over debts, coachmen nursing lame horses—she *knew*. She could not say how, but she did. She knew that one of the brusque suitors she'd refused, Mr. Rackham, would be cruel if he succeeded in winning her; another, Mr. Carroll, would simply ignore her. From the ladies, she felt the gossip about how Elizabeth was proud and odd and would die an old maid if she were not careful. The old men wondered what was wrong with her, that she should turn up her nose at their sons.

She felt herself to be like the ancient Greek oracles, caught up in the torture of ecstatic revelation. Empathy was the word she found— profound, damaging empathy. And she could not tell a soul.

At last, finally, the music ended, and Elizabeth curtseyed with a sigh of relief. Mr. Forester insisted on seeing her to a chair, when all she wanted was to flee.

"Miss Weston, you seem quite flush, do let me bring you a sherry," he said, but he was not concerned with her well-being, only with flattering her so that she might fall in love with him.

"No, I thank you, I only need to sit—"

"Elizabeth! How long since you arrived? I did not see you! Here, come with me, I've been longing to speak with you—oh, pardon me, Mr. Forester, but I must steal Miss Weston away from you, I'm sure you understand." Without further explanation, Amy Brannock swept between them, hooked her arm around Elizabeth's, and pulled her into the next room, leaving Forester staring.

"Thank you," Elizabeth breathed.

"Richard Forester is such a bore, I'm sure you have had quite enough of him. I *knew* my mother was going to waylay you. I had wanted to be there, I was watching for you, but then she sent me off to see that Emma knew to fill the punch bowl—Mother can't leave well enough alone."

Amy looked very well, as she always did, with roses in her cheeks, wearing a pink muslin gown that complemented her light hair and creamy features. Elizabeth wore a gown of blue with lace—it suited her because Amy had helped choose it, and her friend beamed at the compliment Elizabeth paid by wearing it.

In the drawing room they settled on a pair of chairs. Elizabeth could listen contentedly for hours while Amy gossiped. She might not move for the rest of the afternoon.

And then three strange gentlemen entered the drawing room.

The trio stopped at the door to look around, and because they were strangers, everyone else paused to study them.

"Goodness, will you look at them?" Amy said, hand on her breast like some romantic heroine. "Have you ever seen such . . . shapely gentlemen? Is shapely the right word for it?"

"Yes," Elizabeth said. "I think it is."

All three had powerful forms under well-made suits; they possessed broad shoulders and took graceful steps. They . . . *prowled*, looking about with a hooded darkness in their gazes, which scoured every surface, every face. Elizabeth could not take her eyes from them. Mr. Brannock immediately went forward to meet them, shaking hands all around, and the room returned to a normal state of pleasantness, as if a cloud had passed by the sun.

"Who are they, do you think?" Amy asked.

"It's your ball," Elizabeth said. "Do you not know?"

"I'll just go see, then." She flounced up and made her way to where her mother sat with the matrons. Elizabeth felt herself shrinking in her seat, hoping that no one felt the chivalrous need to come and speak with her. She did not mind being a wallflower.

Fortunately, Amy flounced back soon enough. "I've gotten all the news of it from Mother. They are the Misters Wilde, brothers who've come into the neighborhood and have taken the lease at Lilies Park. Father met them in town and invited them, to introduce them to the neighborhood. It never hurts having more beaux among the number, yes? I imagine Father thinks to put them in my way."

"Brothers? They don't look anything alike."

Indeed the tallest of the men was fair; the shortest had a brown complexion, calling to mind the West Indies sun; while the middle had dark hair and striking gray eyes.

Amy furrowed her brow, an expression her mother was always complaining of because it marred her features. "They don't, do they? Ah well, who's to say?"

The middle one, with the gray eyes, caught her staring. She quickly looked away, but knew he still studied her—she felt a focused attention that put her in mind of a hawk.

"That one there has his eye on you, I wager," Amy said, her smile mischievous.

With increasing dread, Elizabeth watched the Wilde brothers make bows to the host, who brightened after a moment's conversation and turned toward her and Amy.

"Oh, you see?" Amy said brightly. Of course she was thrilled. New gentlemen meant new attention.

"Do stay close," Elizabeth said, clutching her friend's hand.

"Of course, but promise me that if he asks you for a dance, you will accept? It's only a dance and perhaps you will like him. Not all men are Mr. Foresters."

That was Amy—every gentleman deserved at least one dance.

Elizabeth looked up and met the gray-eyed gentleman's gaze. This time, she could not look away, though she was sure she ought to. He held her fast, and her heart sped up, like that of a rabbit fleeing the hunt. He offered a polite nod of his head. She had forgotten to breathe.

He was intrigued by her—the same way she could identify arrogance and pity, she knew he was intrigued. But his interest would quickly fade once he actually spoke to her, surely. When she stumbled during their inevitable dance.

"Truly, he will not ask me for a dance," she said to Amy. "Will he?"

"I am certain he means you no harm. Don't be afraid."

She steeled herself as if she were walking into battle. "Then I promise. Because you asked. I may even enjoy it."

"With that one? Oh, please enjoy it!"

At last the gentlemen approached, and the ladies stood to make curtseys as Mr. Brannock presented them.

The tallest one was Vincent Wilde; the shorter, swarthy man was Francis Wilde; and the middle, dark-haired man was Edward Wilde.

Amy's father said, "This is my eldest daughter, Miss Brannock, and her good friend Miss Weston."

"How do you do?" Amy said for them both.

Mr. Brannock said suggestively, "Do you think the music is very good? The quartet came highly recommended."

"It's very good," Amy agreed.

"Indeed," Vincent said.

There was only the slightest pause before Francis Wilde bowed again. "Miss Brannock, will you grant me the next dance?"

Amy's true feelings were as eager as her smile. "Thank you, sir." She took his offered hand.

That left Elizabeth standing before Edward Wilde, whose emotions were plain to her. Though the strangeness of it . . . the gentleman's interest in her was, indeed, for *her*. Not her money, her family, or her brown curls. He might have been as intent as a hunting hound, but the attention was honest. This as much as anything startled her. Perhaps he simply had not been in the neighborhood long enough to hear of her fortune or her oddness.

"Miss Weston, I would not be left behind by my brother, if you will do me the honor?"

She did not think twice before taking his hand. Yes, her stomach might still be roiling. But the feeling was not dread this time. Edward Wilde's touch was light, as if he knew that any pressure on her hand would incite panic. If she wanted to flee, he would not hold her. This comforted her to a degree that surprised her. In turn, Mr. Wilde's feelings also settled.

She would engage him in conversation, if she only knew what to say. She did not have Amy's open nature, alas. The benefit of dancing was that she could pretend to be so engrossed in the music and where she placed her feet that she need not speak.

The couples lined up; Elizabeth repeated steps to herself, watched others for the proper cues.

Mr. Wilde's gaze kept drawing her. In spite of herself, she kept wanting to look at him. To study him. To learn exactly why he was so different from anyone she'd ever met. He and his brothers, really, but he was the one standing before her.

Of course, she stumbled. It was the part of the dance where one crossed over with one's opposite partner, and one was meant to look into his eyes and not at one's feet. She always feared losing her place or running into the other gentleman, and that was what happened—she took a wrong step, saw herself about to collide, and quickly moved to avoid it, which meant she lost the rhythm of the entire sequence and ruined the figure for her partner and the other couple besides.

Mr. Wilde rescued her. He did so deftly and without fuss, when the next bar of music came and it was his and the other lady's turn to cross over, he touched her elbow and pressed her over while nodding to exactly the spot she should have been, next to him, before the music told them to turn half a circle back to their original places. What was more, he did not express contempt or pity, as others before him had done when they tried to dance around her mistakes. He did not leer, did not roll his eyes, and his emotion was . . . sympathy. If he smiled, it was not to laugh at her, but out of understanding, that there was nothing more difficult than remembering where to put one's feet while others were watching you.

The other gentleman, however, chuckled, passing a mocking glance to his lady. The usual behavior that Elizabeth had come to expect.

And Edward Wilde growled at him.

She distinctly heard the burr in his throat. He glared hard at the other man, who stopped, wide-eyed and trembling, before his part-ner pushed him into the next phrase of the dance.

"I beg your pardon," Edward whispered hoarsely, and they crossed over with the next couple in the row. Far from granting him pardon, she wanted to thank him.

She did not make another mistake for the rest of the dance. When Mr. Edward Wilde asked for the next dance as well, she accepted.

Propriety dictated that for the third dance he move to a new partner, and Elizabeth politely declared that she must rest. Much of the company was watching her as she found a chair to sit and catch her breath. She realized this was because she was smiling. Those in attendance had known her since her girlhood, and they were shocked—no, that was too strong a word, more they were all astonishment—because she was not slouching. Might she even be enjoying herself? Because of this new gentleman? When he wasn't dancing, Edward Wilde stalked the edges of the room, glaring at any who dared look at him, until the light-haired brother touched his arm and brought him back to himself.

The music ended, and Elizabeth looked up from her seat to find Mr. Wilde—the dark-haired Wilde, Edward—and Amy approaching.

He said, "Miss Brannock asked me to escort her to sit beside her best friend, so here we are. Might I be so bold as to bring you both refreshment?"

"Oh yes, please, that would be lovely," Amy said, patting Eliza-beth's wrist. "Wouldn't it, Beth?"

"Oh yes," Elizabeth said. "Thank you."

Mr. Wilde made a bow and went away.

Amy took both of Elizabeth's hands in her own and gave her a smile large enough to knock her over. "Well?"

Elizabeth bit her lip. "Well what?"

"What do you think of Mr. Wilde?" she said with mock frustra-tion.

"Which one?"

"Oh, Elizabeth!"

"He is very kind."

Amy seemed to be nonplussed at this. "I will take that to mean you like him."

They had to leave off then, because Mr. Wilde returned—along with his brother, Mr. Wilde. This could become quite confusing, Elizabeth reflected. She couldn't tell by looking who was eldest. They seemed of an age.

The brothers had brought them glasses of punch, and Francis drew Amy off for a conversation—intentionally, Elizabeth was sure, leaving her with Edward Wilde seated attentively beside her. Francis Wilde offered a smile that was not entirely as kind as his brother's.

She made herself sit very straight and proper.

"How do you like the ball, Miss Weston?" Edward Wilde asked in a way that suggested he had practiced this question as a crutch for polite conversation. He was looking about warily as if he expected someone to leap at him.

"I like it very well," Elizabeth said, and meant it, for once. "And you? I mean—you are new to the neighborhood, it must be quite overwhelming meeting so many people. How do you find it all?"

"I believe I find it quite agreeable. I'm not often comfortable in gatherings such as this," he said. "So many . . . people in such a close space."

Would that she could stop blushing. "I understand—about gatherings, that is. They can be very trying. Especially—well. It would all be so much easier if I liked balls and assemblies as much as Amy—Miss Brannock—does."

"Easier?"

She pressed her lips in a sad smile. "At my age I am supposed to be seeking companionship, not avoiding it. And yet, I feel most at ease when I am alone. I am told this will not do for a young lady." His frank interest was startling her into honesty when she should have kept quiet. She rarely talked so much.

"The matrons throw their sons at you in hopes of forming an attachment. I do see how that could be tiring."

She laughed; the sound startled her, and she put a hand over her mouth. "I had three marriage proposals before I turned eighteen. I was able to put them off by claiming my youth, but that excuse no longer serves."

"You are one of those romantic girls who wants to marry for love." The jest was meant kindly. His smile was conspiratorial.

"I want to marry for *trust*, Mr. Wilde. For trust." She lowered her gaze.

He looked thoughtful. "I think I understand you." And he did. Her words had sparked his appreciation.

"I beg your pardon," she said, blushing so fiercely she thought she must faint. "I speak far too freely."

"You do me a great compliment by speaking freely. Thank you."

She was sure that he could hear her heart beating faster. Again, he put her in mind of a hawk—or perhaps a fox.

Because she had said far too much already, she added, "Mr. Wilde, if you are not comfortable in places like this, why tolerate it? You can do whatever you like. You aren't expected to come to assemblies and make a good show of it. You can run free in the woods if you like, and people would merely think you eccentric—"

He looked at her with something like shock, as if she had uncovered some deep truth. She couldn't see the truth itself, only that she had exposed him. She fell quiet because, obviously, she kept saying the wrong thing. His thoughts turned chagrined—he had been working very hard to hide his discomfort, she realized. She had exposed him, and now she was sorry for it.

"My brothers and I," he said, taking a steadying breath, "decided we would like to come in from the woods. There are . . . attractions to drawing rooms and assemblies."

She felt a great welling of desire, and could not tell if it came from him, or from her.

"Edward! My goodness, but people will talk, with you dominating this poor young lady's attentions!" Francis Wilde came over and taunted his brother. Elizabeth couldn't see where Amy had gone to.

She started to say that no, Edward wasn't a bother at all, and then excuse herself to find her friend, but Edward bristled. An emotion that was half annoyance poured from him—the other half was anger. He rose and faced the other. "Francis. Do not interrupt where you're not wanted."

"I'm *saving* you. No—I correct myself. I'm saving the lady *from* you. From the gossip you will incite." He bowed at her, and his smile was mischievous.

She wanted to smile at his playfulness, but Edward's anger confused her. Something more than what was visible was happening here. The two men had both stiffened, and their glares held challenges.

"You are provoking me, sir," Edward said, his voice constrained.

Francis blinked a moment in apparent surprise. "Yes, perhaps I am. And how are you getting on with that?"

The two brothers glared at one another, their expressions fierce.

"Miss Weston, you must pardon my brothers." This was Vincent. He'd deftly stepped between them, grabbed them both by the necks, and glared pointedly until they drew back. The brewing argument vanished. "They are prone to teasing one another."

Francis started, "It was only a conversation—" But Vincent threw him such a look, the small man wilted and ducked his gaze.

Edward, his shoulders still bunched with tension, looked away. "I will remember myself."

"Good," Vincent said to him. "Do endeavor to be pleasant for at least another hour."

Elizabeth could not interpret what she had witnessed—rivalry, authority, uncertainty, all of it. The goading, the reprimand—perhaps it was that they were only brothers, deeply competitive. But there was more than that at work here. *We decided we would like to come in from the woods . . .*

Francis bowed something that was like an apology and went off to another room. Vincent followed him, and she expected Edward to do likewise.

Instead, he turned to her, his expression chagrined. "My deepest apologies. Tell me you will forgive me and grant me one more dance?"

She should have been frightened of him, after what she had seen. But she took his hand and stood before she knew what she was about.

"You like him," her father said, as they sat at supper. She was with her parents near the Brannocks. The brothers Wilde were at the far end of the table. She didn't dare steal a glance at Edward, though she was sure he was stealing glances at her.

Elizabeth gathered herself as well as she could, folding her hands before her. "I don't know that I would use so strong a word," she replied. "Mr. Wilde is very . . . interesting."

"That is more than you have said about any other man who has ever turned an eye toward you, my sweet girl." He kissed her hand and smiled knowingly.

Perhaps she could persuade Edward Wilde to return to whatever woods he had come from, and take her with him. This thought was shocking—and pleasant. She wrapped herself up with it.

While the gentlemen smoked and drank their brandy, Mrs. Brannock led the ladies to the drawing room. The gossip that followed there was mercenary. For once, the thoughts of the women were just as stark as the words they spoke. There were more daughters than available bachelors in the neighborhood, and the arrival of the Wildes was a boon.

"But what of their family? Does no one know anything of them?"

"Clearly, the family made its money in business, this is why no one has heard of them."

"They do have a rough edge to them, don't they?"

"But money forgives many faults, doesn't it?"

A few stray glances went to Elizabeth, who pretended to be occupied with the lace on her sleeve.

"I would know more about them before allowing them to claim one of my daughters."

"Does anyone know if they even *have* this fortune that everyone speaks of? Taking Lilies Park isn't a sure sign of it—"

"They'd have had to prove their credit before taking the estate, surely—"

"I'm sure *I* don't understand such things—"

"But they do seem very fine, don't they? Ah, to be young again, I might try to catch one of them for myself!"

The worry over money was valid, but it had a second function: to raise doubt and thus put off rivals. Whatever they said, the mothers would be happy to have their daughters married to money. None of them were so fine that they could easily refuse anything upward of three thousand a year. If the marriage went poorly years hence, whether because of money or disposition, they would all say that they knew from the first it would be so. None would remember the talk of this evening.

Amy leaned close to Elizabeth. "You are thinking very deep thoughts, my friend."

"Oh? I'm told that thinking in ladies is unattractive."

"Usually it is, but it makes you appear *quite* mysterious. I approve."

"Amy, you're a bad influence on me."

"Good! Now, do share."

She took a deep breath. "I am thinking, what a pack of vultures."

Amy burst out laughing, and the matrons and their daughters turned sharp looks to them, which caused Elizabeth's friend to choke back even more laughter.

The gentlemen joined the ladies soon enough, and there was music and whist. The younger of the company drifted to an adjacent parlor, talking around the fireplace with the illusion of privacy, chaperoned by the company in the other room.

"I think our introduction to the neighborhood has been a great success, brothers," said Francis, the merry one, as Elizabeth thought of him. "What say you, ladies?"

"A triumphant success, I think," Amy exclaimed. "But you will have to hold a ball of your own soon to truly establish yourselves."

"Ah, of course," Francis said. "We cannot escape the balls, can we?"

Vincent and Edward showed sour expressions at this, though they made a good show of fortitude. The drawing room was not their natural habitat, as Edward had indicated. Francis masked discomfort by being forward. Vincent and Edward did not mask it at all.

"But now—I am going to be quite rude," Amy said. "I hope you will not think ill of me for it."

"How could anyone ever think ill of you?" Francis said.

"We know nothing about you," she said. "Where are you from? What can you tell us of the Wilde family? If you do not wish to answer directly, perhaps we can play a game of questions. You need only answer yes or no, then."

"There is nothing to tell, really," Vincent said, eyeing his brothers.

"No, please, a game of questions would be delightful! Are you from the north?"

"Ah . . . no," Vincent said.

"The south, then?"

"No."

The young lady pursed her lips. "Well then, where are you from?"

"Miss Weston," Edward said. He began to pace. "Do you play the pianoforte?"

Elizabeth flinched, startled. "Not very well, I'm afraid."

Francis laughed. "Then we must hear you play, Miss Weston, for all ladies say they do not play well, to better display their genteel humility."

Amy stood and gave a brilliant smile. All the gentlemen must swoon. "Mr. Wilde, we are having such a fine conversation, I'm sure no one wishes to leave it even for a moment just to play something."

Rescue. Elizabeth's relief was physical.

Francis seemed put out. "Really, I thought this was how it was done. The lady is asked to play, she demurs that she does not play well, her assembled friends assure her that she plays very well indeed, and then the lady is allowed to demonstrate her skill without being accused of undue pride." He was teasing. His manner was bright, containing no malice at all, but Elizabeth might wish she weren't the subject of his banter. She was ill equipped to bear it.

"Mr. Wilde, do be still," Edward said, biting the words. Something rose up in him. His lips curled, showing teeth.

Their exteriors were polite. They did not tear into each other with claws—but they wanted to, with the looks they gave one another, raking each other up and down with sharp gazes. Their lips parted hungrily, their teeth were white and sharp.

Elizabeth stood. She did not have to feign an anxious tremor in her voice. "I think . . . I think I should like to take a walk. A turn about the room. To get some air."

The brothers turned to her, still annoyed but they no longer seemed as if they wished to devour one another, and that made a great improvement on Elizabeth's nerves.

"Miss Weston, are you well?" Vincent Wilde asked.

"In truth, the room seems somewhat . . . crowded."

"There are less than a dozen of us here!" one of the other young ladies, one often frustrated with Elizabeth's fragility, exclaimed.

"And yet I think the room is quite full."

"Miss Weston displays a great deal of insight, I think," Edward said. "If I may, I will escort you to the window for some air."

"Thank you, sir."

They went off a little ways, and Edward pushed open the window. The air that came in was cold and damp. Her mother would be horrified of a chill overtaking her, but Elizabeth breathed it in gratefully.

They had some privacy. They could speak alone in quiet voices. It seemed wonderfully illicit. Some of the others might think this had all been a ploy on her part to get Edward alone. Amy might have encouraged her to try such a trick, but she would know this was honest. Elizabeth wasn't very good at ploys.

Edward's concern was genuine. He did not think this was a ploy.

"Thank you," she said softly. "I was quite overwhelmed."

"You are not wrong about the room," Edward said. "It is more full than it appears."

"I think that is because the personalities of you and your brothers are so very large. When you were boys your mother and father must have despaired of ever having peace again. Except—you are not truly brothers, are you?"

"How do you guess that? I know we do not favor one another, but it is very forward of you to say so."

"I have never done a forward thing in all my life but talk to you."

"You—your insight . . . it astonishes me." His whole manner had stiffened.

She had never wanted to understand someone as much as she wanted to understand him. At the moment, he was building walls in his mind to keep her out.

"I am not trying to astonish, truly."

"It makes you all the more intriguing."

She had never before wanted to kiss someone, but she could finally see why one might want to. If she leaned in, if she put her hand on his chest—it was scandalous. She also felt that if she tried to kiss him, he would let her.

He shook his head and took a step back, and she felt as if a chasm opened between them.

"I fear, Miss Weston, that I have misled you. I admire you, but I cannot do more than that. This is for your own safety, please believe me."

He was not lying. But he was disguising the full truth.

"Mr. Wilde—" But he had already walked away.

Amy interrogated her thoroughly.

"But what did he *say*?"

Heads bent together, no one could hear them. The evening was over. Elizabeth was in her coat, waiting in the foyer for the carriages to be drawn up. The brothers Wilde were nowhere to be seen.

"That this was for my own safety, and then he left. He was unhappy, I could see that he was."

"Of course he was, to give you up. My dear, he has used you very ill, to draw you in and then drop you like . . . like a handkerchief." She frowned at her own metaphor.

"I do not know what I did wrong. Perhaps I spoke too freely—"

"Oh, do not blame yourself. Who can understand men?"

They kissed cheeks in farewell and the Westons left in their carriage. When her father asked her how she liked the evening, she only said that she liked it well enough, but that she was tired now and didn't want to speak.

That night, a wolf howled across the valley. She had never before heard such a sound, a plaintive cry, a heart breaking as the piercing note drew long and faded. The tenor of longing, and of uncertainty, was familiar to her. It should not have been. The sound was the frustration of someone who had been unhappily standing in close company all evening, but who no longer felt at home in the woods, either. The cry of someone who would be pleased to dance, if only he could find the right partner.

Because she had danced so much more than she was used to, because she had spoken so freely to Edward Wilde, she was feeling brave, and so she donned her coat and took a lantern and went out to the grounds of the manor.

She did not think to search so much as she meant to let herself be found. But the wolf did not cry again. "Edward!" she called out once, but her voice echoed strangely and she cringed. Perhaps she should go to the edge of the wooded park and wait for him.

Her slippers grew wet with dew, as did the hem of her nightdress. She ought to have put on better clothes; she thought her heavy coat would be enough. This was all madness—but she did not mind so much. It felt honest, in a world of pretense.

Then she saw him, a huge creature loping across the grass of the park. He was gray, the color of slate and steel, with a touch of mist on his muzzle and belly. His fur stood thickly from his body. His long, rangy legs carried him toward her. His eyes were icy. She should have been terrified, but she was not. She should have imagined the creature leaping and biting into her throat. Instead, the wolf slowed, stopped, and watched her.

He was lost, angry, and terribly sad. She wanted very badly to touch him, to say that all would be well.

At the edge of the wooded park, she sat, hugging her coat around her against the dewy grass. The wolf sat, too. They regarded each other as a couple in a dance might, looking across a space just barely too far apart to reach out and touch, not knowing what to say to one another. The wolf—she felt him being oh so careful; he did not trust himself to move any closer.

Moments passed, and she found she was satisfied to sit, and listen. The wolf bowed his head, his ears pressed back. There was apology in the gesture. Shame. She had seen hounds look like this after being scolded.

"Don't be sorry," she assured him. "Oh please, don't be sorry. It is such a pleasant evening, I am happy to sit with you like this." The air was cool, but with her coat she did not feel the damp.

The wolf settled, lying down and resting his head upon his paws. He sighed a breath that sounded like a whine.

Elizabeth waited.

"Bloody hell!" Francis cried out when he came out through the trees. "I beg your pardon, Miss Weston, you startled me."

The wolf had not startled him; she had.

She blinked awake—she had nodded off. The wolf—he was truly asleep, curled up, tail to nose. She flattered herself that she had given him some comfort, to allow him to rest.

Vincent came up behind Francis. Both stood, wearing coats and looking harried. The masks were gone.

"Mr. Wilde . . . and Mr. Wilde," she said, thinking that she ought to stand, but she did not want to disturb the wolf's rest. Something was happening—she did not look away for fear of missing it. The creature's fur seemed to thin; his limbs seemed to lengthen, claws fattening into fingers. The changes happened with the gentleness of mist fading at dawn.

"Miss Weston," Vincent said. He seemed tired; his brother stood wary. "What in God's name are you doing here?"

She hugged herself. "I do not know. A voice drew me."

"Edward—" Vincent said wonderingly, and she nodded. "But how?"

"Again, I do not know."

Francis laughed, and the sound was a relief. The merry version of him was more pleasant. "Do not take this as an insult, my dear lady—but what are you?"

"I might ask the same of you."

The wolf was half man now, a naked face with pointed ears, sharp teeth behind curled human lips. The fur continued to thin.

Vincent said softly, "He spent too long in a crowded ballroom. We . . . we are not so used to polite company."

"He said you had decided to come in from the woods."

"Yes," the taller brother said. "Francis and I have more . . . fortitude. For Edward, it is difficult. He lasted in company longer than I thought he would, and I believe we have you to thank for it."

"Oh?"

"You give him a reason to be civilized."

He does the same for me, she thought.

Edward Wilde lay before them now, nude, back bowed in the curled shape his wolf had lain down in. He seemed tense, muscles taut, as if dreaming some difficult dream.

"He will sleep for some time," Vincent said.

"He is exhausted," she said.

"Yes," he said. "I'm astonished that you understand. You are not at all . . . frightened?"

She smiled. "Assemblies frighten me. Proposals frighten me. This . . . is merely wondrous."

Her limbs had grown stiff and she took some time rising from the ground. Francis rushed forward to assist but was only in time to touch her elbow and bow an apology. She thanked him anyway. Moving then to Edward, she removed her coat and spread it over him. He made a sound, a soft murmur that she couldn't make out, and nestled more deeply into his grassy bed and sighed in comfort.

"I think I should take my leave, sirs. Do have a pleasant evening."

"Miss Weston, we should escort you home—"

"No, it isn't far, I'll be fine, truly. Stay with Edward."

They bowed, and she curtseyed, which seemed ridiculous here under the moon by the shadow of the forest, but it also seemed proper.

Taking her lantern, she hurried back to the house, shivering in her nightdress, to warm herself in her bed. Her maid never asked how her slippers had become so muddy and grass stained.

Several days later she received a parcel wrapped in paper and tied with twine. She took it to her room to unwrap, because she was sure what the package contained: her coat, with a carefully written slip of paper that said, *My thanks.*

This gave her such a warm feeling she was almost overwhelmed, and she held the note to her breast for a long time.

Elizabeth gladly attended the next assembly in town, not for any expectation that the brothers Wilde would be present, but for the hope that they would. Hope, she discovered, was a powerful inducement to feats of bravery.

She refused two dances, with Amy defending her by spreading about that she had a weak ankle, and was sitting in her usual wallflower role in a chair, happy to watch people enter and exit by the foyer.

And there he was. The three brothers entered, much as they had at the Woodfair ball. Edward was in the middle, and his gaze fell on her directly, as a hound on the scent. Elizabeth stood in a bit of a panic. Vincent nodded to her and took a smirking Francis off to another part of the room.

Edward came to stand before her. He bowed; she curtseyed. The emotions pouring from him were tangled, but the strongest thread she felt was happiness.

He asked if she would like to sit; she did, clutching her hands together in her lap. He sat in the chair beside her. He was like the wolf, ears pricked forward, afraid to move lest he startle her.

"May I speak freely with you, Miss Weston?" he asked finally.

"Of course." They sat a little apart from one another. The distance seemed a mile.

"I could smell you, when I woke. Your coat—it smelled of you." He blushed, trying to find the words. "I have never slept so well. I have never slept so soundly and comfortably, after returning from my other self. I fear I must ask you to run after me every full moon, to drape me with your coat."

"I would do it," she said simply.

He chuckled. "You should stay inside where it is safe. But perhaps I can learn to carry your handkerchief with me."

"I would give you a handkerchief right now, if I had one."

"Elizabeth. There is so much you don't know about us."

She smiled. "You and the other Misters Wilde are not brothers—well, you are in spirit, if not by blood. It is most strange."

"Indeed. And yet no one but you questions it."

"Most people are eager to accept what they are told."

"But not you."

"This is my secret, Mr. Wilde: I can feel lies. And almost every word spoken in parlors like this is a lie. I wonder that you are so eager to leave your woods."

"As I said, there are some attractions here."

"I do like the music," she said.

"Miss Weston—will you trust me?" The meaning behind the words was more than what he spoke, and she understood him perfectly.

"Yes, I will," she said.

Unternehmen Werwolf

OCTOBER 31, 1944

The boy, Fritz, had only a few hours to assassinate the collaborator.

He had completed the first part of the mission the night before, crossing over enemy lines into occupied territory. This was the easy part; he'd done it a dozen times before. But this time, he carried a gun in his pack, not the messages and supplies he'd couriered previously.

As usual on these journeys, he awoke in the morning, safe in a copse of autumn shrubs he'd found to hide in, shrouded by fallen leaves and tangled branches. He was naked, but he was used to that. After giving himself a moment to recall where he was, to reacquaint himself with his human limbs, his grasping fingers instead of ripping claws, he untangled himself from his pack, looped around his shoulders so it wouldn't slip off when he was a wolf. Inside, he found a canteen of water, a day's rations, and common workmen's clothes and boots so he could travel unnoticed. And the gun.

Dressed and armed, he set off. He'd memorized the maps and the description of his target. The village had been occupied by Allied forces for several weeks, and the woman, Maria Lang, a nurse, had not only surrendered to enemy forces, she had been assisting in administration of the village, supplying the American soldiers with aid and information. The village might or might not be recaptured in coming battles, that wasn't his concern. Right now, the woman must be punished. Executed.

Not murdered, they told him. Executed.

He balked, when they told him his target was a woman. That did not matter, his superiors in his SS unit told him. She was a collaborator. A traitor, not worthy of mercy. And Fritz was seventeen now, ready for such an important mission. He ought to be more than a letter carrier. And so here he was, trekking across abandoned farmland toward the edge of a wooded stretch where the collaborator's cabin was said to stand, using his preternatural sense of smell to detect the scent of treachery.

A wolf could cross enemy lines when a man in a uniform could not. When even a man in disguise could not. A wolf traveling in a forest did not draw suspicions. And a wolf could be trained to follow a certain route, certain procedures. To return to a certain spot on schedule. A wolf was wild, but the man inside the werewolf could learn.

Fritz had been a shepherd boy, like in one of the old fairy tales, tending sheep in pastures at the edge of a Bavarian forest. Still living the old ways, with the old fears. Then, he cried wolf, and no one heard him.

He survived the attack, and the bite marks and gashes on his legs healed by morning, and everyone knew what that meant. He knew what to do, and on the next full moon he spent several nights in the woods alone. Howled to the sky for the first time. When he returned, friends and family said nothing about it, did not ask him what he felt or what he'd experienced. He learned to live with the monster, but he no longer looked after his family's sheep.

The war came, and he was too young to be recruited as a proper soldier, but a man from the SS found him. Said he was forming a special unit, and that he'd heard rumors about these forests. About the shepherd boy who no longer looked after sheep. Colonel Skorzeny had a job for him, and you did not tell men like that no, so Fritz went with him.

His new home, a compound fenced in with razor wire—steel edged with silver, he was told—had normal barracks and storage buildings and such. There were also cages, for those who had not volunteered, or who had changed their minds. The soldiers carried knives and bayonets laced with silver. Silver bullets loaded their guns. A mere nick from one of those blades, a graze from one of those bullets, would kill him. Fritz did as he was told.

Fritz had never met another werewolf before joining Skorzeny's special unit. The SS colonel had found a dozen of them across Germany, and he made more, finding soldiers who volunteered to be bitten, and a few who didn't. Fritz was the youngest, and his instinct was to cower, to imagine a tail folding tight between his legs, to lower his gaze and slouch before the older, fiercer werewolf soldiers. Skorzeny would yell at him for weakness because he didn't understand, but the others recognized the gestures of a frightened puppy. Some looked after him, as an older wolf in a pack would. Some took advantage and bullied.

Fritz was a monster from a fairy tale. He shouldn't be afraid of anything. What, then, did that say about the SS soldiers he cowered before? Who were the greater monsters? He told himself he deferred to them because he was loyal to the Fatherland, because he fought for the Führer, because he believed. But when he returned from a mission in the pre-dawn gray, lying naked at a rendezvous point as soldiers waited to escort him back to the barracks and the silver razor wire, he knew the truth: he was afraid. Even he, near invulnerable, a monstrous creature haunting dark stories, was afraid. This was the world he lived in.

Tonight was the full moon. He had two choices: to stay human and shoot the woman before night fell, or to wait until the light of the moon transformed him, and let his wolf do the work with teeth and claws.

In the forest some miles outside Aachen, he did not trust his wolf to do what needed to be done. The wolf worked on instinct, on gut feeling, and in the end Fritz could not tell his wolf what to do, especially on a full moon night. He had tried to argue with the colonel, who wasn't a wolf and didn't understand. But the colonel said this mission must happen now, and must be completed tonight. The Allies were gaining ground and a message needed to be sent to other would-be collaborators, that death awaited them.

So Fritz went. *He* would have to complete the mission, not his wolf, because he suspected his wolf would follow his instinct and run to safety. Away from Germany. He and his wolf had been having this argument for months now.

He found the house; it wasn't hard. As the description said, it stood alone, isolated, and the woman lived by herself. She walked to the village several times a week, but she rarely had visitors. The place seemed oddly comforting: an old-fashioned white-washed cottage with a thatched roof, a garden plot that still had a few odd remnants left over from the fall harvest, a well lined with stones and a wooden bucket beside it. He circled the place, smelling carefully, and only smelled a woman, Maria Lang. And she was at home.

He camouflaged himself behind a tree on a small rise some hundred yards away and watched for the next hour until she opened the front door. He had good vision, a wolf's vision, and even from the hilltop he could see his target. Standing on the threshold of her doorway, she wrapped a woven shawl more tightly over her shoulders and looked out. Not searching for anything in particular, not bent toward any chore. Just looking.

When her gaze crossed the hill, her eyes seemed to meet his, and he started.

Smiling before she ducked her face, she went back inside and closed the door. She had seen him—or she had not. If she had, perhaps she believed he wasn't a danger. Some hunter lost in the woods. A boy from the village.

If she did not believe he was a danger, he could simply knock and shoot her when she opened the door. In loyal service to the Fatherland. Keeping low, moving quickly, he made his way toward the cottage.

He could not explain the feeling of dread that overcame him as he left the shelter of the trees and approached the clearing where the garden plot and semi-tamed brambles spread out. The setting still appeared idyllic. A curl of smoke rose from the leaning stone chimney, indicating warmth and comfort inside. These were like the cottages at home. This should be easy. But he took a step, and he could not raise his foot again. As if the ground had frozen, and his boots had stuck to the ice. As if his bones had turned to iron, too heavy to shift. The cottage before him suddenly seemed miles away. The sky grew overcast, shrouded with clouds, and a wind began to murmur through the trees.

His wolf scented magic and told him to run.

The memory of Colonel Skorzeny and his silver bayonet urged him on, and Fritz forced another step. Forward, not away. Only a few steps, a knock on the door, and he could finish this. The gun was already in his hand.

Next came the voices, a scratch-throated chattering descending over him like a fog and rattling his ribs. He put his hands over his ears to cut out the noise, and looked up to see ravens. Glint-eyed, black, wings outstretched and blurred as they flapped over him, and their nearly human croaking seemed to call, *away, away, away*. They banked and swooped and tittered, brushing his hair with wingtips before dodging. He snapped at them, teeth clicking together, and swatted with fingers curled like claws. Wolf would make short work of them. But he had vowed to stay human. The gun sat coldly in his hand.

He ignored the ravens, which settled in surrounding trees and cawed their commentary at him. They smelled like dust and spiders.

He shifted a leg to take another impossible step, but again he could not move. Vines had come, thorny brambles reaching from the solid hedge to take hold of him, to dig into the fabric of his trousers, and under that his skin. The pain pricks of a thousand little needles. A growl caught in the back of his throat. A threat, a show of anger. Wolf, wanting to rise up. Wolf could escape this, if the human was too stupid to.

Teeth bared, Fritz jerked his leg forward, then the next. His trousers ripped, as did his skin. Blood trickled down his legs. Still the brambles climbed, reaching for his middle, grasping for his arms, pulling him away from the cottage. He twisted, lunging one way and another, hoping to break away, and it worked. Vines ripped, he progressed another foot or two, and his momentum carried him full around—and when he faced away from the cottage, the brambles vanished.

For a long time he stood and looked across the clearing to the straight pines of the forest, all quiet, all peaceful. He could move freely—as long as he moved away from the cottage. It was all illusion. His breath caught.

He really had no choice about what path to choose. He could not fail in his mission. He could not take the coward's route. But when he turned back to the cottage, the brambles returned, the battle resumed. His wolf's strength let him fight on when a normal person would have been overwhelmed, succumbing to the blood and pain of the thorny wall. He wrenched, pushed, twisted, and growled, until the last strand of vine broke away, and he was through, close enough to the cottage to touch.

His wolf's agility meant he sensed the ground give way a moment before it did. A hole opened—no, a trench, or a moat even. A cleft in the earth, circling the cottage, splitting open and falling to darkness. Fritz sprang back, balanced as if on a wolf's sure paws, to keep from falling backward into the vines, or forward into the pit. His toes pushed a stone and few bits of brown earth forward, and the pieces rattled down the sides to some unseen bottom.

Colonel Skorzeny had not told him that Maria Lang was a witch.

The cleft widened, the edge nearest him crumbling further, forcing him to inch away until the brambles with their reaching thorns threatened to claw into his back. This was impossible. This also made him furious. He wasn't a boy, a feckless common soldier, he was a wolf. Hitler's werewolves, the colonel called them, and they saluted with their *heils* and expected victory.

Fritz dug his booted toes into the earth, called on wolf's strength, imagined the light of the coming full moon filling him further, giving him power. He took a single running step and jumped. Crashed to the ground on the other side of the pit, rolled once, hit the cottage's front door, and slumped to a rest. His ears were ringing, his muscles ached. He'd only traveled a few feet but felt as if he'd run for miles. For a moment, he couldn't remember why he'd come here at all.

The door opened, and the woman stood on the threshold, looking down on him. His information said she was in her thirties, but he couldn't decide if she looked old or young. Her hair was black, tied under a blue kerchief. Her lips were full, but pale. Laugh lines creased her eyes. Her hands were thin, calloused.

"Boy, would you like some tea?" she said. Her voice was clear, amiable. Something like an aunt, not so much like a grandmother, and nothing like a witch.

"But I am a werewolf," he blurted, perhaps the first time he had ever stated this aloud.

"Yes, I know," she answered.

He looked over his shoulder at the way he'd come. The clearing, the garden, the forest and hill beyond—all were normal, utterly ordinary, the way they had been when he arrived. He looked at the gun in his hand, and the woman who didn't seem at all afraid. Sighing, he climbed up off the ground and followed her inside.

She showed him to a straight-backed, rough-hewn chair, and obediently he sat. She had an old-fashioned open hearth with a fire burning, and already had a kettle set to boiling water. He watched as she used a dish cloth to move the kettle from the fire, pour water into a teapot, and scoop in herbs from an earthenware jar.

He looked around. The place was filled with herbs, jars of them lined up on a shelf, bundles of them hanging from roof beams, mortars and pestles sitting on a work table in the center of the room, all dusted with herbs. The pungent smell, strong as a Christmas dinner, made him sneeze. Stairs led up, probably to an attic bedroom. The whole cottage was as cozy as one could wish for, insulated and warm, filled with signs of home. Fritz was surprised that his wolf wasn't complaining about the closed space and the shut door. His wolf did not feel trapped, but instead had settled, like a puppy curled by a fire.

He blinked up at the woman, confused. "They told me you were a nurse."

"Healer, not a nurse. They couldn't tell the difference, I'm sure."

"You're a witch."

She smirked at him. "You are very young. Here, have some tea."

And just like that she presented him with a teacup and set it in his hands as she slipped the gun away from him. He didn't even notice until he'd taken a long sip. The tea warmed him, and the warmth settled over him. Citrus and cinnamon, and hope.

Then he stared at his hands, his eyes widening. She set the gun on the worktable out of his reach and left it there as she poured herself a cup of tea.

"What have you done to me?" he cried.

"I haven't done anything." Her smile should have been beautiful, full lips on a porcelain face, but the expression held wickedness. Mischievousness. Tricks. "I have nine layers of protection around my home, knowing people like you would come to kill me. You should have dropped dead—even you, with your half-wolf soul—should have dropped dead before you reached my door. Do you know what that means?

"You never truly meant to kill me. You thought you did, perhaps. You might have held the gun in your hands and pressed the barrel to my chest, but you could not have killed me. Everyone would call you a monster if they knew what you were. But you have a good heart, don't you? What of that, boy?"

He didn't know. He took another sip of tea and kept his gaze on the amber surface of the liquid. She wasn't even wolf, and he was showing her signs of submission. He was useless.

"Then what am I to do?" he said. He knew what happened to those the SS no longer had use for. Skorzeny knew how to kill werewolves.

"It's the night of the full moon," she said.

A window in the front of the cottage still showed daylight. The ghosts of his wolf's ears pricked forward. No, it wasn't quite time, not yet.

She said, "They wanted you to come tonight, on the full moon, because they thought your wolf would make you a killer. Make murdering easier."

"I tried to explain to them, it doesn't work like that—"

"Especially when they have made us a world where men are the monsters, and the wolves are just themselves. Would you like one?" She offered him a plate piled with sugar cookies, wonderful, buttery disks sparkling with sugar, and where had she found butter and sugar in the middle of the war? He recalled the story of the witch who fattened children up to eat them.

"No, thank you," he said. Smiling, she set the plate aside.

"Do you know what tonight is, boy? Besides a full moon night?"

He thought for a moment and said, blankly, "Tuesday?"

"All-Hallows Eve. The night when doors between worlds open. And a full moon on All-Hallows Eve? The doors will open very wide indeed. Where would you like to go? This is a night when you might be able to get there."

I want to go home. That was a child's wish, and he was ashamed for thinking it.

She might have read his mind.

"The home you knew, you will never see it again. Even if I could transport you there this moment, home will never mean what it did.

Germany will never be the same. We might as well all have land-ed on another planet, these last years." She went to the table, wiped her hands on her apron, and began to work, chopping up a sprig of some sweet-smelling plant, scooping pieces into a mortar, grinding away, adding another herb, then oil to make a paste. The movements seemed offhand, unconscious. She'd probably done them a thousand times before. She spoke through it all. "They, your masters, are intent on harnessing the powers of darkness, but they do not remember the old stories, do they? The price to be paid. They have forgotten the les-sons. They put werewolves in cages and think because they have a bit of silver, they are safe."

He leaned back in the chair, sipping his tea as worry fell away from him. He was a child again, listening to the stories of his grand-mother, the old ones, about dark woods and evil times, bramble forests and wicked tyrants. He was sure he didn't close his eyes—he remembered the fire in the hearth dancing, he watched her hands move as she chopped, mixed, ground, and sealed her potions up in jars. He saw his gun sitting at the corner of the table and remembered he had come for a reason. But he no longer cared, because for the first time in ages, the wolf inside him was still.

"Some of us still have power, and some of us can fight them," she said. "We do what we can. Your masters, for example. Just seeing you, here, I've learned so much about them. They think their werewolves will save them. Even without the true wolves like you, they think that they can act like wolves to strike at their enemies. They think that they can control the monsters they've created. But I will curse them, and they will fail. Keep this in mind when you decide what to do, and which way to run."

He saw an image in his mind's eye of endless forest, and the strength to run forever, on four legs, wind whispering through his fur. His voice tickled inside him, not a snarl this time, but a howl, a song to reach the heavens.

"Boy." He started at her voice, suddenly close. She stood before him, arms crossed. "The moon's up. It's time for you to fly."

The world through the window was dark, black night. The trees beyond the clearing glowed with the mercury sheen of the rising moon. Both he and his wolf awoke. Marie took the teacup from him before he dropped it.

He could change to wolf anytime he liked, but on this night, this one time each month, he had no choice. The light called, and the monster clawed to get out, ribs and guts feeling as if they might split open, the pinpricks of fur sprouting from his skin, over his whole body. His clothing felt like fire, he had to rip free of it. His breathing quickened, he turned to the door.

She opened it for him. "Goodbye," she said cheerfully as he raced past her.

He ripped off all the clothes before he crossed the clearing, left his satchel behind, never thought again about the gun. By the time he reached the trees he had a hitch in his stride, as his back hunched and his bones slipped and cracked to new shapes. His vision became sharp and clear, and the scents filling his nose made the world rich and glorious. Tail, ears, teeth, a coat of beautiful thick fur, and nothing but open country before him.

The doors of All-Hallows Eve had opened, and the boy's wolf knew where to go, even if he didn't. West. Just west, as far and as fast as he could. Armies and soldiers and checkpoints and spies didn't stop him. No one fired on him. All any of them saw was a wolf, a bit scrawny and the worse for wear perhaps, racing through the night, a gray shadow under a silver moon.

Later, Fritz would remember flashes of the journey, woods and fields, a small stream that he splashed through, the feel of moonlight rising over him. For decades after, the smell of fireworks would remind him of the stink of exploded artillery shells that filled his head as he crossed the site of a recent battle. The memories made him think of a hero in a fairy tale, the boy who had to fight through many hardships to reach the castle and rescue the princess. The knight with his sword, slaying the dragon. Never mind that he was a monster, like the monsters in the stories. Perhaps he didn't have to be a monster anymore. Not like that, at least.

He ran all night, collapsed an hour or so before dawn, not knowing where on the map of Europe's battlefields he'd ended up, not caring. He'd run as far as he could, then he slept, and the wolf crept away again.

He'd run all the way to France.

The American soldiers found him naked, satchel and gun and clothing long gone. Hugging himself, he hid behind a tree trunk, torn between fleeing again or begging for help. When they leveled rifles at him, he didn't flinch. He didn't imagine the Amis had brought silver bullets with them. They could not kill him, but they didn't know that. He waited; they waited.

He read confusion in their gazes. He must have looked like a child to them: thin, glaringly pale against the gray of the woods and overcast sky. Lost and shivering. Ducking his gaze, a sign of submission, he crept out from behind the tree. He licked his lips, needing water, but that could wait. Still, they didn't shoot. He decided to step through the door that had opened.

"I . . . I surrender," he said in very rough English, and raised his arms.

KITTY AND THE FULL SUPER BLOODMOON THING

"SO WHAT ARE WE EXPECTING TO HAPPEN?" Ben asked.

"Same as any other full moon . . . but more so," I said. "I'm kind of hoping we all spontaneously break into a synchronized lip-synch of 'Day-O.'"

Even Shaun gave me an annoyed look from across the clearing. So I guess that only sounded like fun to me.

We were at our spot in the national forest up in the mountains, all of us in the pack, waiting. The place—a clearing by an outcrop of granite, surrounded by miles of pines, usually felt like home. Any other full moon night, the pack would gather, and as dark fell we'd shed our clothes. As the moon rose our skin would sprout fur, our bones break and stretch, our four-legged selves taking control. We'd run, we'd hunt—wolves, summoned by the full moon.

This night, however, we nervously waited and watched the sky.

"Supermoon," Ben said, arms crossed, squinting through the trees. The moon—full, silver—was just starting to rise. "So we should all get X-ray vision or be able to fly or something."

"Listen to you," I said. "Like turning into a wolf every four weeks isn't enough of a superpower."

He frowned, clearly dissatisfied. "You're right. Not enough super-power."

"Well, next time get bit by a radioactive spider instead of a were-wolf."

He gave me this look like he couldn't tell if I was joking.

People kept asking me: Supermoon. Blood moon. Did any-thing change? Was it all different? I didn't know why everyone was worked up. The supermoon happened when the moon's orbit brought it closest to Earth—a pretty regular occurrence. The lu-nar eclipse happened whenever the Earth came between the sun and moon—another pretty regular occurrence. Even both together happened every thirty years or so. I had to be honest—the philo-sophical underpinnings of the whole thing weren't at the forefront of my mind when my fingers were sprouting claws and my mouth stretching to fit a predator's set of teeth.

Which they were about to do right now. My skin itched. I flexed my fingers. Elsewhere in the clearing, others of the pack were strip-ping down, while their backs arched and a sheen of fur grew down along their skin. Ben and I watched our pack, and a shadow took a crescent bite out of one side of the moon.

"It's time," he murmured.

I felt it, too. The animal inside of me pressing at the bars of her cage, waiting to break free.

But there was something else. Something . . . kind of tingly. Weirdly, I felt more relaxed, when at this time during a full moon I ought to be feeling more than tense, like my body was ripping apart.

Then I saw Becky in the shape of her sandy-colored wolf charge across the clearing, stumble, and roll over on her back, paws batting at the air, tongue hanging out the corner of her mouth. Shaun's dusky wolf sat nearby, teeth bared, face pointed upward—almost like he was laughing.

Ben watched, squinting. "Does that look kinda weird to you?" He spoke slowly—his words were almost slurred. I couldn't really focus on what he was saying. Claws sprouted from my fingers. I was Changing. But the whole thing felt kinda . . . blurry.

I looked at Ben, and both of us starting laughing. The laughs turned into lupine whines.

"I think we're drunk," I managed to gasp out.

"So. Less Blood Moon and more 'nice dry, merlot moon'?" Ben said, and it was the last thing he said, because his body slipped and the Change washed over him. His wolf emerged—teeth bared, laughing.

I was about to follow. And you know what? That was all right.

KITTY AND CORMAC'S EXCELLENT ADVENTURE

"I NEED YOUR HELP."

I leaned back in my office chair and stared at the phone for a moment. Cormac never asked for help. "Are you feeling all right?"

He blew out a breath of what sounded like frustration, as if he was just as surprised as I was by this conversation. "Yeah, I'm fine. I just need a favor." His tone was curt. He didn't want a discussion.

"What can I do?"

Each word sounded forced out against his will. "I need to see Rick."

Rick, the Master Vampire of Denver. My brow furrowed, confused. "Why do you need to see Rick?"

"Just a message. Not a big deal."

It was probably a big deal. "You could call him yourself—"

"But he'll actually talk to you."

"Come on, what's this about? You hate vampires."

"Just five minutes."

"He's going to want to know what this is about. He won't open the door to you just because I ask." Cormac was a bounty hunter specializing in supernatural creatures. Vampires, werewolves, a lot of other crazy stuff. At least, he used to be, before he went to prison for manslaughter. Now, he was more of a paranormal investigator, along with the ghost of a Victorian magician who lived in his mind. Long story there. He'd mellowed quite a bit under Amelia's influence, or so I liked to think. But yeah, Rick didn't exactly trust him. It sometimes seemed kind of weird that I did.

"That's why I need to you to ask. Convince him."

I was dying of curiosity. At this point I'd make the meeting happen just to see what it was about. And of course I would be there. "Am I going to regret this?"

The pause told me that yes, there was a good possibility that I would in fact regret this. "It'll be fine."

"Sure," I drawled. "I won't be able to talk to him until nightfall."

"The sooner the better."

"Seriously, Cormac, are you in trouble?"

"It'll be *fine*. Call me when it's set up." He hung up.

What the hell had he gotten into, and why was I just going to dive in after him? I'd better get a good story out of this.

Rick agreed to the meeting, probably because after I told him about Cormac's request, he was just as curious as I was. "What could he possibly be up to?" he asked.

"No idea," I answered. "So, you're in?"

He was in, as long as the meeting happened on his turf at Obsidian, the art gallery that served as the public face of the lair of Denver's vampire Family. Cormac wasn't happy about that when I called him.

"I'd hoped we could do this on neutral territory. Your place, maybe."

"Take it or leave it," I said. "I'll be there, if you think it'll help."

He scowled. "I'd rather keep you out of this."

"Nope, you dragged me in already, I want the story."

I met Cormac in the alley behind the gallery. He was a tall, rugged guy with an easy manner and hard face, dressed in a T-shirt, jeans, and leather jacket. After his felony conviction—he'd been out of prison for a couple of years now—he stopped carrying guns, but he still kept weapons. He usually had a couple of stakes up his sleeve. Now he carried them openly, hanging in a quiver off his belt, along with a spray bottle that was no doubt filled with holy water, and a silver cross hanging around his neck. Had Cormac ever set foot in a church in his life?

"Really?" I said, deadpan, glaring at him.

"Just making a statement," he said. Also, he wore sunglasses to protect against vampires' hypnotic stare.

"All right, wait here," I said. He leaned up against the back of the building while I went down a set of concrete stairs to the basement door and knocked.

Rick himself opened the door. Any other Master would have had minions and gatekeepers, but not Rick.

"Hey," I said, waving a little. "Thanks for doing this."

He smiled. "And how are you this evening?"

"Good, good. Dying of curiosity."

"Any idea what he's up to?"

"Not at all."

"Then let's get this over with." He gestured me up the stairs first.

Where Cormac was rough, Rick was elegant, his dark hair short, swept back, his gaze amused. I hadn't gotten the whole story, but he was probably around five hundred years old. He claimed he'd been part of Coronado's expedition into the southwest. Couldn't guess that about him now. His accent was flat American, and while his looks and manner were refined, they didn't seem particular to any time or place. He must have seen so much, had so many adventures. I wanted to hear all the stories, but he rarely talked about his own history.

When we reached the alley, Cormac straightened, his hand moving to his quiver of stakes. Rick lifted a brow at Cormac's armory. I made sure to stand between the two of them. The posturing was stupid; they both knew better than this.

Rick said, "Well, Mr. Bennett?"

Cormac looked down the alley, along the roofline. Everywhere but at the vampire. His mustache shifted when he pursed his lips. I'd have thought this was the hardest thing he'd ever done.

"I'm supposed to deliver a message," he said finally.

"All right," Rick answered. "What is it?"

"The message isn't for you."

Rick opened his hands. "Then why am I here?"

"Because they told me . . . I was told that you'd know where I'm supposed to go."

"You're delivering a message but you don't know where? What are you talking about?"

I watched the back-and-forth, wide-eyed and intrigued. "Cormac. Maybe you'd better start at the beginning."

He scowled, paced a couple of steps, then seemed to come to a decision. "Yeah. Okay," he said, glancing sidelong at an impatient Rick. Then Cormac told a story.

He'd been hired for a job, he said. An easy job, and he should have known better. If you had to call a job easy it meant there was a catch. For the amount of cash he was offered, he figured he could deal with a catch.

The morning after accepting the job, he found a box outside his apartment door. Inside the box was a padded envelope the size of a magazine, labeled with an address but no name. The address was in Ft. Morgan, a small town about an hour northeast of Denver.

He found the spot on a lane off a dirt county road, and Cormac figured even getting this far was enough to earn his pay. He was careful, he kept a watch out. The job might be easy—feeding sharks was easy—but he didn't trust it'd be safe. All he found at the end of the lane were a couple of sprawling cottonwood trees and an old plank board farmhouse that had fallen in on itself decades before.

No one was here to deliver the message to. He couldn't find a mail-box to put it in.

Maybe he shouldn't have assumed the job would be easy.

Cormac studied his maps to see if maybe he'd come to the wrong place. He'd have sent a message to his client to ask for more details, but he couldn't get a phone connection. The address on the enve-lope was specific. This was the right spot. He hunted around for some clue, maybe a forwarding address. Except clearly no one had lived here for years.

Finally, he found a note on the front door. Had to dig for it around a collapsed wall and splintered shingles. It was as if someone had tacked the note there before the house collapsed, which seemed weird and unlikely. Maybe the note had been put here to protect it from the weather.

On the outside of the folded page, the same address had been written in the same handwriting as on the envelope. He unpinned the note, unfolded it, read.

"Talk to the vampire.
I know this isn't expected, but it's necessary."

What the hell was this about?

We are in the middle of something strange here, Cormac, Amelia observed. He'd met Amelia in prison, where she had been wrongfully hanged for murder more than a hundred years ago. She'd also been something of a wizard and had managed to preserve her conscious-ness inside the prison walls. They'd made a bargain: he'd carry her back into the world, and he would get her powers. In the meantime, they had become something like friends.

Was it weird that he immediately thought of talking to Rick, the Master of Denver? He was used to hunting and staking vampires, not talking to them. He could call Kitty, she was friends with the guy, and maybe he'd know what this was about.

So much trouble over such an innocuous envelope. He thought

about ripping it open, looking inside it for some sort of clue about where it was supposed to go.

That would be rather unethical, Amelia thought at him.

"If they really wanted this delivered, they should have made it easier," he grumbled.

If it had been easy they would have done it themselves. I'm telling you, this is odd. I want to know more.

He'd gotten the job via email. He didn't know anything about who had hired him. It had seemed so *simple.*

"I guess we have to go talk to the vampire, then," he said, searching the ruined homestead as if someone might pop out of the broken timbers and explain everything.

Really, it won't be so bad, will it? Master Rick is a gentleman.

He called Kitty.

"I know it sounds crazy, but here I am. I don't know if you're the right vampire, but I had to start somewhere," Cormac said and handed the note from the farmhouse to Rick, shrugging like he was surrendering all responsibility for their current situation. Cormac was a patient guy, but I'd never known him to like puzzles.

Rick read the page. His gaze narrowed. Then he read it again, and glanced at Cormac, his brow furrowed. Finally he handed the note back. "Wait here a minute."

He vanished. In actuality, he moved so quickly he seemed to fly down the steps in a blur, his vampiric speed and power disguising him. Returning after just a couple of minutes, Rick walked up the steps at normal speed, holding a small item in his hand. A key.

"I think you need this," he said. The key wasn't old, but it wasn't new. The size of his thumb, steel maybe. Small, simple, for luggage or a strong box. He held it out. Seemingly in a daze, Cormac took it from him, studied it. Rick explained, "Fifty years ago, I was asked to keep this safe. I was told that I would know who to give it to when the time was right, and that I would be told, 'I know this isn't expected, but it's necessary.'"

Cormac lifted his sunglasses to study the key more closely, vampire or no. "Fifty years ago?" Rick nodded solemnly.

"Who?" I burst in. "Who does that? Who keeps something safe for a stranger for fifty years?"

"Vampires," Cormac and Rick said at the same time. Cormac scowled, but Rick quirked a smile.

I said. "So, fifty years ago, some stranger came to you out of the blue and said, 'Hey, take this for me,' and you were like, 'Yeah, sure'?"

Rick added, "You'll have to trust me when I say this isn't the strangest thing that's ever happened to me."

"Oh, I trust you," I said. "The person who gave this to you—were they human? Mortal?"

"At the time I thought he was perfectly normal. White guy, short hair, about this tall. Seemed intense. But now, I'm not sure. My memory isn't perfect."

"Cormac, what's your client look like?"

"Don't know, they set up the job over email."

"So it could be the same person," Rick said. "But why?"

I pointed at Cormac's hand. "I want to know what that key opens."

Cormac blew out a breath. "This is starting to be more trouble than it's worth."

"You can't quit, not now. I want to know what that opens, who that message is for, why—"

"No," Cormac said. "You should stay out of this."

"Oh no," I said, crossing my arms. "You asked for help. I'm helping."

"This is why I don't ask for help," he muttered.

"I bet you need me. I bet before this is all over, you'll be calling me again, so I might as well see it to the end now."

"I think you're stuck with her for this round," Rick said. "Cat's out of the bag."

Cormac rolled his eyes, and I glanced at the vampire sidelong. "Did you really just say that? Really?"

118

Cormac's gaze turned inward, which meant he was probably having a discussion with Amelia. I bet she was arguing for my side. Cormac was a loner. Strangely, Amelia didn't seem to be. She made him act downright human sometimes.

"Fine," he said finally.

This was a mystery. A quest. An epic. It was awesome. "Cool," I said, grinning.

"Sorry I couldn't do more to help," Rick said. "You'll let me know how it all turns out?"

"I'm anxious to find that out myself," I said. "Have a good night, anyway." Rick made a slight bow and returned down the stairs to his lair.

Cormac was already walking back to his Jeep, and I hurried after him. He settled in the front seat, studying the key close-up by the interior light.

"It doesn't really look like a door or car key," I said, trying to be helpful.

"Amelia thinks she can scry, maybe get some clue where it came from."

"Is that an inscription?" I said, peering at the tiny letters engraved on the key's head. He handed the key over for me to look at with my werewolf vision. I had to squint at it, tip it one way and another a couple of times—partly to make out the letters, partly because I didn't quite believe what I was reading.

"Foothills Savings and Loan? Is that a real bank?" I pointed out the number stamped on it.

"Safe-deposit box, maybe?" he asked, then chuckled.

"What?" I asked.

"Amelia. Why use magic when you can just *look*?"

"Aw," I said, sympathizing. "I have a feeling we're going to need some magic before we get to the end of this."

Cormac didn't seem happy about that. He tapped on his phone, doing a web search, it looked like. "Huh. It's in Golden."

"So it is a real place."

"Guess so. Have to wait until morning to check it out."

"Should I meet you there or do you want to pick me up?"

"Kitty—"

"Come on, please let me tag along. You can't open a secret safe-deposit box without me."

"Okay. Fine. I'll pick you up."

"Yes!" I did a tiny fist pump.

"This is weird. You're not supposed to enjoy this."

"You want to get there right when the place opens, or what?"

At home that night, I tried to explain all this to Ben. He was skeptical. "Should I be worried about him?"

"Probably, but at least if I'm with him I can watch out for him," I answered.

He gave me *a look.*

"It'll be fine," I insisted. "It's just . . . a puzzle."

"I'm in court all day or I'd go with you."

"I'll text you. Don't worry."

"I promise not to worry if you promise not to get into trouble."

I furrowed my brow, because I didn't think either of us could make good on those promises.

Foothills Savings and Loan was a small building with an aging parking lot set back from a busy street, away from the highway and box stores on the newer side of town. It must have been built in the seventies, with that particular style of stucco exterior and wood shakes over the eaves of a flat roof. The name of the bank was painted on a nondescript sign hanging by the door. No other cars were in the lot.

We stood by the Jeep and stared at the building for a moment. "This looks like it should be a dentist's office," I said.

"Let's get this over with." He walked to the door, held it open for me, and we stepped in.

The interior matched the exterior, with burnt umber carpet and brown wood paneling. A Muzak version of "Do You Know the Way to San Jose" played on a staticky P.A. I felt like I'd stepped through a time warp.

"Is this a real bank?" I murmured. "This can't be a real bank." This was the set of a Tarantino film, surely.

The woman at one of two teller counters seemed modern and real enough, dressed in a contemporary blouse and slacks, her dark hair pulled back in a ponytail, wearing just a bit of makeup. She looked to be in her thirties.

"Hi," she said, smiling widely. "Can I help you?"

Cormac showed her the key. "Do you have safe-deposit boxes?"

She studied the key for a moment. "Oh yes, that's one of ours. If you'll come this way, I can get the box for you." We followed her to a small conference room off the main lobby. "It'll just take me a moment," she said pleasantly. "Can I get you coffee, tea?"

"No thanks," I said, my smile frozen, while Cormac studied the room like he expected to find a bomb. I whispered to him, "Don't they usually need to see ID or something before they'll get out a box?"

"No idea," he said. "I'm not going to bring it up."

My pulse was racing, waiting for the teller to bring in the box. What would we find? How amazing was this, a real-live treasure hunt? Cormac's expression never changed. Could he at least *pretend* to be excited?

We both twitched when the door opened again and the teller came in with a metallic box in her arms, about the size of a shoe box, locked tight. She set it on the table and turned back to the door with hardly a second glance. "Let me know when you're finished, or if you need anything else." She must have practiced that smile in the mirror every morning.

The conference room door closed, and Cormac considered the box.

"Open it, open it!" I urged, bouncing in place a little.

Instead, he studied it, feeling along all the edges, turning it over. It seemed heavy.

"Well?" I didn't know how much longer I could stand the suspense.

"Just wondering if there's anything magical going on here," he said.

That set me back. "Oh. How do you tell?"

He reached into his jacket pocket and drew out a small iron nail tied to a string. This was Amelia's work. I still wasn't sure I entirely understood what had happened with the two of them, but I had learned to recognize when she was the one in charge. His movements became more careful, his diction more precise. Cormac had given up his guns, but Amelia's magic was more powerful.

He held the end of the string and let the nail dangle, balanced horizontally. A makeshift pendulum. This was *so exciting*, but I held my breath and tried not to interrupt.

Nothing happened.

We waited. Still nothing, until finally Cormac bundled the string and nail back in his pocket.

"So. No magic?" I asked.

"Not that we can tell from outside."

"Is this going to be like Al Capone's vault? There's not going to be anything in it, is there?" He hesitated, tilted his head. "What?"

"I had to explain Al Capone's vault to Amelia."

I wanted to scream. "Here. Give me the key. I'll open it."

Cormac smirked at me and slipped the key into the box's lock.

So, it wasn't Al Capone's vault. The box wasn't empty, but it also didn't release a puff of stale, ancient, intriguing air like I was hoping it would. My wolfish nose took a long breath just to be sure. And . . . it smelled like an animal.

Cormac opened the lid all the way and we peered inside. The box contained two items: a chunk of fur tied with a string, and a postcard.

"Well, that's satisfyingly cryptic," I said.

He took out the postcard first. It showed a historic Western main street against the backdrop of snow-capped peaks. LEADVILLE, COLORADO, was printed across the scene in friendly letters. The back of the card was blank.

The fur was tawny colored, rough. "Can you tell what that came from?" he asked.

I leaned in to get a better smell. It smelled familiar, but not. Canine, I thought. But . . . I wrinkled my nose, tried again. Then leaned back.

"That came from a lycanthrope," I said.

"One of yours?" he asked.

"No, I don't know who it is. Just . . . it's not entirely canine, it's got that little bit of human in it, you know? No, I guess you wouldn't. I don't think it's wolf. I don't know what it is."

"Huh," he said, frowning.

I took the card from him, thinking maybe I could get a scent off it too, but it had been stored with the fur so long both items just smelled like each other. I studied the picture, looked over the back. Blinked. Looked again, just to be sure. Held the card up to Cormac.

"This . . . this is newer than fifty years old." I pointed out the copyright date on the postcard. Ten years ago. The postcard, and probably the fur, were no more than ten years old.

"So?"

"Rick said he got the key fifty years ago. How can the key be older than the thing it locks? How did this get locked in here ten years ago if Rick already had the key?"

"I'm not here to ask questions. I'm just trying to do this job."

"Maybe there was a second key? A master key?"

"See, logical explanation," he said.

I wasn't convinced. "This is a really weird job, Cormac."

"Yeah, I've noticed."

"So I guess we're going to Leadville?"

"Shit," he muttered.

We told the clerk we were finished with the box. We didn't tell her we'd emptied it. I had a few questions for her. "Just out of curiosity, do you have information on file about when the box was rented and who rented it?"

She went to her computer terminal. It seemed to be a modern computer with a flat-screen monitor, so at least that was up to date. She typed for a minute, then another minute. "Hmm," she murmured intriguingly.

"It's rented under the name of Mr. Crow, and the rent on it was paid in advance . . . well, for a good many years, it looks like."

"Do you have contact information for Mr. Crow?" I asked.

She gave me her best, most professional customer service smile. It was soothing. "Nothing I'm allowed to give out, I'm sorry." She really did seem to be sorry.

"Thanks anyway," I said. "You have a great day!"

"Thank you so much, you too!"

We fled.

I texted Ben to let him know we were going to Leadville, and told him to call Cormac with any questions. When Cormac's phone rang a minute later, the hunter shut it off.

"He's just going to call back," I said. We were already on I-70 west out of Denver. This trip was going to take the rest of the day, at least.

"Then you talk to him, he's your husband," he said curtly.

So I called him. "Hey there, you're on speaker," I said, and held the phone between me and Cormac.

"Why are you going to Leadville?" Ben asked in a frustrated tone.

I answered, "Because we found a postcard for Leadville in the safe-deposit box." A long pause followed. "Ben?" Maybe we'd lost the connection.

"This doesn't make any sense," he said. "Why is your client sending you on a scavenger hunt?"

"I'd like to know," Cormac said. "This message is starting to feel like a grenade. I want to get rid of it before it goes off." The original envelope was tucked in next to the driver's seat.

Ben muttered a curse under his breath. "I hope you're getting paid *really well* for this."

"I even got half up front."

"Well, that's something, anyway. I don't have to tell you to be careful, do I? This feels really off."

"We'll be careful," Cormac said.

"Kitty? Call me the minute you're headed back home. Or if you need help. Or if you get arrested. Or—"

"I'll call. I promise. Love you."

"I love you, too. Be careful!"

I ended the call and blushed a little, with all that emotion out in the open and Cormac looking on, stone-faced. If he cared, I'd never know it.

"Sorry about the mush," I said.

We probably went another mile before he said, quickly, like he was worried he couldn't get it all out, "You two are the best people I know. I'm glad you're together."

In an incautious moment I asked, "So, no regrets?"

He hesitated. Just for a minute. "A few. But it's okay."

"It might have been fun. You and me."

"Maybe. And it would have ended the minute you tried to bring me home to meet your parents."

"Wait. You still haven't met my parents, have you? You really should come over sometime. Maybe Thanksgiving."

"No."

"You wouldn't have to stay long, just have some pie or something—"

"No."

"Oh, come on—"

"I am not going to meet your parents."

I grinned.

Leadville was touted as having the highest elevation of any town in the U.S. Over ten thousand feet. The thin air had a crisp, heady chill to it. I filled my lungs.

"Now what?" I asked.

He pulled the postcard out of a pocket, tapped it on his hand. "I don't know. Smell anything?"

"Rocky Mountain high," I said, drawing another deep breath. "Let's walk around a little bit."

We went down the old main street, a picturesque stretch of turn-of-the-century brick and stone buildings. Lots of people wandering around like us, looking up and around, checking out the shops.

"Maybe I should get a pound of fudge to take back to Ben, to make up for being all mysterious." Or maybe I just wanted to buy a pound of fudge because it was there.

Cormac wasn't paying attention. He stopped, stepped off the curb between parked cars, and studied the front of the postcard. Flipped it over, then back. Held it up at arm's length, then seemed to sight along it.

"What?"

"Check it out." He handed the card over, pointing out a little hole that might have been made by a thumbtack. I had only noticed it before as standard wear and tear.

When I held it up, the image in the photo lined up with the scene in front of us. And the pinhole—I squinted, peered through it. I moved the card away just to be sure of what I was looking at, checked the makeshift viewfinder again. It pointed toward a spot on a distant hillside, a small clearing in the pine forest.

"X marks the spot?" I asked.

"Sure, why not?"

Cormac stopped the Jeep a couple of times to double check landmarks as we took one dirt road after another, passing occasional homesteads tucked back in the trees. Finally, we turned onto a two-track path and he got to practice his off-roading skills. I held tight to the doorframe as we rocked and bounced over stones and hillocks. I looked back once to see a great view of the town, and yes, we seemed to be headed to the right place. Finally, he parked.

We'd come to a small mountain meadow, bounded on one side by a patch of aspens, bright green among the darker conifers. This was how he'd identified the spot back in town, the landmark he'd used to guide us. The clearing was maybe fifty yards across, quiet and isolated. Elk came here to graze—lots of droppings lay scattered, and their scent was everywhere.

A small cabin sat tucked up against the trees, almost invisible. Made of rough-cut logs, its low roof was covered in pine boughs. The whole thing was barely big enough to count as a closet. But someone was living here, I could smell it.

Cormac stalked forward, studying the cabin's exterior and the space around it. On a bare patch of ground, he found a fire circle, ashes ringed by scorched stones. A blackened stick still had a shred of burnt meat on it.

"Fire's still warm," he said. "Whoever it is was just here."

"Is this who you're supposed to deliver the message to, or another clue?"

He looked around, agitated, like he was searching for the hidden camera.

I settled myself. Breathed deep, took in the calm of the forest, the hush of a soft breeze through the trees. Let my Wolf side out, just a little. Her senses, hearing, vision, and sense of smell that could track a rabbit across a prairie. Felt the itch across my shoulders of invisible hackles rising. This was a hunt, and Wolf was ready.

The firepit. The door. The wall outside—and a pile of clothes, army surplus camo pants and a ratty sweatshirt. The scent was all over them. And it wasn't entirely human. I didn't know what it was, except . . . lycanthrope. Canine.

I looked back at Cormac. "It's the same scent as the fur in the box. It's a guy, he's shapeshifted."

He pulled the fur out of his jacket pocket, and I held it to my nose. It had lost some of its strength and had taken on some of Cormac's own smells of leather jacket and maleness. But yeah, it was the same.

"He headed into the woods. Probably saw us coming. I can track it. Or Wolf can track it." If I shifted, Wolf would able to follow that smell anywhere.

"You don't have to do that."

I was already taking off my shirt. I wanted to see this through to the end, to find who that fur had come from. Cormac looked away, frustrated, as I shoved my jeans down around my ankles.

"It's too dangerous," he said.

"Yeah, probably. I'll be careful. We've come too far to not keep going."

Cormac turned his back as I stripped off the rest of my clothes. He'd seen this before, and I'd been a werewolf too long to be self-conscious. But he would never be comfortable with it.

The chill mountain air felt good on my skin, and Wolf was ready.

Werewolves had to change on nights of the full moon, but we could shift voluntarily whenever we wanted. Sometimes, I wanted to an awful lot. To be Wolf was to be strong, free. To flee worry. Wolf was always there, just under the surface.

I imagined my ribs were a cage, holding her in. Most of the time, except for full moon days, she slept. A presence, but not obtrusive, unless I was angry or scared or in danger. Then, she woke up. Then, I could feel her pressing against the bars of the cage, fighting to get out. Claws pressing at the tips of my fingers, ready to burst through the skin.

Most of the time she slept. But when I called her, she was always ready.

"Kitty," Cormac said. I glanced over my shoulder. "I'm right behind you."

"Thanks," I said.

I knelt, put a hand on the ground, my fingers digging into the earth, and I imagined a door opening, the bars of a cage dissolving. And she was *there*. Hundreds of pinpricks stabbed my skin, fur bursting through. My back arched, and I grunted as bones melted, broke, reformed, my whole body wrenching into something else. This pain was familiar, and the best way to cope was to let it happen, let it wash through, fast, fierce—

—blinks at the sun, she so rarely sees daylight, she is a nighttime creature, a child of the moon. She shakes out her fur, remembers . . . she has a job. The scent. Strange, mysterious, like her but not. Muzzle to ground, her nose lights up and she finds the trail. Runs.

She is followed, two-legged footfalls. Hesitates, glances over her shoulder. She knows him, his scent, he is pack, so she continues on. A true hunt, friend at her back, quarry ahead.

The trail is strong, growing stronger. The prey flees, weaving around trees but moving constantly uphill. So wonderful to run, free, surrounded by wild, soft earth under her paws, cool air through her fur, she can keep running, just keep going—

No. Remember the job. Her other self drives her.

She catches sight of her target. Pushes harder. Closes. Her quarry wheels, dances in place. Curious, she pulls up. Studies it, nose flaring. Doesn't bare her teeth because she doesn't feel threatened. It has four gangly legs, scraggily tawny coat, narrow face, smaller nose.

Wary, tail straight out, she waits for a challenge. Braced to spring if she needs to. The other paws the ground, backs up. Isn't staring but isn't backing down. Offers a yip, an uncertain greeting. And then she has a name for him.

Coyote.

A thrill. She—her other self—wants to meet him, speak to him. But he is wary. She circles. He springs. She dashes ahead, cuts him off. He whirls on hind legs and again she blocks his way. He's bigger, but she's faster. She is no threat, her hackles are down. If she can show him that she only wants to talk—

She sits. So does he, some distance away. She licks her snout. Her other self, the daytime, two-legged self is struggling, she wants words to explain, but she only has this body, so she lies down, tucks her tail, waits.

And so does he. Rest, just rest.

She is uncertain, confused, curious, not sure this is safe. But his manner is calm. Her other self urges her, sleep, sleep . . .

Rubbing my face, I woke from strange dreams. I didn't always remember my time running as Wolf. Images, the taste of blood on my tongue after a hunt, flashes of vision. This time felt particularly odd, unreal. Then I remembered a name: Coyote.

I sat up, forest dirt covering my naked side. My hair was a tangle, and I itched.

A young man sat across from me, leaning up against a beetle-eaten pine tree with sparse boughs and dried-out needles. He wore a blanket over his shoulders but was otherwise naked. I took a breath, and yes, he was my quarry, the coyote. Were-coyote. I'd never met one before.

"Hi," I said, sitting up, hugging my knees to my chest. About twenty feet separated us. Just enough to really look at each other, far enough away to not feel threatened.

"Hi," he said back, without enthusiasm. His straight black hair fell to his ears. He was lean, muscular. His dark eyes were wary.

"I'm Kitty," I said, and waited for him to introduce himself.

He stared. "Of course you are."

Cormac jogged up, then stopped, looking back and forth between the two of us. The coyote flinched, but held his ground.

"Who are you?" Cormac demanded, and I was sure the were-coyote would flee again, so I interrupted.

"Cormac, I think that envelope is for him." He had the envelope tucked under one arm, he'd gone back for it, as if he suspected he might need it. Under his other arm, he held a bundle of clothes. "Are those my clothes? May I have them, please?"

He handed them over. I dressed as quickly and smoothly as I could, which wasn't very, wiggling to pull up my jeans. I just shoved the bra in my pocket.

"You haven't been a lycanthrope very long, have you?" I asked the coyote. He glanced away, picked at the edge of the blanket. "That's why you're out here, hiding. While you figure out how to keep it together."

"Feels safer here," he said.

"We have a message for you," I said. "I think. Cormac?"

"Fine. Take it off my hands." He tossed the envelope to the guy, who fumbled with the blanket for a moment but managed to catch it.

Warily, he opened it. Inside, several folded sheets formed a letter. The guy held it up. The outside of the sheaf of pages had one word written on it in block letters: COYOTE. Brow furrowed, confused, he unfolded the pages and started reading.

Cormac's face was expressionless, as if he was just done having opinions about the whole thing. I went to stand next to Cormac, scuffing my bare toes in the dirt. He'd forgotten my sneakers when he'd picked up the rest of my clothes.

"What do you think this means?" I asked softly.

"I don't really care anymore, as long as the check clears."

Well, deciding not to think about it was certainly one solution.

The coyote kept reading. Then he glanced up at us.

"Well?" I asked. "What's it say?"

"I can't tell you," he said. "But . . . thank you. This is important."

"But what is it?" I pleaded, almost whining.

"Sorry." The young man seemed more at ease than he had a moment ago. He leaned back against the tree, snugged under the blanket, and regarded the pages of the message like it had told him something wonderful. Maybe if I was fast enough I could grab it from it. Run away with it just long enough to see what it said. Maybe.

"Well. What's your name, then?"

He offered half a grin. "Can't tell you that, either."

A key from fifty years ago. A safe-deposit box from ten years ago. A guy who wasn't born yet in the first case and would have been just a teenager in the second, and certainly not living anywhere near where the postcard had marked his location . . . "None of this makes sense. It's not, like, time travel—"

"I'll say this much," the were-coyote said. "Mr. Crow sends his regards."

I fumed. Clenched my hands into fists and set my jaw. I wanted to yell. "And who is Mr. Crow?"

He just grinned, for all the world like a coyote yipping in mockery.

I glared a challenge. "My Wolf could have totally taken you, if she'd wanted to."

"I'm sure she would," Coyote said, grinning.

"Kitty, we should go," Cormac said.

But I hadn't gotten the whole story. I wanted to know. I said, "My pack runs in the foothills south of Boulder. You know, if you ever want to come visit."

"Maybe I will. But he's right, you should get going."

Cormac was already walking away. In the end, I knew a wall when I saw one. And this guy . . . he had a big story, I could tell. As much as him not telling me might drive me crazy, I couldn't do much about it. So I followed Cormac back to the tiny cabin, found my shoes, and we left.

We spent the drive back in silence, at least until we hit I-70. Returning to the reality of big highways and traffic seemed to break a spell.

"It's not time travel," he said, abruptly.

"No," I confirmed. "It's not time travel, because if time travel existed, then it would always already exist and would never not exist and we would know about it."

He stared at me. "I don't think I understood a word of what you just said."

"It's not time travel," I reiterated.

"So what was it?"

"Coyote and Crow," I said softly. "Tricksters. We're in someone else's story."

He tilted his head, as if listening. Amelia, explaining to him, maybe. "It's probably for the best we don't know more," he said finally.

"Probably, yeah."

"It's probably messy. Messier."

"Yeah."

"We don't really want to know."

"That's right."

"Goddammit," he muttered.

We stared ahead, driving away from the westering sun.

SEALSKIN

RICHARD'S HAND WAS SHAKING. The noise, the closed space, the lack of easy access to the door were all getting to him. He pressed the hand flat on the polished, slightly sticky surface of the bar. The webbing between his fingers, mutant stretches of skin reaching to the middle joints, stood out. The hand closed into a fist.

Doug noticed him staring at his own hand. "Ready for another one?"

"No, I think I'm done." Richard pushed away the tumbler that had held Jack and Coke.

"This is supposed to be a celebration. I'm supposed to be congratulating you."

"I'm thinking of getting out." He hadn't said the words out loud before now.

Richard appreciated that Doug didn't immediately start arguing and cajoling.

"Can I ask why?" Doug finally asked.

He offered a fake grin. "Well, my knees aren't going to last forever."

"Fuck that. Why?"

He shrugged. "I don't deserve the promotion."

"Richey, that's exactly why you deserve it. Nothing's worse than an entitled asshole in command."

It was nice of him to say so, but Doug had been on that last mission; he knew what had happened. Richard stared at the empty tumbler, trying to figure out what to say to make his friend understand.

Doug kept talking. "You didn't screw up. It could have happened to anyone. Besides, what'll you do if you get out? You have some kind of plan?"

He didn't. His skill sets were highly developed, but highly specialized. He could spend ten minutes underwater on one breath. He could infiltrate and escape any country on Earth undetected. He could snipe a Somali pirate on a life raft from a hundred yards on rough seas.

He said, "Private sector? Make a fortune while the joints still work, then find a beach somewhere to retire to?"

Doug gave him that "bullshit" look again. "Sounds like a waste of meat to me. Maybe you can buy an ice cream stand." He smiled, indicating he'd meant to tell a joke. But he kept studying Richard. "That last trip out really spooked you."

His team was on call to mobilize for rescue operations. The four weeks of boredom and two days of terror routine. This time they'd been tasked with rescuing hostages from pirates in the Arabian Sea. The target he'd shot had been fifteen years old. At the time, all Richard cared about was that the guy had an AK-47 pointed at a boatful of civilians.

The people he was killing were younger and younger, while he was feeling older and older. He didn't know where it ended. When it was his turn, he supposed. So what was the point? Just do as much good as he could until then. By shooting teenagers.

Yeah, it had probably spooked him.

Doug's phone rang. "I have to take this. My sister's been in labor all day and Mom said she'd call with news. I'm going to be an uncle." He grinned big as a sunrise.

"Congratulations," Richard said as Doug trotted out the door. Richard was happy for Doug, and Doug's sister, the whole family. But that left him sitting alone, staring at the rows of bottles on the back wall.

"Can I get you something else?" The bartender was an older woman—Richard couldn't guess her age, either a worn fifty or a youthful sixty-something. Not the usual young and hip type of bartender. She might have been doing this her whole life.

He gestured with the empty tumbler. "Naw, I'm good."

"Looks like you got left."

"He had a phone call. He'll be back."

He must have looked like he was in need of conversation, because she kept going. "You stationed out at Coronado?"

"That obvious?" he said.

"We get a lot of you boys out here. You have the look."

"What look is that?"

"Let's just say we don't get a lot of trouble here, when you and your friends are around."

It wasn't his build, because he wasn't that big. It was the attitude. You spotted guys like him not by the way they looked, but by the way they walked into a room. Surveyed the place, pegged everyone there, and didn't have anything to prove.

Doug came back in and called out to the room, "It's a girl! Seven pounds eight ounces!" Everyone cheered, and he ducked back out with his phone to his ear.

"Well, isn't that nice?" the bartender said.

"I wouldn't know." It just slipped out.

"No siblings? No kids in the family?"

"No family," he said. "Mom died last year, I never knew my dad."

"Well, I'm sorry."

"It's just how it is." He shrugged, still staring at his empty glass, trying to decide if he needed another. Probably not.

"Then you're all alone in the world. The soldier seeking his fortune."

Is that what it looked like? He smiled. "I know that story. You're supposed to give me some kind of advice, aren't you? Some magical doodad? Here's an invisible cloak, and don't drink what the dancing princesses give you. Or a sack that'll trap anything, including death." He'd have a use for a sack like that.

"Got nothing for you but another Jack and Coke, hon. Sorry."

"That's okay. I'll tip big anyway."

"You change your mind about the drink?"

"Sure, I'll take one more."

Doug came back in then. Richard expected him to start handing out cigars, but he just slapped his shoulder.

"I'm an uncle! I'm going to head up to L.A. this weekend to see them. Can't wait. I have no idea what to bring—what do you give baby girls?"

"Blankets and onesies," the bartender said. "You can never have too many blankets and onesies."

"What's a onesie?"

Richard raised his fresh drink in a toast. "Congratulations, brother."

"You know what you should do?" Doug said, and Richard got a sinking feeling. "You should come with me. You're going on leave—get the hell out of San Diego, come to L.A. with me."

"I am not going to hang around while you visit a baby." He couldn't borrow someone else's family.

"You have to do something," he said. "You can't just stay around here. You'll go crazy. *More* crazy."

A soldier seeking his fortune. He didn't even know where to start. He didn't want to look at his hands.

"You think I'm crazy?"

"I'd be lying if I said we weren't worried about you."

God, it was the whole team, then. "Right, okay, I'll find a place to go on vacation. Do something normal."

"Good."

Normal. As if it could be that easy.

He didn't remember learning to swim—he always knew. He did remember the day he noticed that none of the other kids at the pool had webbed feet and hands. He counted it a stroke of profound good luck that he never got teased about it. But everyone wanted him to hold his hands up, to look at them, to touch his fingers, poke at the membranes of skin, thin enough that light showed through, highlighting blood vessels. He loved to swim, and for a long time didn't notice how sad his mother looked whenever he asked to go to the pool of their low-end apartment complex.

They didn't have much money growing up, and he joined the military because it seemed like a good way out, a good way up to better things. He was smart. ROTC, active duty, advanced training, special forces—it all came easily to him, and he thrived. He was one of those masochistic clowns who loved SEAL school. They trained underwater—escape and survival. One time, their hands were tied behind their backs; they were blindfolded, weighted, and dumped into the pool. They had to free themselves and get to their scuba gear. Terrifying, a test of calm under pressure as much as skill. Richard had loved it. He'd gotten loose and just sat there on the bottom of the pool for a long minute, listening to the ambient noise of everyone else thrashing, taking in the weight and slowness of being submerged. He'd been the last one out, but he'd been smiling, and his pulse wasn't any faster when he finished than it had been when he started.

"He's half fish," the trainer had declared, holding up Richard's hand. "Your feet like that too, Fishhead?" They were. He'd graduated top of his class. His teammates still called him Fishhead.

Richard got on a discount travel website and searched under "Last Minute Deals." Belize—intriguing, but sounded too hot and too much like the equatorial places he'd been to recently for professional reasons. San Diego, ironically. Las Vegas, not on a dare. Ireland—ten days, rock bottom airfare and rental car.

Cool, green, quiet. He could have sworn he heard his dead mother whisper, "Do it. Go."

Luck had gotten him back into the country in time to be at her bedside when the cancer finally took her. That was enough to make him believe in miracles. It wasn't much of a stretch to imagine her spirit pushing him on. He booked the trip and wondered why doing so made his heart race.

His mother only ever said two things about his father: he was Irish, and he was like something out of a fairy tale. Richard had figured this was a metaphor, that she'd had a wild fling in Dublin or Galway with some silver-tongued Celt who'd looked like a prince or a Tolkienesque elf. Gotten knocked up and came home. When Richard was young, he'd urged her to go look for him, to try to find him. He'd desperately wanted to meet this fairy-tale father. When his mother said it was impossible, he'd taken that mean to the man was dead.

Ireland, then. Not because he thought he could find his father or get sentimental at some gravesite, or even because he wanted to. But because his mother must have been there, once upon a time.

It would be going back to where he started.

What he loved most about Ireland: how green this country was, and how close the sea was, no matter where he went.

Dublin was a city like any city, big and cosmopolitan, though he found himself having to adjust his thinking—a hundred years was not old here. History dripped from every corner. He didn't stay long, ticking off the tourist boxes and feeling restless. He picked up the rental car and headed down the coast on his third day.

Ireland was having a heat wave. He rolled down the windows, let the smell of the ocean in, and arrived in Cork. Found a B&B at the edge of town, quiet. Went for a walk—these towns were set up for walking in a way few American towns were, a central square and streets twisting off it, all clustered together. Cork was a tourist town, shop fronts painted in bright colors, signs in Gaelic in gold lettering, just like in all the pictures. He still somehow found himself at a bar. Pub, he supposed. The patrons here were older. Locals, not tourists. No TV screens in sight. Low conversation was the only background noise. He ordered a Guinness, because everything he'd read had been right about that: Guinness was better in Ireland.

"You American?" the barman asked. Two stooped, grizzled men who must have been in their seventies were sitting at the bar nearby and looked over with interest.

Richard chuckled. Everyone had been able to spot him before he even opened his mouth. Maybe it was his jeans or his haircut or something. "Yeah."

"You looking for your roots? Family? Americans always seem to show up looking for their ancestors. Every single American has an Irish great-uncle, seems like."

"I'm just on vacation," he said. "Enjoying the scenery."

One of the old men said, "What's your name, son? Your family name?"

"My mother's name was Green."

"Huh. English. Could be from anywhere. Your father?"

"I don't know." He gave a good humored shrug. "He was supposed to be Irish. But I don't know his name."

The barman snorted. "Most folk looking for family at least have a name to go on."

"Sorry. Mom liked being mysterious."

"Hey," the second grizzled old man said. "Hold up your hand there, son."

He got a sudden thudding feeling in his heart. The back of his neck tingled, the sort of thing that would normally have him reaching for his sidearm and checking on his teammates. But it was just him and the curiosity of some old men.

He lifted a hand, spreading his fingers to show the webbing.

The room fell quiet. Richard squeezed his hand shut and took a long drink of beer.

"Son," the second old man said, his voice gone somber. "You're in the right place."

"The right place for what?" Richard muttered.

"You know the stories, don't you?" A couple had come over to the bar, the same age as the two men, their eyes alight; the woman had spoken. "The stories about hands like yours?"

"It's a genetic mutation."

The woman, short white hair pressed close to her head, shook her head. "It's the *stories*."

"Can I get you another?" the barman said. He'd finished his drink.

"No, it's okay. I think I'd better get going—"

The first old man put a hand on his arm. Richard went still. He felt trapped, but he couldn't exactly shove the guy off. The man said, "Go south from here, past Clon and out to Glandore Harbour. That's where you start."

"But what's there—"

"It's very pretty," the woman said.

Nobody would say more than that.

He knew the stories. He got a degree in English with his ROTC scholarship, he'd taken classes in folklore and mythology. Maybe looking for that fairy-tale father.

It was a genetic mutation.

Irish back roads were harrowing in ways Richard thoroughly enjoyed. Barely enough room for cars to pass, no markings, curving right up against hedgerows or stone walls, or to the edge of cliffs, promising a rolling plunge down if he missed the turn. Never a dull moment.

The landscape was searing green, and the sea beyond was a roiling, foam-capped gray. He kept having to draw his gaze back to the road ahead.

He approached Glandore, and the directions he'd gotten from

the man at the bar and the actual available roads he encountered didn't quite match up. But he could see the ocean the whole way down.

That gave him his compass.

The town itself was ridiculously picturesque, a perfect sleepy fishing village. Sailboats dotted the harbor. Richard kept driving to the far side of the harbor. Anticipation welled up. He thought he was going to keep his eyes open for a B&B, one of the cute little houses-turned-inns that seemed to cover the island. But he kept going. He wanted to see if the roads ever stopped.

He wanted to get away from people, away from buildings and boats and civilization. Go someplace where he could be sure to be the only person for miles around. Then maybe he'd be able to think clearly. But the farmland, cultivated squares of fields and pastures, went all the way to the coast. People had lived on this island for a very long time.

Eventually, he parked the car on the verge and walked out to where the roads and farmland couldn't get to—broken cliffs where the waves had eaten away at the rock. There wasn't any room for him to move, between the water and the land. That was all right. He made his way over stone ridges and crevices where he could, letting the spray of breaking waves soak him. A big one would wipe him right off the cliff side. He wouldn't even mind. He could get washed away here and no one would ever know what happened to him. No one knew where he was, no one would look for him—

Instead of letting himself fall toward the comforting waves, he inched further along the rocks until he found a spot where he could lean back, rest a moment, think.

There were seals in the water. They were smaller, sleeker than the hulking sea lions living off the California coast. These creatures were elusive, blending into the color of the water. Domed heads would peek up from the surface, revealing liquid dark eyes and twitching, whiskered noses, then vanish. This—this was what the world might have looked like a million years ago, before people.

A little further on, the cliff curved sharply into an inlet. He'd continue on, explore what was there, then maybe climb up to the top to see where he'd ended up. Maybe find a village and start asking around to see if anyone knew of a guy who'd knocked up an American tourist some thirty-five years ago.

A hopeless quest for the fortune-seeking soldier.

In the inlet, cut not more than twenty feet back, he found a boat. It must have been set on a narrow ledge of rock during high tide and left dry when the tide went out. A standard aluminum rowboat, the kind you'd take fishing on a lake. A niggling in the back of his mind was sad that it wasn't one of the hide-bound *currachs* Ireland was famous for. Just as well. That would have been too perfect.

He looked around for the boat's owner, thinking maybe someone had come out here to fish, had gotten in trouble and needed help. Nothing—just him, the waves, and a couple of seals glaring at him from afar. He got to the boat and looked it over—it had been here a while. A pool of brownish water filled the bottom; a film of green scum clung to the sides. Algae, along with salt and water stains, discolored the outside of the hull.

But a pair of oars still lay inside. The pool of water suggested the thing didn't have leaks and was still seaworthy. However it had gotten here, the boat now looked to him like a challenge.

With a lot of awkward bumping and banging, he managed to get the thing unwedged from the rocks and let it slide down to the water. He kept hold of the edge, scrambling over the crumbling outcrop to hang on to it while nearly falling over, and in, getting smashed up by the waves in the process. It was a fight, but a satisfying fight, and in the end the boat was in the water, drifting away from the cliff, and he was inside.

No oarlocks for the oars, but that didn't matter. First thing was to get away from the cliff. The waves helped. Once he was out and drifting, he made a perfunctory effort to bail out some of the water. He was already soaking wet; sitting in the stale pool didn't seem to make much difference.

Felt good to be out on the water, though. Out on the water with no job to do, just the sun and sky and the gentle rocking. He stretched out on what passed for a bench, lay back with his arms under his head. Maybe he'd take a little nap, see where the waves took him.

That would be an adventure.

The boat thudded, and he started awake. That was a collision, something hitting the hull from underneath. Doug or one of the other guys playing a prank during training, he thought. Except he wasn't off Coronado; he was in the Celtic Sea off the coast of Ireland.

It happened again, something slamming into the hull hard enough to make the boat jump. Dolphins playing? Maybe some of those seals. Some whale species lived in these waters as well. He leaned over the edge to look.

Just gray water, chilled and opaque. He touched the surface, splashing his fingers in the sea.

Hands reached up and grabbed hold of him.

The hands came with powerful arms that pulled him over the side before he could take a breath. He splashed into the water.

There were more of them, many hands grabbing his shirt, clamping around his arms and legs, and brushing fingers through his hair. He could just make them out underwater, like looking through a fogged window. Women, muscular and graceful, with flowing hair fanning around them in the water like seaweed. They surrounded him, curling their long, scaled tails around him in weird embraces.

One of them, black hair rippling in streamers, wrapped her fists in the front of his T-shirt and pulled him close. He squinted to see her, but human eyes weren't meant to see underwater. All he could see were their shapes, and feel them diving and circling, rubbing against him as they passed.

He was dreaming. He'd fallen asleep and was dreaming. Or had fallen overboard and was drowning. That was okay, too.

When she kissed him, he didn't really care what happened next, but as his arms closed around her, the kiss turned into a bite, sharp pain on his lower lip that stopped being fun awfully quick. He made a noise; heard laughter, like the chittering of dolphins. When she pulled away, he tasted blood. Bubbles from his last breath streamed from him.

She shoved him away and dived straight down. Her sisters followed her, ivory and silver bodies falling into the depths, propelled by muscular tails, stray bubbles trailing behind them. Then they were gone. Loose, limp, his body drifted up of its own accord. He broke the surface and took a reflexive breath.

He didn't appear to be dreaming. His lungs burned, and his eyes stung with salt water.

He had no clue how far out he was. Treading water at the surface, bobbing with the waves, he looked around to get his bearings. That far-off strip of land, dark cliff topped with an edge of green, was where he'd been climbing. The boat was gone. Like it had been set out as bait and he'd taken it.

In the other direction lay the low, rocky profile of an island, a spit of rock so low he couldn't see it from the mainland, of a slate gray that blended with the color of the ocean, the skin of seals. This was closer, so this was what he aimed for, just to get out of the water and catch his breath.

The rock wasn't comfortable. It wasn't even that dry—likely, high tide would submerge it. At least the sun felt warm. He peeled off his T-shirt and wrung it out. Pausing, he looked around.

The rock inlet was covered with seals. Writhing bodies humped across the rocks, slipping into the water then lurching back out, grunting, squeaking, barking. Dozens of seals, all looking across the rocks at him, blinking with large wet eyes, studying him. Out across the water, heads bobbed among the rippling waves, eyes and nostrils just above the surface. The mermaids were there too, black- and brown-haired, mischievous smiles flashing.

He was sure if he tried to make a swim for it, the mermaids would force him back if the seals didn't. He was trapped. Captured. He smiled a little because training never covered a situation quite like this. Maybe he could wait them out. If he could hunt for a weapon, maybe he could make them back off.

Then, the seals on the inlet parted. With raucous barking, the crowd of them moved away, some of them sliding into the water, some of them waddling aside and looking back, as if staying to watch.

Three men appeared, standing on the inlet's highest point. There wasn't a boat around. They might have been hiding behind the rock outcrops. They couldn't have swum here; they were dry—and naked, unselfconscious about their lean, tanned bodies. They looked like California surfers without the swim trunks. Muscular, rough hair, pompous smirks. Young guys with something to prove. And they held weapons—spears of pale wood tipped with what might have been broken shells, the jagged edges threatening, and bound with green fibers of seaweed.

Richard wondered exactly what he'd fallen into here.

"Hi," he said, making the word a challenge.

Two of the guys dropped their spears and ran at him. So that probably meant they didn't want to kill him, at least not right off. Small comfort.

Richard was ready. They would go for his arms, hoping to restrain him, so at the last minute he swerved, shoved the first aside, twisted to get out of the reach of the other. Threw his shoulder into a punch at the closest, rushed to tackle the second. They were strong, and fast, dodging and countering all his moves. He'd underestimated them.

But they'd underestimated him as well.

One stuck out his leg to trip Richard, a move he should have seen coming. He fell on the rocks and felt a cut open on his cheek, blood running. From the ground, he grabbed a loose stone, big enough to fit in his hand, with sharp edges. He saw his target's eyes widen as Richard swung up. The guy ducked, which meant Richard caught his chin instead of the forehead he'd been aiming for. The spatter of blood was still satisfying, and the target had to pause a moment to clear his head. This guy's partner was smart enough to stay out of range, so Richard threw the rock at him instead. He didn't think he could lay the guy out, but it might buy him time.

He was reaching for another rock, his only available weapon, when the first guy grabbed his arm—his right arm; they'd paid attention to which arm was his strongest. Richard changed direction, tried to leverage himself free—didn't work. The second guy grabbed his left arm and pulled the other direction. They stretched him out between them, forced him to his knees. He made a token struggle but he had nothing to fight against from this position. When he tried to swing a kick at one of the guy's naked, unprotected genitals, the man swerved out of the way. Their muscles were taut, straining— at least they had to work to keep hold of him.

The third guy hadn't joined in, not even when Richard did damage to his companions. He stood before them, leaning on his spear, regarding Richard with a clear sense of victory. He was the leader of the gang—and he had an agenda, a reason for all this. He was studying Richard. Sizing him up.

"Think he'll do, then?" one of the henchmen said in the thickest brogue Richard had heard since arriving in Ireland. The man might have grown up not speaking English at all. "He can surely fight." He sounded impressed, but the compliment only annoyed Richard. If they'd wanted a fight they could have asked for one.

The leader, Richard assumed—the one who'd kept his hands clean—said in an equally thick brogue, "What are you, then? Not so big as all that, not so tough. And I'd heard you were a big, bad man." Richard grinned back in an attempt to piss the guy off but the man ignored him. "There's some that think we can use you—a strong man with the sea in his veins, even if it's just a little of it. A warrior with skills that none of us have, that might be useful in our battles. There's some that think that blood calls to blood and if I called, you'd answer."

Richard's mind raced to keep up with the words and the tangle of meanings. "Who are you?" he demanded.

"Show me your hand," the leader said. Richard didn't move, because he couldn't.

Clamping his arm against his side to keep him still, the goon on the right forced Richard's hand up, squeezing his palm to straighten and spread his fingers.

"Webbed," the leader observed. "You know the stories?"

Richard struggled, mostly on principle, and the two guards gripped him even harder. His hands were growing numb. "Yeah."

"Tell me the story."

His mother met a handsome stranger under circumstances she never talked about. He'd always lived by the sea, and his mother would always look out at the waves as if she was searching for something. It was just the waves, he thought. How could anyone not look at the waves with a sense of longing? It was just the way things were.

"Tell me the story," the naked man repeated, stepping forward and lifting his spear to threaten.

Richard was sure the guy wouldn't actually hurt him. *Pretty* sure. "The story goes, the child of a selkie and a human will have webbed feet and hands."

"You believe that? You think it's real, those stories you've heard?" the man asked.

Just a mutation. Richard's jaw tightened. "Yes."

The man smiled like he'd won something. "Well, then. Why are you here, selkie's child?"

"I don't know," Richard said, suddenly tired. "I don't even know." He'd wanted to find something, but he hadn't known that he'd been looking. He'd wanted an answer, an origin—but this wasn't quite it.

"I think it's fate." The leader nodded, and his two guards let go. Richard's arms dropped. He wiped blood from his cheek and stared up at this man with salt-crusted hair. "Do you know who you are, selkie's child?"

"I have a feeling you're going to tell me." Richard chuckled, letting go of good judgment, of trying to make sense of this. He ought to be thinking of escape—he was sure he could swim to shore. But he couldn't swim faster than seals or mermaids.

"You're the son of the seal king. And so am I."

The statement was no more outlandish than the fact of him sitting on these rocks, talking to these men in the first place, all of them slipped out of time and reality. He studied the man standing before him, trying to find any part of himself: eyes, nose, build, or manner. He couldn't see it.

"How do you know?"

"The sea hears. The sea tells stories. You know it. You've listened."

He'd been watching the sea the whole drive down the coast. He parked because it seemed like a good spot. He'd been looking for something, or following something. He'd been trying to drown.

He spread his hands, felt the membrane of the webbing stretch. A crowd of seals had gathered, staying a respectful distance off, but they watched, looking back and forth between them with an eerie awareness.

The man—who somehow seemed at home on the rocky outcrops, even as he seemed terribly out of place, bare-skinned and primal in a modern world—moved to a spot and reached into a hidden depression. With his free hand he drew out an object, a folded weight of something, thick and wide, almost too large for him to lift. He held it up like a prize. It was gray, sunlight reflected off a rubbery sheen.

Sealskin.

Richard almost reached out to touch it, but stopped himself. His hand was shaking again.

"My father—our father—sent me to find you," the leader said. "I don't like it at all—there should only be one Seal Prince. But I see why he did. I see the wisdom of it. We need warriors—"

"Why?" Richard said, laughing outright. "What kind of wars can you possibly have to fight, when all you have are spears and seaweed—"

The Seal Prince's two guards tensed, and the damp seals around them grumbled and shifted.

The Prince merely smiled. "There are other tribes of our kind. They raid our fishing grounds and we raid theirs. We defend our territory. But you—you don't understand what it is to have a home, do you, selkie's child? Would you like to learn? I can give you this." The sealskin was a limp, still version of the creatures gathered around him.

Richard had a flash of a vision, a lifetime encompassed in a beautiful moment, sunlight streaming through green-gray waters, nudged by a current as he dived along rocks, his body curving and twisting with the shape of the surf, clothed in the smoothness of the skin he'd been given, the second skin he'd longed for all his life without knowing—

But it would be a borrowed skin, an act of charity. He wasn't born to the water, not like these men were. He was born at the edges, in the surf, half of him in each world. He could swim like a fish and hold his breath for ten minutes. He could fight and kill—and was that all they needed him for? What then, when the war was over?

"He left us. My mother and I—*he left us*. Why should I think that he, that any of you, care about me now?"

"He's been listening for you all this time, hasn't he? We know about the boy you shot, the hostages you didn't save. The feeling of fear and of failure, and how you haven't had a good day since."

He didn't need to be told. Being told made him angry, and it put him back there. That chaotic moment when your thinking brain didn't know what the hell was going on but your training knew exactly what to do, and you already had the target in your sights. Enemy shots fired, and when your captain yelled, "Take it, take it!" you were already breathing out and squeezing the trigger. The Somali boy's head whipped back. A crack shot on rough seas and a rush of triumph. This was the kind of shot they gave medals for. He didn't really see the kid when he shot him. He saw the gun, he saw the enemy, he'd felt very rational about the whole thing. When it was all over, the water he'd swum in looked just like this. When they arrived at the skiff and examined the aftermath, the rush died. The pirates were dead. So were the three hostages. The pirates had been trapped so they lashed out, taken a stand the only way they could, and if Richard had made the shot two seconds earlier, the aid workers he'd been trying to save would have survived. Nobody's fault, no reprimands needed. Just the bad odds of a bad situation. Two sides with guns face off, people get killed. But he should have taken that shot two seconds earlier. And this shouldn't be a world where fifteen-year-old kids carried AK-47s and killed hostages for a living. That moment your training takes over becomes the moment you play in your memory over and over again, wondering what happened and if you could have done it differently.

"The sea is in our blood, and our blood is your blood. We felt the shock, even so far away," the Seal Prince said. "We felt you return home, felt you swimming straight out from shore as far as you could, thinking you'd swim so far out you couldn't get back and so not have to make a decision to keep going at all. You thought maybe one of the white sharks would take you, but they know better than to hunt the son of the Seal King. And now here you are 'cause you've nowhere left to go.

"Take it, Richard. Come with us." He knelt, touched the skin, nudged it forward.

Well, he'd told Doug he might try going freelance.

The water was the only place he felt safe. He was born for the water, webbed hands that worked best when he was swimming. But he wouldn't be a true seal any more than he was a true human.

A mutant in both worlds.

At least when his teammates called him Fishhead, they did it with love. What would they call him here?

Richard chuckled. "I know this story, too. The soldier home from war, who gets advice not to drink what the dancing princesses offer him. He doesn't drink, so he stays awake, and he sees where they really go at night."

The Seal Prince snorted. "Do I look like a princess to you, then? Does this look like poison?"

"No. Are you really my brother?"

"I could say yes or no and you wouldn't believe me either way."

He was right. Richard smirked. "I have a place waiting for me back home." He wasn't born for land or sea. He wanted to keep a foot in each place. That, he could do. He wanted to go home.

The Seal Prince studied him, and Richard couldn't read his expression, if he was surprised or disappointed or full of contempt. He had a feeling he could have known this man his whole life and he still wouldn't be able to read him, to understand him.

"Don't you even want to meet your father?" the Seal Prince asked.

"If he'd wanted to meet me he would have come himself," Richard said. His half-brother didn't deny this.

"Go then, selkie's child," the prince said, gathering up the borrowed sealskin. "Go back to your world. We'll be watching you."

Richard said, "Tell the Seal King—tell him that my mother died last year. She never stopped looking at the waves."

The Prince's smile fell. The two guards, henchmen, whatever they were—they looked to their leader. None of them had expected him to say what he'd said. His news had shocked them. They might have known many secrets, but they hadn't known this.

"I'm sorry for your loss," the Seal Prince said.

"Thanks."

The three men, tanned bodies shining, disappeared behind the same outcrop of rocks they'd emerged from. As a mass, a rippling mob of shining mottled skin, the barking seals lifted themselves, scooted on blubber and flippers and heaved into the waves, splashing a wall of water and mist behind them.

And suddenly the world was quiet. The barking and belching ceased, leaving only waves lapping against the rocks. Richard looked back to the mainland. The audience of seals and mermaids were all gone. The stretch of waves between here and where he'd started was unbroken. He sat there, nothing more than a man who'd lost his boat in an ordinary world. He turned his face to the sun and grinned.

He had a long swim ahead of him.

THE ARCANE ART
OF MISDIRECTION

THE CARDS HAD RULES, but they could be made to lie.

The rules said that a player with a pile of chips that big was probably cheating. Not definitely—luck, unlike cards, didn't follow any rules. The guy could just be lucky. But the prickling of the hairs on the back of Julie's neck made her think otherwise.

He was middle-aged, aggressively nondescript. When he sat down at her table, Julie pegged him as a middle-management type from flyover country—cheap gray suit, unimaginative tie, chubby face, greasy hair clumsily combed over a bald spot. Now that she thought about it, his look was so cliché it might have been a disguise designed to make sure people dismissed him out of hand. Underestimated him.

She'd seen card-counting rings in action—groups of people who prowled the casino, scouted tables, signaled when a deck was hot, and sent in a big bettor to clean up. They could win a ridiculous amount of money in a short amount of time. Security kept tabs on most of the well-known rings and barred them from the casino. This guy was alone. He wasn't signaling. No one else was lingering nearby.

He could still be counting cards. She'd dealt blackjack for five years now and could usually spot it. Players tapped a finger, or sometimes their lips moved. If they were that obvious, they probably weren't winning anyway. The good ones knew to cut out before the casino noticed and ejected them. Even the best card counters lost some of the time. Counting cards didn't beat the system, it was just an attempt to push the odds in your favor. This guy hadn't lost a single hand of blackjack in forty minutes of play.

For the last ten minutes, the pit boss had been watching over Julie's shoulder as she dealt. Her table was full, as others had drifted over, maybe hoping some of the guy's luck would rub off on them. She slipped cards out of the shoe for her players, then herself. Most of them only had a chip or two—minimum bid was twenty-five. Not exactly high rolling, but enough to make Vegas's Middle-America audience sweat a little.

Two players stood. Three others hit; two of them busted. Dealer drew fifteen, then drew an eight—so she was out. Her chubby winner had a stack of chips on his square. Probably five hundred dollars. He hit on eighteen—and who in their right mind ever hit on eighteen? But he drew a three. Won, just like that. His expression never budged, like he expected to win. He merely glanced at the others when they offered him congratulations.

Julie slid over yet another stack of chips; the guy herded it together with his already impressive haul. Left the previous stack right where it was, and folded his hands to wait for the next deal. He seemed bored.

Blackjack wasn't supposed to be boring.

She looked at Ryan, her pit boss, a slim man in his fifties who'd worked Vegas casinos his whole life. He'd seen it all, and he was on his radio. Good. Security could review the video and spot whatever this guy was doing. Palming cards, probably—though she couldn't guess how he was managing it.

She was about to deal the next hand when the man in question looked at her, looked at Ryan, then scooped his chips up, putting stack after stack in his jacket pockets, then walked away from the table, wearing a small, satisfied grin.

He didn't leave a tip. Even the losers left tips.

"Right. He's gone, probably heading for the cashiers. Thanks." Ryan put his radio down.

"Well?" Julie asked.

"They can't find anything to nail him with, but they'll keep an eye on him," Ryan said. He was frowning, and seemed suddenly worn under the casino's lights.

"He's got to be doing something, if we could just spot it."

"Never mind, Julie. Get back to your game."

He was right. Not her problem.

Cards slipped under her fingers and across the felt like water. The remaining players won and lost at exactly the rate they should, and she collected more chips than she gave out. She could tell when her shift was close to ending by the ache that entered her lower back from standing. Just another half hour and Ryan would close out her table, and she could leave. Run to the store, drag herself home, cobble together a meal that wouldn't taste quite right because she was eating it at midnight, but that was dinnertime when she worked this shift. Take a shower, watch a half hour of bad TV and finally, finally fall asleep. Wake up late in the morning and do it all again.

That was her life. As predictable as house odds.

There's a short film, a test of sorts. The caption at the start asks you to watch the group of people throwing balls to one another, and count the number of times the people wearing white pass the ball. You watch the film and concentrate very hard on the players wearing white. At the end, the film asks, how many times did people wearing white pass the ball? Then it asks, Did you see the gorilla?

Hardly anyone does.

Until they watch the film a second time, people refuse to believe a gorilla ever appeared at all. They completely failed to see the person in the gorilla suit walk slowly into the middle of the frame, among the ball-throwers, shake its fists, and walk back out.

This, Odysseus Grant knows, is a certain kind of magic.

Casinos use the same principles of misdirection. Free drinks keep people at the tables, where they will spend more than they ever would have on rum and Cokes. But they're happy to get the free drinks, and so they stay and gamble.

They think they can beat the house at blackjack because they have a system. Let them think it. Let them believe in magic, just a little.

But when another variable enters the game—not luck, not chance, not skill, not subterfuge—it sends out ripples, tiny, subtle ripples that most people would never notice because they're focused on their own world: tracking their cards, drinking free drinks, counting people in white shirts throwing balls. But sometimes, someone—like Odysseus Grant—notices. And he pulls up a chair at the table to watch.

The next night, it was a housewife in a floral print dress, lumpy brown handbag, and overpermed hair. Another excruciating stereotype. Another impossible run of luck. Julie resisted an urge to glance at the cameras in their bubble housings overhead. She hoped they were getting this.

The woman was even following the same pattern—push a stack of chips forward, hit no matter how unlikely or counterintuitive, and win. She had five grand sitting in front of her.

One other player sat at the table, and he seemed not to notice the spectacle beside him. He was in his thirties, craggy-looking, crinkles around his eyes, a serious frown pulling at his lips. He wore a white tuxedo shirt without jacket or bow tie, which meant he was probably a local, someone who worked the tourist trade on the Strip. Maybe a bartender or a limo driver? He did look familiar, now that she thought about it, but Julie couldn't place where she might have seen him. He seemed to be killing time, making minimum bets, playing conservatively. Every now and then he'd make a big bet, a hundred or two hundred, but his instincts were terrible, and he never won. His stack of chips, not large to begin with, was dwindling. When he finally ran out, Julie would be sorry to see him go, because she'd be alone with the strange housewife.

The woman kept winning.

Julie signaled to Ryan, who got on the phone with security. They watched, but once again, couldn't find anything. Unless she was spotted palming cards, the woman wasn't breaking any rules. Obviously, some kind of ring was going on. Two unlikely players winning in exactly the same pattern—security would record their pictures, watch for them, and might bar them from the casino. But if the ring sent a different person in every time, security would never be able to catch them, or even figure out how they were doing it.

None of it made sense.

The man in the tuxedo shirt reached into his pocket, maybe fumbling for cash or extra chips. Whatever he drew out was small enough to cup in his fist. He brought his hand to his face, uncurled his fingers, and blew across his palm, toward the woman sitting next to him.

She vanished, only for a heartbeat, flickering in and out of sight like the image on a staticky TV. Julie figured she'd blinked or that something was wrong with her eyes. She was working too hard, getting too tired, something. But the woman—she stared hard at the stone-faced man, then scooped her chips into her oversized handbag, rushing so that a few fell on the floor around her, and she didn't even notice. Hugging the bag to her chest, she fled.

Still no tip, unless you counted what she dropped.

The man rose to follow her. Julie reached across the table and grabbed his arm.

"What just happened?" she demanded.

The man regarded her with icy blue eyes. "You saw that?" His tone was curious, scientific almost.

"It's my table, of course I saw it," she said.

"And you see everything that goes on here?"

"I'm good at my job."

"The cameras won't even pick up what I did," he said, nodding to the ceiling.

"What *you* did? Then it did happen."

"You'd be better off if you pretended it didn't."

"I know what I saw."

"Sometimes eyes are better than cameras," he said, turning a faint smile.

"Is everything all right?" Ryan stood by Julie, who still had her hand on the man's arm.

She didn't know how to answer that and blinked dumbly at him. Finally, she pulled her arm away.

"Your dealer is just being attentive," the man said. "One of the other players seemed to have a moment of panic. Very strange."

Like he hadn't had a hand in it.

Ryan said, "Why don't you take a break, Julie? Get something to eat, come back in an hour."

She didn't need a break. She wanted to flush the last ten minutes out of her mind. If she kept working, she might be able to manage, but Ryan's tone didn't invite argument.

"Yeah, okay," she murmured, feeling vague.

Meanwhile, the man in the white shirt was walking away, along the casino's carpeted main thoroughfare, following the woman.

Rushing now, Julie cleaned up her table, signed out with Ryan, and ran after the man.

"You, wait a minute!"

He turned. She expected him to argue, to express some kind of frustration, but he remained calm, mildly inquisitive. As if he'd never had a strong emotion in his life. She hardly knew what to say to that immovable expression.

She pointed. "You spotted it—you saw she was cheating."

"Yes." He kept walking—marching, rather—determinedly. Like a hunter stalking a trail before it went cold. Julie followed, dodging a bachelorette party—a horde of twenty-something women in skin-tight mini-dresses and overteased hair—that hadn't been there a moment ago. The man slipped out of their way.

"How?" she said, scrambling to keep close to him.

"I was counting cards and losing. I know how to count—I don't lose."

"You were—" She shook the thought away. "No, I mean how was she doing it? I couldn't tell. I didn't spot any palmed cards, no props or gadgets—"

"He's changing the cards as they come out of the shoe," he said.

"*What?* That's impossible."

"Mostly impossible," he said.

"The cards were normal, they felt normal. I'd have been able to tell if something was wrong with them."

"No, you wouldn't, because there was nothing inherently wrong with the cards. You could take every card in that stack, examine them all, sort them, count them, and they'd all be there, exactly the right number in exactly the number of suits they ought to be. You'd never spot what had changed because he's altering the basic reality of them. Swapping a four for a six, a king for a two, depending on what he needs to make blackjack."

She didn't understand, to the point where she couldn't even frame the question to express her lack of understanding. No wonder the cameras couldn't spot it.

"You keep saying 'he,' but that was a woman—"

"And the same person who was there yesterday. He's a magician."

The strange man looked as if he had just played a trick, or pushed back the curtain, or produced a coin from her ear. Julie suddenly remembered where she'd seen him before: in a photo on a poster outside the casino's smaller theater. The magic show. "You're Odysseus Grant."

"Hello, Julie," he said. He'd seen the name tag on her uniform vest. Nothing magical about it.

"But *you're* a magician," she said.

"There are different kinds of magic."

"You're not talking about pulling rabbits out of hats, are you?"

"Not like that, no."

They were moving against the flow of a crowd; a show at one of the theaters must have just let out. Grant moved smoothly through the traffic; Julie seemed to bang elbows with every single person she encountered.

They left the wide and sparkling cavern of the casino area and entered the smaller, cozier hallway that led to the hotel wing. The ceilings were lower here, and plastic ficus plants decorated the corners. Grant stopped at the elevators and pressed the button.

"I don't understand," she said.

"You really should take a break, like your pit boss said."

"No, I want to know what's going on."

"Because a cheater is ripping off your employer?"

"No, because he's ripping off *me*." She crossed her arms. "You said it's the same person who's been doing this, but I couldn't spot him. How did you spot him?"

"You shouldn't be so hard on yourself. How would you even know what to look for? There's no such thing as magic, after all."

"Well. *Something's* going on."

"Indeed. You really should let me handle this—"

"I want to help."

The doors slid open, and Julie started to step through them, until Grant grabbed her arm so hard she gasped. When he pulled back, she saw why: the elevator doors had opened on an empty shaft, an ominous black tunnel with twisting cable running down the middle. She'd have just stepped into that pit without thinking.

She fell back and clung to Grant's arm until her heart sank from her throat.

"He knows we're on to him," Grant said. "Are you sure you want to help?"

"I didn't see it. I didn't even look."

"You expected the car to be there. Why should you have to look?"

She would never, ever take a blind step again. Always, she would creep slowly around corners and tread lightly on the ground before her. "Just like no one expects a housewife or a businessman from the Midwest to cheat at table games in Vegas."

"Just so."

The elevator doors slid shut, and the hum of the cables, the ding of the lights, returned to normal. Normal—and what did that mean again?

"Maybe we should take the stairs," Julie murmured.

"Not a bad idea," Grant answered, looking on her with an amused glint in his eye that she thought was totally out of place, given that she'd almost died.

Down another hallway and around a corner, they reached the door to the emergency stairs. The resort didn't bother putting any frills into the stairwell, which most of its patrons would never see: The tower was made of echoing concrete, the railings were steel, the stairs had nonskid treads underfoot. The stairs seemed to wind upward forever.

"How do you even know where he is? If he knows you're looking for him, he's probably out of town by now."

"We were never following *him*. He's never left his room."

"Then who was at my table?"

"That's a good question, isn't it?"

This was going to be a long, long climb.

Grant led, and Julie was happy to let him do so. At every exit door, he stopped, held before it a device that looked like an old-fashioned pocket watch, with a brass casing and a lumpy knob and ring protruding. After regarding the watch a moment, he'd stuff it back in his trouser pocket and continue on.

She guessed he was in his thirties, but now she wasn't sure—he seemed both young and old. He moved with energy, striding up the stairs without pause, without a hitch in his breath. But he also moved with consideration, with purpose, without a wasted motion. She'd never seen his show, and thought now that she might. He'd do all the old magic tricks, the cards and rings and disappearing box trick, maybe even pull a rabbit from a hat, and his every motion would be precise and enthralling. And it would all be tricks, she reminded herself.

After three flights, she hauled herself up by the railing, huffing for air. If Grant was frustrated at the pauses she made on each landing, he didn't let on. He just studied his watch a little longer.

Finally, on about the fifth or sixth floor, he consulted his watch and lifted an eyebrow. Then he opened the door. Julie braced for danger—after the empty elevator shaft, anything could happen: explosions blasting in their faces, ax-wielding murderer waiting for them, Mafioso gunfight—but nothing happened.

"Shall we?" Grant said, gesturing through the doorway as if they were entering a fancy restaurant.

She wasn't sure she really wanted to go, but she did. Leaning in, she looked both ways, up and down the hallway, then stepped gingerly on the carpet, thinking it might turn to quicksand and swallow her. It didn't. Grant slipped in behind her and closed the door.

This wing of the hotel had been refurbished in the last few years and still looked newish. The carpet was thick, the soft recessed lighting on the russet walls was luxurious and inviting. In a few more years, the décor would start to look worn, and the earth-tones and geometric patterns would look dated. Vegas wore out things the way it wore out people. For now, though, it was all very impressive.

They lingered by the emergency door; Grant seemed to expect something to happen. Consulting his watch again, he turned it to the left and right, considering. She craned her neck, trying to get a better look at it. It didn't seem to have numbers on its face.

"What's that thing do?" she asked.

"It points," he said.

Of course it did.

He moved down the hallway to the right, glancing at the watch, then at doorways. At the end of the hall, he stopped and nodded, then made a motion with his hands.

"More magic?" she said, moving beside him.

"No. Lockpick." He held up a flat plastic key card. "Universal code."

"Oh my God, if the resort knew you were doing this—and I'm right here with you. I could lose my job—"

"They'll never find out."

She glanced to the end of the hallway, to the glass bubble in the ceiling where the security camera was planted.

"Are you sure about that? Am I supposed to just trust you?"

His lips turned a wry smile. "I did warn you that you probably ought to stay out of this. It's not too late."

"What, and take the elevator back down? I don't think so."

"There you go—you trust me more than the elevator."

She crossed her arms and sighed. "I'm not sure I agree with that logic."

"It isn't logic," he said. "It's instinct. Yours are good, you should listen to them."

She considered—any other dealer, any *sane* dealer, would have left the whole problem to Ryan and security. Catching cheaters once they left the table was above her pay grade, as they said. But she wanted to *know*. The same prickling at her neck that told her something was wrong with yesterday's businessman and today's housewife, also told her that Odysseus Grant had answers.

"What can I do to help?" she asked.

"Keep a look out."

He slipped the card in the lock, and the door popped open. She wouldn't have been surprised if an unassuming guest wrapped in a bath towel screamed a protest, but the room was unoccupied. After a moment, Grant entered and began exploring.

Julie stayed by the door, glancing back and forth, up and down the hallway as he had requested. She kept expecting guys from security to come pounding down the hallway. But she also had to consider: Grant wouldn't be doing this if he didn't have a way to keep it secret. She couldn't even imagine how he was fooling the cameras. *The cameras won't even pick up what I did,* he'd said. Did the casino's security department even know what they had working under their noses?

She looked back in the room to check his progress. "You expected that watch, that whatever it is, to lead you right to the guy, did you?"

"Yes, it should have," Grant said, sounding curious rather than frustrated. "Ah, there we are." He opened the top bureau drawer.

"What?" She craned forward to see.

Using a handkerchief, he reached into the drawer and picked up a small object. Resting on the cloth was a twenty-five dollar chip bound with twine to the burned-down stub of a red candle. The item evoked a feeling of dread in her; it made her imagine an artifact from some long-extinct civilization that practiced human sacrifice. Whatever this thing was, no good could ever come of it.

"A decoy," Grant said. "Rather clever, really."

"Look, I can call security, have them check the cameras, look for anyone suspicious—they'll know who's been in this room."

"No. You've seen how he's disguising himself; he's a master of illusion. Mundane security has no idea what they're looking for. I'll find him." He broke the decoy, tearing at the twine, crumbling the candle, throwing the pieces away. Even broken, the pieces made her shiver.

Then they were back in the hallway. Grant again consulted his watch, but they reached the end of the hallway without finding his quarry.

They could be at this all day.

"Maybe we should try knocking on doors. You'll be able to spot the guy if he answers."

"That's probably not a good idea. Especially if he knows we're coming."

"How long until you give up?" she said, checking her phone to get the time. The thing had gone dead, out of power. Of course it had. And Grant's watch didn't tell time.

"Never," he murmured, returning to the emergency stairs.

She started to follow him when her eye caught on an incongruity, because the afternoon had been filled with them. A service cart was parked outside a room about halfway down the hallway. Dishes of a picked-over meal littered the white linen table cloth, along with an empty bottle of wine, and two used wineglasses. Nothing unusual at all about seeing such a thing outside a room in a hotel. Except she was absolutely sure it had not been there before.

"Hey—wait a minute," she said, approaching the cart slowly. The emergency stair door had already shut, though, and he was gone. She went after him, hauling open the door.

Which opened into a hallway, just like the one she'd left.

Vertigo made her vision go sideways a moment, and she thought she might faint. Shutting the door quickly, she leaned against it and tried to catch her breath. She'd started gasping for air. This was stupid—it was just a door. She'd imagined it. Her mind was play-ing tricks, and Grant was right, she should have stayed back in the casino.

No, she was a sensible woman, and she trusted her eyes. She opened the door again, and this time when she saw the second, iden-tical—impossible—hallway through it, she stayed calm, and kept her breathing steady.

Stepping gently, she went through the door, careful to hold it open, giving her an escape route. Her feet touched carpet instead of concrete. She looked back and forth—same hallway. Or maybe not—the room service cart wasn't here.

"Odysseus?" she called, feeling silly using the name. His stage name, probably, but he hadn't given her another one to call him. His real name was probably something plain, like Joe or Frank. On sec-ond thought, considering the watch, the universal lockpick, his talk of spells, his weird knowledge—Odysseus might very well be his real name.

"Odysseus Grant?" she repeated. No answer. Behind one of the doors, muted laughter echoed from a television.

She retreated to the original hallway and let the door close. Here, the same TV buzzing with the same noise, obnoxious canned laughter on some sitcom. She could believe she hadn't ever left, that she hadn't opened the door and seen another hallway rather than the stairs that should have been there. This was some kind of optical illusion. A trick done with mirrors.

The room service cart was gone.

She ran down the hall to where it had been, felt around the spot where she was sure she had seen it—nothing. She continued on to the opposite end of the hallway, past the elevators, which she didn't dare try, to the other set of emergency stairs. Holding her breath, she opened the door—and found herself staring into another hallway, identical to the one she was standing in. When she ran to the opposite end of *that* corridor, and tried the other door there, she found the same thing—another hallway, with the same numbers outside the rooms, the same inane voices from the television.

Bait. The room service cart had been bait, used to distract her, to draw her back after Grant had already left. And now she was trapped.

Casinos, especially the big ones on the Strip, are built to be mazes. From the middle of the casino, you can't readily find the exit. Sure, the place is as big as a few football fields lined up, the walkways are all wide and sweeping to facilitate ease of movement. The fire codes mean the casino can't actually lock you in. But when you're surrounded by ringing slot machines and video poker and a million blinking lights, when the lack of windows means that if you didn't have your watch or phone you'd have no way to tell the time, when the dealer at the blackjack table will keep dealing cards and taking your chips as the hours slip by—you leave by an act of will, not because the way out is readily apparent.

More than that, though, the resort is its own world. Worlds within worlds. You enter and never *have* to leave. Hotel, restaurants, shopping, gaming, shows, spas, all right here. You can even get married if you want, in a nice little chapel, tastefully decorated in soft colors with pews of warm mahogany, nothing like those tawdry places outside. You can get a package deal: wedding, room for the weekend, and a limo to the airport. The resort makes it easy for you to come and spend your money. It's a maze, and as long as your credit card stays good they don't much care whether you *ever* get out.

That, too, was a certain kind of magic.

Grant climbed two flights of stairs, the single hand on his pocket watch giving no indication that anything untoward lay beyond the door at each landing, before he noticed that the earnest blackjack dealer was no longer with him.

He paused and called down, "Julie?" His voice echoed, and he received no response. He thought he'd been cautious enough. He looked around; the staircase had suddenly become sinister.

One of the notable characteristics of a very tall staircase like this one was that it all looked the same, minimalist and unwelcoming. This landing was exactly like the last, this flight of stairs like the first six he'd climbed up.

The number painted on the door at this landing was five. He turned around, descended a flight, looked at the door—which also read five. And the one below it. Climbing back up, he returned to where he'd stopped. Five again, or rather, still. Five and five and five. Somewhere between this floor and the last, his journey had become a loop. Which meant he was in trouble, and so was Julie.

There were still doorways, which meant there was still a way out.

Five was one of the mystic numbers—well, any number could be mystic to the right person under the right circumstances. Go to the casino and ask people what their lucky numbers were, and every number, up to a hundred and often beyond, would be represented. But five—it was a prime number, some cultures counted five elements, a pentagram had five points. It was the number of limbs on the human body, if you counted the head. A number of power, of binding.

What kind of power did it take to bend a stairwell, Escher-like, upon itself? This magician, who'd orchestrated all manner of tricks and traps, was drawing on an impressive source of it. And that was why the culprit hadn't fled—he'd built up a base of power here in the hotel, in order to initiate his scheme. He was counting on that power to protect himself now.

When turning off a light without a switch, unplugging the lamp made so much more sense than breaking the light bulb. Grant needed to find this magician.

He pocketed his watch and drew out a few tools he had brought with him: a white candle, a yard of red thread, and a book of matches.

Julie paced in front of the doorway. She thought it was the first one, the original one that she and Grant had come through, but she couldn't be entirely sure. She'd gotten turned around.

How long before Grant noticed she was missing? What were the rules of hiking in the wilderness? Stay still, call for help, until someone finds you. She took out her phone again and shook it, as if that kind of desperate, sympathetic magic would work. It didn't. Still dead. She'd be trapped here forever. She couldn't even call 911 to come and rescue her. Her own fault, for getting involved in a mess she didn't know anything about. She should never have followed Grant.

No, that hadn't been a mistake. Her mistake had been panicking and running off half cocked. This—none of this could be real. It went against all the laws of physics. So if it wasn't real, what was it? An illusion. Maybe she couldn't trust her eyes after all, at least not all the time.

She closed her eyes. Now she didn't see anything. The TV had fallen silent. This smelled like a hotel hallway—lint, carpet cleaner. A place devoid of character. She stood before a door, and when she opened it, she'd step through to a concrete stairwell, where she'd walk straight down, back to the lobby and the casino, back to work, and she wouldn't ask any more questions about magic.

Reaching out, she flailed a bit before finding the doorknob. Her hand closed on it, and turned. She pushed it open and stepped through.

And felt concrete beneath her feet.

She opened her eyes, and was in the stairwell, standing right in front of Odysseus Grant. On the floor between them sat a votive candle and a length of red thread tied in a complicated pattern of knots. Grant held a match in one hand and the book it came from in the other, ready to light.

"How did you do that?" he asked, seeming genuinely startled. His wide eyes and suspicious frown were a little unnerving.

She glanced over her shoulder, and back at him. "I closed my eyes. I figured none of it was real—so I just didn't look."

His expression softened into a smile. "Well done." He crouched and quickly gathered up items, shoving thread, candle, and matches into his pockets. "He's protecting himself with a field of illusion. He must be right here—he must have been here the whole time." He nodded past her to the hallway.

"How do you know?"

"Fifth floor. It should have been obvious," he said.

"Obvious?" she said, nearly laughing. "Really?"

"Well, partially obvious."

Which sounded like "sort of pregnant" to her. Before she could prod further, he urged her back into the hallway and let the door shut. It sounded a little like a death knell.

"Now, we just have to figure out what room he's in. Is there a room 555 here?"

"On the other end, I think."

"Excellent. He's blown his cover." Grant set off with long strides. Julie scurried to keep up.

At room 555, Grant tried his universal key card, slipping it in and out of the slot. It didn't work. "This'll take a little more effort, I think.

No matter." He waved a hand over the key card and tried again. And again. It still didn't work.

A growl drew Julie's attention to the other end of the hallway, back the way they'd come.

A creature huddled there, staring with eyes that glowed like hot iron. At first, she thought it was a dog. But it wasn't. This thing was slate gray, hairless, with a stout head as big as its chest and no neck to speak of. Skin drooped in folds around its shoulders and limbs, and knobby growths covering its back gave it an armored look. Her mind went through a catalog of four-legged predators, searching for possibilities: hyena, lion, bear, badger on steroids, dragon.

Dragon?

The lips under its hooked bill seemed to curl in a smile.

She could barely squeak, "Odysseus?"

He glanced up from his work to where she pointed. Then he paused and took a longer look.

"It's a good sign," Grant said.

"How is that a good sign?" she hissed.

"A guardian like that means we've found him."

That she couldn't argue his logic didn't mean he wasn't still crazy.

"Can you distract it?" he said. "I'm almost through."

"Distract it? How on Earth—"

"This magician works with illusions. That thing is there to frighten us off. But most likely it's not even real. If you distract it, it'll vanish."

"Just like that, huh?"

"I imagine so."

He didn't sound as confident as she'd have liked.

She tried to picture the thing just vanishing. It looked solid enough—it filled most of the hallway. It must have been six feet tall, crouching.

"And you're absolutely sure it's not real." She reminded herself about the hallways, the room service cart. All she had to do was close her eyes.

"I'm reasonably sure."

"That's not absolutely."

"Julie, trust me." He was bent over the lock again, intent on his work.

The beast wasn't real. All right. She just had to keep telling herself that. Against her better judgment, Julie stepped toward the creature.

"Here, kitty kitty—" Okay, that was stupid. "Um, hey! Over here!" She waved her hands over her head.

The beast's red eyes narrowed; its muscles bunched.

"Remember, it's an illusion. Don't believe it."

The thing hunched and dug in claws in preparation of a charge. The carpet shredded in curling fibers under its efforts. *That* sure looked real.

"I—I don't think it's an illusion. It's *drooling*."

"Julie, stand your ground."

The monster launched, galloping toward her, limbs pumping, muscles trembling under horny skin. The floor shook under its pounding steps. What did the magician expect would happen? Was the creature supposed to pass through her like mist?

Julie closed her eyes and braced.

A weight like a runaway truck crashed into her, and she flew back and hit the floor, head cracking, breath gusting from her lungs. The great, slathering beast stood on her, kneading her uniform vest with questing claws. Its mouth opened wide, baring yellowing fangs as it hissed a breath that smelled like carrion. Somehow, she'd gotten her arms in front of her and held it off, barely. Her hands sank into the soft, gray flesh of its chest. Its chunky head strained forward. She punched at it, dug her fingernails into it, trying to find some sensitive spot that might at least make it hesitate. She scrabbled for its eyes, but it turned its head away, and its claws ripped into her vest.

She screamed.

Thunder cracked, and the creature leaped away from her, yelping. A second boom sounded, this time accompanied by a flash of light.

Less like a lightning strike and more like some kind of explosion in reverse. She covered her head and curled up against the chaos of it. The air smelled of sulfur.

She waited a long time for the silence to settle, not convinced that calm had returned to the hallway. Her chest and shoulders were sore, bruised. She had to work to draw breath into complaining lungs. Finally, though, she could uncurl from the floor and look around.

A dark stain the size of a sedan streaked away from her across the carpet and walls, like soot and ashes from an old fireplace. The edges of it gave off thin fingers of smoke. Housekeeping was going to love this. The scent of burned meat seared into her nose.

Grant stood nearby, hands lifted in a gesture of having just thrown something. Grenade, maybe? Some arcane whatsit? It hardly mattered.

She closed her eyes, hoping once again that it was all an illusion and that it would go away. But she could smell charred flesh, a rotten taste in the back of her throat.

From nearby, Grant asked, "Are you all right?"

Leaning toward the wall, she threw up.

"Julie—"

"You said it was an illusion."

"I had every—"

"I trusted you!" Her gut heaved again. Hugging herself, she slumped against the wall and waited for the world to stop spinning.

He stood calmly, expressionless, like this sort of thing happened to him every day. Maybe it did.

She could believe her eyes. Maybe that was why she didn't dare open them again. Then it would all be real.

"Julie," he said again, his voice far too calm. She wanted to shake him.

"You were right," she said, her voice scratching past her raw throat and disbelief. "I should have stayed behind."

"I'm glad you didn't."

When she looked up, the burned stain streaking across the hall and the puddle of vomit in front of her were still there, all too real. Grant appeared serene. Unmoved.

"Really?"

"You have a gift for seeing past the obvious. You were the kid who always figured out the magic tricks, weren't you?"

She had to smile. For every rabbit pulled out of a hat there was a table with a trapdoor nearby. You just had to know where to look.

"You *are* all right?" he asked, and she could believe that he was really concerned.

She had to think about it. The alternatives were going crazy or muddling through. She didn't have time for the going crazy part. "I will be."

"I'm very sorry," he said, reaching out to help her up. "I really wasn't expecting that."

She took his hand and lurched to her feet. "You do the distracting next time." She didn't like the way her voice was shaking. If she thought about it too much she'd run screaming. If Grant could stand his ground, she could, too. She was determined.

"I was so sure it was an illusion. The players at your table—they had to have been illusions."

"The guy from yesterday was sweating."

"Very good illusions, mind you. Nevertheless—"

She pointed at the soot stain. "That's not an illusion. Those players weren't illusions. Now, maybe they weren't what they looked like, but they were *something*."

His brow creased, making him look worried for the first time this whole escapade. "I have a bad feeling."

He turned back to the door he'd been working on, reaching into both pockets for items. She swore he'd already pulled more out of those pockets than could possibly fit. Instead of more lockpicks or key cards or some fancy gizmo to fool the lock into opening, he held a string of four or five firecrackers. He tore a couple off the string, flattened them, and jammed them into the lock on the door.

Her eyes widened. "You can't—"

"Maybe the direct approach this time?" He flicked his hand, and the previously unseen match in his fingers flared to life. He lowered the flame to the fuse sticking out of the lock.

Julie scrambled back from the door. Grant merely turned his back.

The black powder popped and flared; the noise seemed loud in the hallway, and Julie could imagine the dozens of calls to the hotel front desk about the commotion. So, security would be up here in a few minutes, and one way or another it would all be over. She'd lose her job, at the very least. She'd probably end up in jail. But she'd lost her chance to back out of this. Only thing to do was keep going.

Grant eased open the door. She crept up behind him, and they entered the room.

This was one of the hotel's party suites—two bedrooms connected to a central living room that included a table, sofa, entertainment center, and wet bar. The furniture had all been pushed to the edges of the room, and the curtains were all drawn. Light came from the glow of a few dozen red pillar candles that had been lit throughout the room. Hundreds of dull shadows seemed to flicker in the corners. The smoke alarms had to have been disabled.

The place stank of burned vegetable matter, so many different flavors to it Julie couldn't pick out individual components. It might have been some kind of earthy incense.

A pattern had been drawn onto the floor in luminescent paint. A circle arced around a pentagram and dozens of symbols, Greek letters, zodiac signs, others that she didn't recognize. It obviously meant something; she couldn't guess what. Housekeeping was *really* not going to like this.

Two figures stood within the circle: a man, rather short and very thin, wearing a T-shirt and jeans; the other, a hulking, red-skinned being, thick with muscles. It had a snout like an eagle's bill, sharp reptilian eyes, and wings—sweeping, leathery-bat wings spread behind it like a sail.

Julie squeaked. Both figures looked at her. The bat-thing—another dragon-like gargoyle come to life—let out a scream, like the sound of tearing steel. Folding its wings close, it bowed its head as a column of smoke enveloped it.

Grant flipped the switch by the door. Light from the mundane incandescent bulbs overpowered the mystery-inducing candle glow. Julie and the guy in the circle squinted. By then, the column of smoke had cleared, and the creature had disappeared. An odor of burning wax and brimstone remained.

The guy, it turned out, was a kid. Just a kid, maybe fifteen, at that awkward stage of adolescence, his limbs too long for his body, acne spotting his cheeks.

"You've been summoning," Grant said. "It wasn't you working any of those spells, creating any of those illusions—you summoned creatures to do it for you. Very dangerous." He clicked his tongue.

"It was *working*," the kid said. He pointed at the empty space where the bat-thing had been. "Did you see what I managed to summon?"

He was in need of a haircut, was probably still too young to shave, and his clothes looked ripe. The room did, too, now that Julie had a chance to look around. Crumpled bags of fast food had accumulated in one corner, and an open suitcase had been dumped in another. The incense and candle smoke covered up a lot of dorm-room smells.

On the bed lay the woman's purse with several thousand dollars in casino chips spilled around it.

"I think you're done here," Grant said.

"Just who *are* you?" the kid said.

"Think of me as the police. Of a certain kind."

The kid bolted for the door, but Julie blocked the way, grabbing his arm, then throwing herself into a tackle. He wasn't getting away with this, not if she could help it.

She wasn't very good at tackling, as it turned out. Her legs tangled with his and they both crashed to the floor. He flailed, but her weight pinned him down. Somebody was going to take the blame for all this, and it wasn't going to be her.

Finally, the kid went slack. "It was *working*," he repeated.

"Why would you even try something like this?" she said. "Cheating's bad enough, but . . . this?" She couldn't say she understood anything in the room, the candles or paint or that gargoylish creature. But Grant didn't like it, and that was enough for her.

"Because I'm underage!" he whined. "I can't even get into the casino. I needed a disguise."

"So you summoned demon doppelgangers?" Grant asked. Thoughtfully he said, "That's almost clever. Still—very dangerous."

"Screw you!"

"Julie?" Grant said. "Now you can call security." He pulled the kid out from under Julie and pushed him to the wall, where he sat slouching. Grant stood over him, arms crossed, guard-like.

"Your luck ran out, buddy," Julie said, glaring at him. She retrieved her phone from her pocket. It worked now, go figure.

Grant said, "His luck ran out before he even started. Dozens of casinos on the Strip, and you picked mine, the one where you were most likely to get caught."

"You're just that stupid stage magician! Smoke and mirrors! What do you know about anything?" He slumped like a sack of old laundry.

Grant smiled, and the expression was almost wicked. The curled lip of a lion about to pounce. "To perform such summonings as you've done here, you must offer part of your own soul—as collateral, you might think of it. You probably think you're strong enough, powerful enough, to protect that vulnerable bit of your soul, defending it against harm. You think you can control such monstrous underworld creatures and keep your own soul—your own self— safe and sound. But it doesn't matter how protected you are, you will be marked. These creatures, any other demons you happen to meet, will know what you've done just by looking at you. *That* makes you a target. Now, and for the rest of your life. Actions have consequences. You'll discover that soon enough."

Julie imagined a world filled with demons, with bat-wing creatures and slavering dragons, all of them with consciousness, with a sense of mission: to attack their oppressors. She shivered.

Unblinking, the kid stared at Grant. He'd turned a frightening, pasty white, and his spine had gone rigid.

Grant just smiled, seemingly enjoying himself. "Do your research. Every good magician knows that."

Julie called security, and while they were waiting, the demon-summoning kid tried to set off an old-fashioned smoke bomb to stage an escape, but Grant confiscated it as soon as the kid pulled it from his pocket.

Soon after, a pair of uniformed officers arrived at the room to handcuff the kid and take him into custody. "We'll need you to come with us and give statements," one of them said to Julie and Grant.

She panicked. "But I didn't do anything wrong. I mean, not really—we were just looking for the cheater at my blackjack table, and something wasn't right, and Grant here showed up—"

Grant put a gentle hand on her arm, stopping her torrent of words. "We'll help in any way we can," he said.

She gave him a questioning look, but he didn't explain.

The elevators seemed to be working just fine now, she noticed, as they went with security to their offices downstairs.

Security took the kid to a back room to wait for the Las Vegas police. Grant and Julie were stationed in a stark, functional waiting room, with plastic chairs and an ancient coffee maker. They waited.

They only needed to look at the footage of her breaking into the rooms with Grant, and she'd be fired. She didn't want to be fired— she liked her job. She was good at it, as she kept insisting. She caught cheaters—even when they were summoning demons.

Her foot tapped a rapid beat on the floor, and her hands clenched into fists, pressed against her legs.

"Everything will be fine," Grant said, glancing sidelong at her. "I have a feeling the boy'll be put off the whole idea of spell-casting, moving forward. Now that he knows people are watching him. He probably thought he was the only magician in the world. Now he knows better."

One could hope.

Now that he'd been caught, she didn't really care about the kid. "You'll be fired too, you know, once they figure out what we did. You think you can find another gig after word gets out?"

"I won't be fired. Neither will you," he said.

They'd waited for over a half hour when the head of security came into the waiting room. Grant and Julie stood to meet him. The burly, middle-aged man in the off-the-rack suit—ex-cop, probably—was smiling.

"All right, you both can go now. We've got everything we need."

Julie stared.

"Thank you," Grant said, not missing a beat.

"No, thank *you*. We never would have caught that kid without your help." Then he shook their hands. And let them go.

Julie followed Grant back to the casino lobby. Two hours had passed, for the entire adventure, which had felt like it lasted all day—all day and most of the night, too. It seemed impossible. It all seemed impossible.

Back at the casino, the noise and bustle—crystal chandeliers glittering, a thousand slot and video machines ringing and clanking, a group of people laughing—seemed otherworldly. Hands clasped behind his back, Grant regarded the patrons filing back and forth, the flashing lights, with an air of satisfaction, like he owned the place.

Julie asked, "What did you do to get him to let us go?"

"They saw exactly what they needed to see. They'll be able to charge the kid with vandalism and destruction of property, and I'm betting if they check the video from the casino again they'll find evidence of cheating."

"But we didn't even talk to them."

"I told you everything would be fine."

She regarded him, his confident stance, the smug expression, and wondered how much of it was a front. How much of it was the picture he wanted people to see.

She crossed her arms. "So, the kind of magic you do—what kind of mark does it leave on your soul?"

His smile fell, just a notch. After a hesitation he said, "The price is worth it, I think."

If she were a little more forward, if she knew him better, she'd have hugged him—he looked like he needed it. He probably wasn't the kind of guy who had a lot of friends. But at the moment he seemed as otherworldly as the bat-winged creature in that arcane circle.

She said, "It really happened, didn't it? The thing with the hallway? The . . . the thing . . . and the other . . ." She moved her arms in a gesture of outstretched wings. "Not smoke and mirrors?"

"It really happened," he said.

"How do you do that? Any of it?" she said.

"That," he said, glancing away to hide a smile, "would take a very long time to explain."

"I get off my second shift at eleven," she said. "We could grab a drink."

She really hadn't expected him to say yes, and he didn't. But he hesitated first. So that was something. "I'm sorry," he said finally. "I don't think I can."

It was just as well. She tried to imagine her routine, with a guy like Odysseus Grant in the picture . . . and, well, there'd be no such thing as routine, would there? But she wasn't sure she'd mind a drink, and a little adventure, every now and then.

"Well, then. I'll see you around," she said.

"You can bet on it," he said, and walked away, back to his theater.

Her break was long over and she was late for the next half of her shift. She'd give Ryan an excuse—or maybe she could get Grant to make an excuse for her.

She walked softly, stepping carefully, through the casino, which had not yet returned to normal. The lights seemed dimmer, building shadows where there shouldn't have been any. A woman in a cocktail dress and impossible high heels walked past her, and Julie swore she had glowing red eyes. She did a double take, staring after her, but only saw her back, not her eyes.

At one of the bars, a man laughed—and he had pointed teeth,

fangs, where his cuspids should have been. The man sitting with him raised his glass to drink—his hands were clawed with long, black talons. Julie blinked, checked again—yes, the talons were still there. The man must have sensed her staring, because he looked at her, caught her gaze—then smiled and raised his glass in a salute before turning back to his companion.

She quickly walked away, heart racing.

This wasn't new, she realized. The demons had always been there, part of an underworld she had never seen because she simply hadn't been looking. Until now.

And once seen, it couldn't be unseen.

The blackjack dealer returned to the casino's interior, moving slowly, thoughtfully—warily, Grant decided. The world must look so much different to her now. He didn't know if she'd adjust.

He should have made her stay behind, right from the start. But no—he couldn't have stopped her. By then, she'd already seen too much. He had a feeling he'd be hearing from her again, soon. She'd have questions. He would answer them as best he could.

On the other hand, he felt as if he had an ally in the place, now. Another person keeping an eye out for a certain kind of danger. Another person who knew what to look for. And that was a very odd feeling indeed.

Some believe that magic—real magic, not the tricks that entertainers played on stage—is a rare, exotic thing. Really, it isn't, if you know what to look for.

What Happened to Ben in Vegas

T HE PAIR OF THUGS cornered Ben outside the men's room.
His first thought: Kitty's paranoia was rubbing off on him. Then:
Damn, she was right all along.

He spotted the type right off and knew they were up to no good.
Late twenties, bulky, hired muscle. Suits, no ties. Slicked back hair.
One of them was the lookout: back to the wall, scanning the area. His
hand never moved very far from his waistband—within easy reach of
the gun holstered under the jacket. The other one got in Ben's face.

"Hey there," he said, pressing close, herding him to the wall, moving him away from the crowd. His breath smelled of mint and cigarettes. His accent was some flavor of New York City.

Ben didn't bother responding. Nothing he could say would change
what was about to happen. He did think about telling them they had
the wrong guy. A flare of anger, a thread of pissed-offedness, made
him stand his ground. Match the guy's stare, and not blink.

The heavy was about the same height. He tried looking down on
Ben, but it didn't work.

"Friend of ours wants to talk to you," the guy said.

Ben's nose flared, taking in the guy's aftershave, the scent of gun
oil. The odor of seedy bars and backroom shakedowns.

"Why?" Ben said, wondering if it sounded like a growl. He wanted to growl, but that would be a bad idea.

The thug, the talker, opened his suit jacket briefly to show the gun inside, in the shoulder holster. "No arguments."

"He couldn't just call me?" Ben said. Arguing. The flame inside was growing. He was getting angry, and a beast with claws was waking up.

The thug put a hand on his shoulder and pushed him. "Come on. Walk normal. Don't draw attention." The lookout led them to a side hallway.

God, he really was being kidnapped out of a Vegas casino.

"What happens if I knock you down and shout right now? You going to shoot me?"

"Maybe not. But we may find a way to draw a bead on that pretty little girl of yours."

That shut him up. They moved out of sight of the poker room and the main casino floor. Empty corridor now, and straight ahead to a set of doors leading to the outside. The lookout was still scanning, ready to jump at a sign of trouble. Ben could almost hear his body quivering. His own escort was steady, methodical, and kept his anxiety tamped down. A pro. Didn't make Ben feel any better.

"How does this friend of yours even care about me?" he asked.

The thug gave a sly smile. "He had a game going. Pretty good game. His boys had a system and would have cleaned up. But you ratted them out. You've made yourself a person of interest. Congratulations."

So much for being a good citizen.

"You can't do this," he said, realizing it was a stupid thing to say. They certainly could do this. They had. Ben could whine all he wanted—they still had the guns. But were the bullets silver? Did he risk getting shot in the back on the streets of Vegas to prove a theory?

"I'm getting married in a couple of hours." As if that kind of argument held any weight with people like this.

"If she really loves you, she'll wait. So—she really love you, or what?"

God, what a question. The worst part about it was the cold lump in the pit of his stomach at the thought the answer might be no.

"I don't know what this is about. Your boss wants to talk to me, that's fine. But at least let me call my girlfriend. Just to tell her I'm going to be late—"

The muscle patted him down, found the phone, tossed it on the concrete sidewalk.

A car was waiting outside. The quiet one opened the door; the New York thug pointed Ben inside. Ben didn't fight, didn't argue, didn't resist—he didn't want to get punched or pounded. That really would wake up the monster. And while that might get him out of this immediate situation, he couldn't see how it would help in the long run. So he waited.

The windows in the sedan were tinted. They blindfolded him anyway. Only then did he start to lose it: heart fluttering, breaths coming in gasps. He curled his hands into fists and dug them into his thighs—and the creature inside him snarled, from a place like a cage, deep in his gut.

He had to keep it together himself this time. Kitty wasn't here to hold his hand.

What was she going to think? What if she thought he'd run off, stood her up? Part of her would. Part of her was still an insecure pup. Amazing, considering what she'd been through, how well she stood up for herself under the gun—and she hardly realized it.

Thinking of her steadied him. Just like holding her hand would have. He had to get through this for her. She often talked about her wolf side like it was a separate entity. Like the two sides argued, conversed. The metaphor was useful. He'd adopted it. It let him say, *Down, boy.*

He pressed his lips together to keep from smiling at that thought. He didn't imagine the tough guys would take his smiling too well. The thug beside him was the kind of guy who would think it was all about him.

They arrived. The car stopped, and the blindfold came off. The location was seedy. Seedier than seedy. The kind of old industrial neighborhood where the windows were smashed out of the warehouses and weeds grew a foot high out of cracks in the asphalt. By the distance they'd traveled, Ben judged they were on the outskirts of town—the deadbeat, dried-up outskirts, not the gentrified suburbs. The building they'd parked by was concrete, wind-blasted and pockmarked. Tiny windows had bars over them anyway. It was the kind of place that didn't have a sign—didn't need one. The line of motorcycles out front said it all. This was the kind of bar that didn't want tourists snooping around. He could hear music pounding from within.

His escort brought him through the front door, then straight through the bar and pool tables and bikers. Didn't give him a chance to look around; not that he needed one. He knew the stereotypes well enough, and the smirk he wore came naturally. But maybe it would give him some armor. Keep him from looking a little less like a hopeless guy in over his head.

They next passed through a door in back, and into another world. Ben's protective smirk fell.

From the outside, this had all looked like more concrete warehouses, auto body shops, and so on. Here, the interior was straight out of a bordello in a Victorian novel. Red plush carpeting, burgundy curtains held back by gold tasseled cords—not that there were any windows to cover. Sofas, chaise lounges, wingback chairs. Men in suits, smoking cigarettes and cigars like chimneys, gathered around poker games at several green felt tables. He wrinkled his nose to keep from sneezing at the odor. Draped over all—men and furniture both—were a dozen women in lingerie. Like they were part of the decoration. In the back, a beaded curtain marked the entrance to a hallway. Ben could make out a row of doors. So this wasn't just a bar.

It was like something out of a bad movie. *Kitty has got to see this.* He shut down the pang that came with the thought.

In the middle of it all sat the guy who had to be the boss. The guy who was the source of all this ostentatious bad taste. Thin, weedy, hair obviously dyed black because he hadn't bothered touching up his graying eyebrows. Old, weathered. Like he'd moved up through the ranks and spent a lot of time laughing at pain. That's what the hard look in his eyes said.

An old-school gangster. Pure and simple.

Ben's escorts—one on each side—brought him to stand before the table where this guy was shuffling cards and nursing a bourbon on ice. The boss didn't look at Ben for what seemed like a long time. Making him wait, making him sweat. Ben concentrated on breathing, and not sweating. He could wait. He had to, didn't he? But the smell of the women—the musky, wet smell of sex that edged the room's atmosphere—was making him nervous. Making him want to be with Kitty even more than he already did.

The boss shuffled the cards, slowly, like it was the most important task in the world. Taking a deep breath, almost a sigh, he said, "So you're the joker who spotted my ring. Ratted me out."

God, *straight* out of a bad movie. Could this get any cheesier?

"I guess I am," Ben said.

Then, the guy looked at him. His hands paused. Brown eyes studied him. "You know who I am?"

Ben suppressed a smile, because wasn't that just the right level of arrogance? "I'm afraid not. I think I got into this by accident."

"I'm Samuel Faber. And you are—"

"Ben." He thought, pretend this is a movie. Just play it cool. Keep his hindbrain from panicking—at least any more than it already was.

Faber cut the deck and set the cards aside. "I want to know how you did it."

"I just have a nose for these things."

"Sit down. Show me." One of the goons pulled a chair out and glared at Ben until he sat in it.

How was he going to explain this? His guys smelled funny. They twitched when there weren't any cards in play, giving signals. They had a spotter, and he could feel them listening. When he looked, he saw the earpieces. It was all sleight of hand and he only saw it because he was a werewolf.

Nothing for it but to play poker. Faber called over one of the girls, a bottled redhead in a black satin teddy, silk robe, and spike heels. He handed her the cards and told her to deal.

"We're playing for real," Faber said. At a silent signal, a mere glance around the room, four other guys gathered until the table was full. "Play to win—I'll know if you're throwing the game to try to make me feel better."

The boss slid over a rack of chips, which was rather nice of him, not requiring Ben to put up his own stake.

"Drink?" Faber asked, as the redhead dealt the first hand.

"Just water," Ben said.

"Wuss."

Ben just smiled.

Mr. New York, the thug who'd first shown his gun to Ben back at the casino, went over to Faber and leaned on the back of the chair to whisper a conference to the boss. He probably thought he was whispering, and none of the others could probably hear him. But Ben tilted his ear, held his breath, and listened.

"This is a bad idea. The cops are going to be looking for him, Mr. Faber," the thug said.

Faber turned to whisper back, "You were supposed to stay out of sight."

"Yeah, right, in this town?"

Faber glared at him. "Enough, Vince. Go away."

The thug, Vince, straightened, regarded the boss a moment, scowling, then went back to his guard post.

Ben didn't flinch, didn't glance, didn't give a sign that he'd heard. In fact, he tried to ignore them, because it didn't mean anything. Would anyone even notice he'd gone missing? Sure, Kitty would. At six o'clock, when he was due at the chapel.

He looked at his pair of cards. An ace and an eight. Start of a dead man's hand. Swell.

They played.

"So. Ben. What is it you do?" Faber asked. Small talk. Real small.

"I'm a lawyer," Ben said, and this was just like any other party, the way people reacted. The raised eyebrows, the twitches. It was like lawyers were their own species. People made so many assumptions, these guys probably even more than most.

Faber didn't flinch, didn't change his expression. "Yeah? You some kind of hot shot assistant DA type? Prosecuting the lowlifes, cleaning up the streets?" The thugs chuckled. What did you call a group of thugs, anyway? A crowd? A flock? A brute—a brute of thugs.

"Criminal defense," Ben said, deadpan. And that got the guys to look up. A couple of the bodyguard thugs even nodded to each other, like, *Yeah, he's all right.* Ben wanted to tell them, don't get that idea. *I'm not one of you.* But he knew all about guys like them. He knew what made them tick.

The four extra guys Faber brought in were either pros or near enough to it not to make a difference. They watched the table with stone cold gazes, pretended they weren't looking at each other. Never glanced at their cards a second time. One of them spun a chip between his fingers, a complicated bit of fidgeting that drew Ben's eye. Distracted him. They were playing mind games with their intimidating fronts. They'd won just about every pot, and Ben's stack of chips was dwindling.

They all deferred to Faber. Subtly, the way they let him make the calls, waited for him to signal the next round, didn't call for drinks until he did. Faber was the alpha in this room. Ben suppressed a smile at the thought—and had to suppress another one when a couple of gazes turned his way, noticing the change in expression.

They thought they caught something. They thought they'd spotted his tell. They were all sitting there thinking Ben was in way over his head. But that wasn't a big secret—anybody could tell that just by looking.

He tried to avoid the beginner mistakes. Threw out more hands than he bet on, played tight but not too tight, tried not to walk into any traps, and so on. At the same time, he wondered what Faber was hoping to discover with all this. Did he think Ben was some kind of poker genius?

And again, his mind wandered from the game.

He shouldn't be able to win at poker at all. He hadn't studied the game, never put together any real strategy. It was an excuse to drink beer and socialize. He hadn't gotten any better at the game, really. But he was so much more *aware*. He didn't have to know what the cards were doing because this was all about the people. The way Faber didn't seem to look at anyone. The way his flunky only looked at Faber—hungrily, with his hands opening and closing. Ben thought he knew what that meant. Knew a look of tightly masked challenge. Mr. New York thug wasn't happy being the enforcer. Wanted to maybe move up the ranks like Faber had.

The girls here were messing everything up. Their smell—too much perfume, hairspray, sex. The way two of them brushed his shoulders every time they walked behind his chair. They were supposed to be distracting him. His shoulders grew more tense. Back at the casino, when he'd been focused, everything had been so clear. Now—he might as well have been wrapped in cotton. His mind wasn't on the game at all.

Kitty was going to think he stood her up.

Amazing, that he'd discovered advantages to being a werewolf. The most obvious: shacking up with Kitty. They'd have never hooked up if he hadn't become a werewolf. He'd have never had the courage to ask her out if she hadn't jumped him while they were naked in the woods. Not to mention, you didn't ask out clients. Well, that wasn't true. He might have asked her out, eventually. If he'd had a chance to get to know her like he did now. But so many things could have gotten in the way of that . . .

He wasn't the kind of guy to believe that things happened for a reason. He'd seen too much random shit in his life for that, too many good people gone bad, too many bad people getting a free ride. Chaos, all of it.

But maybe this had happened for a reason.

Six p.m. came and went, and oddly enough, Ben's anxiety lessened. The time for the wedding, here and gone. People definitely knew he was missing by now. Assuming Kitty didn't think he'd gotten cold feet and left town. She had to know he wouldn't do that. Right? He hoped she'd know.

He'd see her again soon. He kept telling himself that. Had to believe it.

On the other side of the table, a hand flinched where there shouldn't have been any movement at all. Ben caught the flicker of movement. Like a rabbit twitching in a forest.

"You just palmed a card. Probably an ace," he said to Faber. He didn't look up from the cards under his hand, from the modest stack of chips in front of him.

Faber paused; the other players looked at him, then at Ben, until they were all staring at Ben, who didn't look back at any of them. He's going to shoot me, Ben thought. Right here, just on principle. It was like nobody breathed, the room was so still.

Then Faber turned his hand over, and there it was, the ace of diamonds, nestled out of sight.

If this had been a real poker game, there'd be a fight. Shouting, at least, righteous demands for their money back. But this was Faber's game, and nobody argued. Who the other players looked at with more suspicion was up for grabs: Faber, or Ben.

"How'd you do that?" Faber said.

"I told you, I just have a knack."

"I've been doing this for years and no one's ever caught me. How does some two-bit tourist figure it out?"

He was never going to be able to explain this. Even if he came right out and said, *I'm a werewolf,* Faber would never believe it. Ben shrugged. "Really, I can't explain it." Which wasn't even a lie.

"You psychic?" Faber was grasping, now. Ben smiled, like it was a joke. The gangster turned to his pretty dealer. "Keep going. It's just a fluke, I'm sure of it."

The other players settled in, their well-practiced, bored poker faces firmly in place, but Ben smelled their sweat, their anxiety. They didn't want to be doing this, when they could be playing a real game, or spending time with the women—or not sitting in the line of fire of Faber's bad mood. Ben just kept thinking about Kitty. He had a little bit of hope: If he could just convince Faber he was for real, that he really could spot the fix and there wasn't a big conspiracy, maybe the gangster would just let him go.

Ben called it the next time Faber palmed a card. The guy grumbled at the dealer, "Again."

This wasn't playing a game, this was a death march.

At one point, after another dozen hands, Vince left the room and came back looking nervous. Even more nervous. A little later, he left again, came back again. This time, he didn't bother leaning in to keep the conference secret. In front of them all, in the middle of a hand—they were waiting for the redhead to deal out the river—he launched in with a tone that was almost reprimanding.

"The casino reported him missing and the cops got tape of the two of us," Vince said. "They got descriptions of me and Mikey, police band has APBs out, Faber."

The room went quiet, like it always did when anyone confronted Faber, like they expected him to explode. A couple people even leaned forward, just a little, like they were waiting for a fight to break out. Ben wondered what the guy had been like in his younger days, to warrant that kind of reputation. More temper than brains, he was betting. Guys like him were a dime a dozen, building up their little ponds so they could be the only big fish around.

Kinda fun, watching the medium-sized fish thrash around in that kind of environment.

"I told him he was being sloppy," Ben muttered at his cards.

"You stay out of this," Vince said. He was still glaring at Faber.

Faber looked at Vince, bored-like. "What is it you expect me to do? Hand him a lollipop and let him go?"

"Jesus, Faber. At least let us dump him. He doesn't know where the place is—he won't talk if we threaten him good enough. Do it before the cops trail him here!"

"You have too much faith in the cops," Faber said. "You scare too easy."

Might as well have told him his dick was small. Vince seethed, but uselessly. He couldn't do anything.

"Maybe not scared," Ben said, wondering how far he could push. "Careful. Or worried. Perfectly understandable."

Vince said, "Stay out of it."

"Sorry," Ben said, in a tone that wasn't sorry at all. Wolf had settled because this was a game those instincts understood: Teasing. Distracting. Keep cool, and they'd get out of this.

Vince was seething. Not playing it cool. "We have to do something, if we want to go back to the game."

"The game's over," Faber explained carefully, as if to a small child. "The casinos talk to each other, the security guys take each other out for beers. By the end of the weekend, they'll all know, and the con's finished. Got it? Now, you going to let me satisfy my curiosity?"

"And what are you going to do with him? You just going to dump him somewhere?"

Ben closed his eyes, took a breath, steadied his heart.

"What I oughta do is lay it all on you and hang you out to dry," Faber said.

Ben expected a fight by now. Faber would have to pound this guy in or lose face. But he saw what was happening: Faber was sending a message that Vince wasn't worth the effort. And Vince knew it. The guy was sweating buckets.

Ben pushed. A tiny little shove, just to see what would happen. "Can I offer you a little legal advice? There's no way you're getting out of this on your own—"

"I said stay out of it!" Vince drew his gun and aimed square at Ben.

Well, he'd been trying to get a reaction.

Another long, stony silence, but this time Ben could hear his heart thudding in his ears. Wolf was thrashing; he kept his breathing steady.

Faber chuckled low. "Well, Vinnie. You really are going to get yourself in trouble."

"I'm just trying to clean up *your* mess!"

"That ain't your job. Now put the gun away."

"That's right," Ben murmured. "Put the gun away."

Vince didn't like being told what to do. Was especially tired of a two-bit hood like Faber telling him what to do. He didn't put the gun away. Instead, Ben sensed his trigger finger tighten. Just a little.

What were the odds? This was Vegas, this town dealt in nothing but odds. So what were the odds that gun had silver bullets? What were the odds the guy would actually shoot him?

He had to get out of this. He had to take the chance. Had to believe his odds were pretty good—he'd made it this far, hadn't he? Maybe he'd become a werewolf for a reason.

"Go ahead." He stood from the table and spread his hands, presenting himself as an offering. "But I don't think you have the guts."

When the guy snarled, Ben knew he'd tipped him over the edge, knew that finger was about to squeeze on the trigger the moment before it did. Knew it was too late even as Faber shouted, "Vince, put the goddamn gun down!"

Do it, Ben mouthed the words.

The guy shot him.

The bullet slammed into his chest. Ben took a step back against the impact. He paused, eyes shut with shock, body hesitating, trembling. So this was what it felt like. Dead on his feet. Except—it stopped hurting. He could feel his heart pound, but it was with anger now, howling with the voice of his wolf rising. He clamped down on this tight. Had to stay in control if he was going to get through the next few seconds. He kept his eyes shut tight. Focused on breathing. Slowly, now.

The bullet wasn't silver. He wasn't going to die.

He remained standing, considering.

"Hey," the other thug said. First time he'd spoken all evening. "He ain't falling down. Why ain't he falling down?"

Ben's lip curled. He was a goddamn superhero. And he was going to make it out of this alive.

"You can't get rid of me that easy," Ben said. The look on Vince's face—sheer, blank terror. Everyone else had paled, staring wordlessly.

"I shot you! I got you in the heart! You're dead. *Dead!*"

Ben jumped on the table, then over it. Plowed straight into the guy and kept going, found the gamble paid off, because they were all so shocked they couldn't react. And he was *strong.* Lupine blood roared in his veins. Vince fell, and the rest of Faber's gang were shouting and running. But the only thing Ben had to think about was getting out of there.

The world fell out of focus, and he was sure he'd lost it, that he was shifting.

"No, no, no . . ." he muttered, because he had nowhere to go, no safe place to hide. Vegas was far too human a city to cope with.

Besides, he was starting to think the city had it in for him.

Two legs, not four. He clenched human hands and tried not to think about claws. But the wolf in his blood helped him run faster. Just put your head down, stretch out, and go. He left the fight. Slammed through the door to the outside. Heard gunshots behind him; couldn't stop. Kept running, down a very dark street lined with cracked concrete buildings, an industrial park of some kind, old and worn. Under a dark night sky, washed out by the city's blazing lights.

He'd been at that game for hours. All night—and where was Kitty? What had she been doing all this time? He wondered what would happen if he never saw her again—

No—he crashed to a stop by a wall, slid down 'til he was sitting, panting for breath. Had to get his bearings. Had to figure out where he was and how to get back to the hotel.

The street was very quiet. Motionless. Ben listened for cars, gunfire, for anyone who might be following. Maybe he'd left them behind; he wasn't sure how far he'd gone.

Then he heard police sirens. A lot of police sirens, moving quickly, speeding. Instinctively, he huddled in a shadow, out of sight. He had no reason to hide from the cops, but he didn't want them to find him like this, blood covering his shirt, on the verge of turning wolf. Too much to explain. They'd want to take him to a hospital. All he wanted to do was see Kitty.

The sirens seemed to be converging behind Ben, blocks away—Faber's hideout. Vince was right all along, the cops tracked him there, and Faber's arrogance was going to get the better of him.

But the cops wouldn't find Ben. They'd find blood, they'd get the story—would they even believe it, that Ben had been shot in the heart then run off?

Maybe he ought to go back.

No. Because he couldn't fight it anymore, he let the instinct him carry him: don't get caught, just run. Go back to town, find Kitty.

Exhausted but driven, he set off.

The lights of the Strip guided him like a beacon. He had to have been jogging for miles, he shouldn't have had the strength for it—he was going to pay for it later, he was sure. Sleep for a week. But this was wolf's gig now. Just run, or the animal side was going to fight him, take over, and *make* him run.

He kept going, rather than let that happen.

About half a mile from Fremont Street, he managed to flag down a cab. Finally—and why didn't taxis regularly cruise the run-down, mob-run bad parts of town anyway? The taxi pulled over, and Ben leaned toward the door—and the cab took off, tires squealing, as soon as the driver got a look at his shirt, which was drenched with blood. Ben stood on the curb, abandoned, staring down at himself. The blood had mostly dried in the desert air. Didn't look too good, him walking around with half his chest stained red.

But it looked like he didn't have much of a choice in the matter.

Only another couple of miles to the Olympus Hotel and Casino. His feet were starting to drag.

When he finally came within view of the gleaming, spotlit neo-classical façade of the Olympus, Ben stopped, sighed, and smiled. Never had cheesy, overhyped architecture looked so good. He moved a little faster.

Then, ahead, just outside the driveway of the hotel, he saw her. He'd recognize that profile, that stance anywhere: slender body, legs up to *there*, floppy blond hair, tilt to her head like she was just about to say something funny.

She was getting out of a car—was that Odysseus Grant in the driver's seat? That thread of jealousy . . . worry . . . that was always there, that always asked what Kitty saw in a guy like him, flared, and Ben stilled it. Wait for the explanation. But he wondered: what kind of adventure had *she* been having? When she moved, she seemed as tired as he was.

Finally, she looked up and saw him. He'd stopped. He didn't remember stopping. He just had to, to take her all in.

And he thought, Almost home. A few more steps and I'll be home.

KITTY AND THE
SUPER BLUE BLOOD
OR WHATEVER MOON THING

"**Y**OU KNOW, IT'S EXHAUSTING," Ben said, and took a long draw on his bottle of beer. "It's like every other month there's this new 'Once every hundred years' super special moon-related event we're supposed to be paying attention to. How do we know? How do we really know if it's important? Are we really letting Facebook decide this stuff for us?"

We were naked, sitting next to each other, backs propped up against rock, part of a pile of boulders slumped up on the hillside. He offered the bottle. I took a drink and handed it back. The beer wasn't cold anymore, but it was still bubbly and sent calm through my limbs as it went down.

"Yeah," I said. "Before social media no one really paid attention to this stuff. But it's not like it isn't *interesting*."

"Interesting, sure, but is it *relevant*?"

Across the clearing a wolf howled. The sky wasn't full dark yet but had that rich deep-blue edging to twilight. Soon, the fat full moon would rise. Our werewolf pack had gathered, like we did every month—or every now and then, on a blue moon, twice a month. A few of us had already turned, and the wolves yipped and played.

Others were still in human form, pacing, resisting the call of their other selves demanding to burst free.

We were waiting to see what it meant, this super blood moon thing or whatever the hell they were calling it this time. What supernatural forces we'd be subjected to, out of our control and knowledge. Ben was right, it really was exhausting.

He continued. "What if Earth had five moons, hm? What if we were on, like, Jupiter, with thirty moons? Then what would happen? What would it be like being a werewolf on Jupiter?"

"We'd be crushed under the massive pressure of its atmosphere and tremendous gravitational forces," I answered.

"Oh. Yeah. I suppose so. So everyone who's ever talked about a cure for lycanthropy—has anyone suggested just blowing up the moon?"

I looked at him, his scruffy brown hair and his scrunched-up, thoughtful expression. He was awfully cute.

"No, honey, I don't think they have."

We were waiting for something—something else, apart from the usual full-moon madness, to happen. A few more of us shapeshifted. The clearing had more wolves than people now. Another howl burst out.

"Are you really worried?" I said, turning so I was curled up next to him. Ben set down the bottle and put his arms around me.

"I'm always worried."

Yeah. Couple of werewolves in this crazy world? A lot to worry about.

I said, "Maybe . . . what if . . . just this once . . . we didn't worry about it?"

An oversized wolf raced up to us, yipped eagerly, and darted away again. The moon was rising. It was time to go.

Ben bent his forehead to mine. "You know what? That's so crazy it just might work."

And then we all howled at the moon, the inconstant moon, together.

DEFINING SHADOWS

T HE WINDOWLESS OUTBUILDING near the property's back fence wasn't big enough to be a garage or even a shed. Painted the same pale green as the house twenty feet away, the mere closet was a place for garden tools and snow shovels, one of a thousand just like it in a neighborhood north of downtown Denver. But among the rakes and pruning shears, this one had a body.

Half a body, rather. Detective Jessi Hardin stood at the open door, regarding the macabre remains. The victim had been cut off at the waist, and the legs were propped up vertically, as if she'd been standing there when she'd been sliced in half and forgotten to fall down. Even stranger, there didn't seem to be any blood. The gaping wound in the trunk—vertebrae and a few stray organs were visible in a hollow body cavity from which the intestines had been scooped out—seemed almost cauterized, scorched, the edges of the flesh burned and bubbled. The thing stank of rotting meat, and flies buzzed everywhere. She could imagine the swarm that must have poured out when the closet door was first opened. By the tailored trousers and black pumps still in place, Hardin guessed the victim was female. No identification had been found. They were still checking ownership of the house.

"Told you you've never seen anything like it," Detective Patton said. He seemed downright giddy at stumping her.

Well, she had seen something like it, once. A transient had fallen asleep on some train tracks, and the train had come by and cut the poor bastard in half. But he hadn't been propped up in a closet later. No one had seen anything like *this*, and that was why Patton had called her. She got the weird ones these days. Frankly, if it meant she wasn't on call for cases where the body was an infant with a dozen broken bones, with deadbeat parents insisting they never laid a hand on the kid, she was fine with that.

"Those aren't supported, are they?" she said. "They're just standing upright." She took a pair of latex gloves from the pocket of her suit jacket and pulled them on. Pressing on the body's right hip, she gave a little push—the legs swayed, but didn't fall over.

"That's creepy," Patton said, all humor gone. He'd turned a little green.

"We have a time of death?" Hardin said.

"We don't have shit," Patton answered. "A patrol officer found the body when a neighbor called in about the smell. It's probably been here for days."

A pair of CSI techs were crawling all over the lawn, snapping photos and placing numbered yellow markers where they found evidence around the shed. There weren't many of the markers, unfortunately. The coroner would be here soon to haul away the body. Maybe the ME would be able to figure out who the victim was and how she'd ended up like this.

"Was there a padlock on the door?" Hardin said. "Did you have to cut it off to get inside?"

"No, it's kind of weird," Patton said. "It had already been cut off, we found it right next to the door." He pointed to one of the evidence markers and the generic padlock lying next to it.

"So someone had to cut off the lock in order to stow the body in here?"

"Looks like it. We're looking for the bolt-cutters. Not to mention the top half of the body."

"Any sign of it at all?" Hardin asked.

"None. It's not in the house. We've got people checking dumpsters around the neighborhood."

Hardin stepped away from the closet, caught her breath, and tried to set the scene for herself. She couldn't assume right away that the victim had lived in the house. But maybe she had. She was almost certain the murder had happened somewhere else, and the body moved to the utility closet later. The closet didn't have enough room for someone to cut a body through the middle, did it? The murderer would have needed a saw. Maybe even a sword.

Unless it had been done by magic.

Her rational self shied away from that explanation. It was too easy. She had to remain skeptical or she'd start attributing everything to magic and miss the real evidence. This wasn't necessarily magical, it was just odd and gruesome. She needed the ME to take a crack at the body. Once they figured out exactly what had killed the victim—and found the rest of the body—they'd be able to start looking for a murder weapon, a murder location, and a murderer.

The half a body looked slightly ridiculous laid out on a table at the morgue. The legs had been stripped, and a sheet laid over them. But that meant the whole body was under the sheet, leaving only the waist and wound visible. Half the stainless steel table remained empty and gleaming. The whole thing seemed way too clean. The morgue had a chill to it, and Hardin repressed a shiver.

"I don't know what made the cut," Alice Dominguez, the ME on the case, said. "Even with the burning and corrosion on the wound, I should find some evidence of slicing, cutting movements, or even metal shards. But there's nothing. The wound is symmetrical and even. I'd have said it was done by a guillotine, but there aren't any metal traces. Maybe it was a laser?" She shrugged, to signal that she was reaching.

"A laser—would that have cauterized the wound like that?" Hardin said.

"Maybe. Except that it wasn't cauterized. Those aren't heat burns."

Now Hardin was really confused. "This isn't helping me at all."

"Sorry. It gets worse. You want to sit down?"

"No. What is it?"

"It looks like acid burns," Dominguez said. "But the analysis says salt. Plain old table salt."

"Salt can't do that to an open wound, can it?"

"In large enough quantities salt can be corrosive on an open wound. But we're talking a lot of salt, and I didn't find that much."

That didn't answer any of Hardin's questions. She needed a cigarette. After thanking the ME, she went outside.

She kept meaning to quit smoking. She really ought to quit. But she valued these quiet moments. Standing outside, pacing a few feet back and forth with a cigarette in her hand and nothing to do but think, let her solve problems.

In her reading and research—which had been pretty scant up to this point, granted—salt showed up over and over again in superstitions, in magical practices. In defensive magic. And there it was. Maybe someone *thought* the victim was magically dangerous. Someone *thought* the victim was going to come back from the dead and used the salt to prevent that.

That information didn't solve the murder, but it might provide a motive.

Patton was waiting at her desk back at the station, just so he could present the folder to her in person. "The house belongs to Tom and Betty Arcuna. They were renting it out to a Dora Manuel. There's your victim."

Hardin opened the folder. The photo on the first page looked like it had been blown up from a passport. The woman was brown skinned, with black hair and tasteful makeup on a round face. Middle-aged, she guessed, but healthy. Frowning and unhappy, for whatever reason. She might very well be the victim, but without a face or even fingerprints they'd probably have to resort to DNA testing. Unless they found the missing half. Still no luck with that.

Ms. Manuel had immigrated from the Philippines three years ago. Tom and Betty Arcuna, her cousins, had sponsored her, but they hadn't seemed to have much contact with her. They rented her the house, Manuel paid on time, and they didn't even get together for holidays. The Arcunas lived in Phoenix, Arizona, and this house was one of several they owned in Denver and rented out, mostly to Filipinos. Patton had talked to them on the phone; they had expressed shock at Manuel's demise, but had no other information to offer. "She kept to herself. We never got any complaints, and we know all the neighbors."

Hardin fired up the Internet browser on her computer and searched under "Philippines" and "magic." And got a lot of hits that had nothing to do with what she was looking for. Magic shows, as in watch me pull a rabbit out of my hat, and Magic tournaments, as in the geek card game. She added "spell" and did a little better, spending a few minutes flipping through various pages discussing black magic and hexes and the like, in both dry academic rhetoric and the sensationalist tones of superstitious evangelists. She learned that many so-called spells were actually curses involving gastrointestinal distress and skin blemishes. But she could also buy a love spell online for a hundred pesos. She didn't find anything about any magic that would slice a body clean through the middle.

Official public acknowledgement—that meant government recognition—of the existence of magic and the supernatural was recent enough that no one had developed policies about how to deal with cases involving such matters. The medical examiner didn't have a way to determine if the salt she found on the body had had a magical effect. There wasn't an official process detailing how to investigate a magical crime. The Denver PD Paranatural Unit was one of the first in the country, and Hardin—the only officer currently assigned to the unit, because she was the only one with any experience—suspected she was going to end up writing the book on some of this stuff. She still spent a lot of her time trying to convince people that any of it was real.

When she was saddled with the unit, she'd gotten a piece of advice: The real stuff stayed hidden, and had stayed hidden for a long time. Most of the information that was easy to find was a smoke screen. To find the truth, you had to keep digging. She went old school and searched the online catalog for the Denver Public Library, but didn't find a whole lot on Filipino folklore.

"What is it this time? Alligators in the sewer?"

Hardin rolled her eyes without turning her chair to look at the comedian leaning on the end of her cubicle. It was Bailey, the senior homicide detective, and he'd given her shit ever since she'd first walked into the bureau and said the word "werewolf" with a straight face. It didn't matter that she'd turned out to be right, and that she'd dug up a dozen previous deaths in Denver that had been attributed to dog and coyote maulings and gotten them reclassified as unsolved homicides, with werewolves as the suspected perpetrators—which ruined the bureau's solve rate. She'd done battle with vampires, and Bailey didn't have to believe it for it to be true. Hardin could at least hope that even if she couldn't solve the bizarre crimes she faced, she'd at least get brownie points for taking the jobs no one else wanted.

"How are you, Detective?" she said in monotone.

"I hear you got a live one. So to speak. Patton says he was actually happy to hand this one over to you."

"It's different, all right." She turned away from the computer to face the gray-haired, softly overweight man. Three hundred and forty-nine days to retirement, he was, and kept telling them.

He craned around a little further to look at her computer screen. "A tough-nut case and what are you doing, shopping for shoes?"

She'd cultivated a smile just for situations like this. It had gotten her through the Academy, it had gotten her through every marks-manship test with a smart-ass instructor, it had gotten her through eight years as a cop. But one of these days, she was going to snap and take someone's head off.

"It's the twenty-first century, Bailey," she said. "Half the crooks these days knock over a liquor store and then brag about it on Myspace an hour later. You gotta keep on top of it."

He looked at her blankly. She wasn't about to explain Myspace to him. Not that he'd even dare admit to her that he didn't know or understand something. He was the big dick on campus, and she was just the girl detective.

At least she had a pretty good chance of outliving the bastards.

Donning a smile, he said, "Hey, maybe it's a vampire!" He walked away, chuckling.

If that was the worst ribbing she got today, she'd count herself lucky.

Canvassing the neighborhood could be both her most and least fa-vorite part of an investigation. She usually learned way more than she wanted to and came away not thinking very highly of people. She'd have to stand there not saying anything while listening to people tell her over and over again that no, they never suspected anything, the suspect was always very quiet, and no, they never saw anything, they didn't know anything. All the while, they wouldn't meet her gaze. They didn't want to get involved. She bet if she'd interviewed the Arcunas in person, they wouldn't have looked her in the eyes.

But this was often the very best way to track down leads, and a good witness could crack a whole case.

Patton had already talked to the neighbor who called in the smell, a Hispanic woman who lived in the house behind Manuel's. She hadn't had any more useful information, so Hardin wanted to try the more immediate neighbors.

She went out early in the evening, after work and around dinner-time, when people were more likely to be home. The neighborhood was older, a grid of narrow streets, eighty-year-old houses in various states of repair jammed in together. Towering ash and maple trees pushed up the slabs of the sidewalks with their roots. Narrow drives led to carports, or simply to the sides of the houses. Most cars parked along the curbs. A mix of lower-class residents lived here: kids living five or six to a house to save rent while they worked minimum-wage jobs; ethnic families, recent immigrants getting their starts; blue-collar families struggling at the poverty line.

Dora Manuel's house still had yellow tape around the property. When she couldn't find parking on the street, Hardin broke the tape away and pulled into the narrow driveway, stopping in front of the fence to the back lot. She put the tape back up behind her car.

Across the street, a guy was on his front porch taking pictures of the house, the police tape, her. Fine, she'd start with him.

She crossed the street and walked to his porch with an easy, non-threatening stride. His eyes went wide and a little panicked anyway.

"I'm sorry, I wasn't hurting anything, I'll stop," he said, hiding the camera behind his back.

Hardin gave him a wry, annoyed smile and held up her badge. "My name's Detective Hardin, Denver PD, and I just want to ask you a few questions. That okay?"

He only relaxed a little. He was maybe in his early twenties. The house was obviously a rental, needing a good scrubbing and a coat of paint. Through the front windows she could see band posters on the living room walls. "Yeah . . . okay."

"What's your name?"

"Pete. Uh . . . Pete Teller."

"Did you know Dora Manuel?"

"That Mexican lady across the street? The one who got killed?"

"Filipina, but yes."

"No, didn't know the lady at all. Saw her sometimes."

"When was the last time you saw her?"

"Maybe a few days ago. Yeah, like four days ago, going inside the house at dinnertime."

Patton's background file said that Manuel didn't own a car. She rode the bus to her job at a dry cleaners. Pete would have seen her walking home.

"Did you see anyone else? Maybe anyone who looked like they didn't belong?"

"No, no one. Not ever. Lady kept to herself, you know?"

Yeah, she did. She asked a few more standard witness questions, and he gave the standard answers. She gave him her card and asked him to call if he remembered anything, or if he heard anything. Asked him to tell his roommates to do the same.

The family two doors south of Manuel was also Filipino. Hardin was guessing the tired woman who opened the door was the mother of a good-sized family. Kids were screaming in a back room. The woman was shorter than Hardin by a foot, and brown-skinned, and her black hair was tied in a ponytail. She wore a blue T-shirt and faded jeans.

Hardin flashed her badge. "I'm Detective Hardin, Denver PD. Could I ask you a few questions?"

"Is this about Dora Manuel?"

This encouraged Hardin. At least someone around here had actually known the woman. "Yes. I'm assuming you heard what happened?"

"It was in the news," she said.

"How well did you know her?"

"Oh, I didn't, not really."

So much for the encouragement. "Did you ever speak with her? Can you tell me the last time you saw her?"

"I don't think I ever talked to her. I'm friends with Betty Arcuna, who owns the house. I knew her when she lived in the neighborhood. I kept an eye on the house for her, you know, as much as I could."

"Then did you ever see any suspicious activity around the house? Any strangers, anyone who looked like they didn't belong?"

She pursed her lips and shook her head. "No, not really, not that I remember."

A sound, like something heavy falling from a shelf, crashed from the back of the house. The woman just sighed.

"How many kids do you have?" Hardin asked.

"Five," she said, looking even more tired.

Hardin saw movement over the mother's shoulder. The woman looked. Behind her, leaning against the wall like she was trying to hide behind it, was a girl—a young woman, rather. Sixteen or seventeen. Wide-eyed, pretty. Give her another couple of years to fill out the curves and she'd be beautiful.

"This is my oldest," the woman said.

"You mind if I ask her a few questions?"

The young woman shook her head no, but her mother stepped aside. Hardin expected her to flee to the back of the house, but she didn't.

"Hi," Hardin said, trying to sound friendly without sounding condescending. "I wondered if you could tell me anything about Ms. Manuel."

"I don't know anything about her," she said. "She didn't like kids messing in her yard. We all stayed away."

"Can you remember the last time you saw her?"

She shrugged. "A few days ago, maybe."

"You know anyone who had it in for her? Maybe said anything bad about her or threatened her? Sounds like the kids around here didn't like her much."

"No, nothing like that," she said.

Hardin wasn't going to get anything out of her, though the girl looked scared. Maybe she was just scared of whatever had killed Manuel. The mother gave Hardin a sympathetic look and shrugged, much like her daughter had.

Hardin got the names—Julia Martinal and her daughter Teresa. She gave them a card. "If you think of anything, let me know."

Two houses down was an older, angry white guy.

"It's about time you got here and did something about those Mexicans," he said when Hardin showed him her badge.

"I'm sorry?" Hardin said, playing dumb, seeing how far the guy would carry this.

"Those Mexican gang wars, they got no place here. That's what happened, isn't it?"

She narrowed her gaze. "Have you seen any Mexican gangs in the area? Any unusual activity, anything you think is suspicious? Drive-bys, strange people loitering?"

"Well, I don't get up in other people's business. I can't say that I saw anything. But that Mexican broad was killed, right? What else could have happened?"

"What's your name, sir?" Hardin said.

He hesitated, lips drawing tight, as if he was actually considering arguing with her or refusing to tell. "Smith," he said finally. "John Smith."

"Mr. Smith, did you ever see anyone at Dora Manuel's house? Anyone you'd be able to pick out of a lineup?"

He still looked like he'd eaten something sour. "Well, no, not like that. I'm not a spy or a snitch or anything."

She nodded comfortingly. "I'm sure. Oh, and Mr. Smith? Dora Manuel was Filipina, not Mexican."

She gave him her card, as she had with the others, and asked him to call her. Out of all the people she'd left cards with today, she bet Smith would be the one to call. And he'd have nothing useful for her.

She didn't get much out of any of the interviews.

"I'm sorry, I never even knew what her name was."

"She kept to herself, I didn't really know her."

"She wasn't that friendly."

"I don't think I was surprised to hear that she'd died."

In the end, rather than having any solid leads on what had killed her, Hardin walked away with an image of a lonely, maybe even os-tracized woman with no friends, no connections, and no grief lost at her passing. People with that profile were usually pegged as the killers, not the victims.

She sat in her car for a long time, letting her mind drift, wondering which lead she'd missed and what connection she'd have to make to solve this thing. The murder wasn't random. In fact, it must have been carefully planned, considering the equipment involved. So the body had been moved, maybe. There still ought to be evidence of that at the crime scene—tire tracks, foot prints, blood. Maybe the techs had come up with something while she was out here dithering.

The sun was setting, sparse streetlights coming on, their orange glow not doing much to illuminate past the trees. Not a lot of activity went on. A few lights on in a few windows. No cars moving.

She stepped out of the car and started walking.

Instead of going straight through the gate to the backyard, she went around the house and along the fence to the alley behind the houses, a narrow path mostly haunted by stray cats. She caught movement out of the corner of her eye; paused and looked, caught sight of small legs and a tail. She flushed and her heart sped up, in spite of herself. She knew it was just a cat. But her hindbrain thought of the other creatures with fur she'd seen in back alleys. The monsters.

She came into Manuel's yard through a back gate. The shed loomed before her, seeming to expand in size. She shook the image away. The only thing sinister about the shed was her knowledge of what had been found there. Other houses had back porch lights on. She could hear TVs playing. Not at Manuel's house. The lights were dark, the whole property still, as if the rest of the street had vanished, and the site existed in a bubble. Hardin's breathing suddenly seemed loud.

She couldn't see much of anything in the dark. No footprints, not a stray thread of cloth. She didn't know what she was hoping to find.

One thing she vowed she'd never do was call in a psychic to work a case. But standing in the backyard of Manuel's residence at night, she couldn't help wondering if she'd missed something simply because it wasn't visible to the mundane eye. Could a psychic stand here and see some kind of magical aura? Maybe follow a magical trail to the person who'd committed the crime?

The real problem was—how would she know she was hiring an actual psychic? Hardin was ready to believe just about anything, but that wouldn't help her figure out what had happened here.

The next day, she made a phone call. She had at least one more resource to try.

Hardin came to the supernatural world as a complete neophyte, and she had to look for advice wherever she could, no matter how odd the source, or how distasteful. Friendly werewolves, for example. Or convicted felons.

Cormac Bennett styled himself a bounty hunter specializing in the supernatural. He freely admitted he was a killer, though he claimed to only kill monsters—werewolves, vampires, and the like. A judge had recently agreed with him, at least about the killer part, and sentenced Bennett to four years for manslaughter. It meant that Hardin now had someone on hand who might be able to answer her questions. She'd requested the visit and asked that he not be told it was her because she didn't want him to say no to the meeting. They'd had a couple of run-ins—truthfully, she was a little disappointed that she hadn't been the one who got to haul him in on charges of attempted murder, at the very least.

When he sat down and saw her through the glass partition, he muttered, "Christ."

"Hello," she said, rather pleased at his reaction. "You look terrible, if you don't mind me saying." It wasn't that he looked terrible; he looked like any other con, rough around the edges, tired, and seething. He had shadows under his eyes. That was a lot different than he'd looked the last time she'd seen him, poised and hunting.

"What do you want?"

"I have to be blunt, Mr. Bennett," she said. "I'm here looking for advice."

"Not sure I can help you."

Maybe this had been a mistake. "You mean you're not sure you *will*. Maybe you should let me know right now if I'm wasting my time. Save us both the trouble."

"Did Kitty tell you to talk to me?"

As a matter of fact, Kitty Norville had suggested it. Kitty the werewolf. Hardin hadn't believed it either, until she saw it. It was mostly Kitty's fault Hardin had started down this path. "She said you might know things."

"Kitty's got a real big mouth," Bennett said wryly.

"How did you two even end up friends?" Hardin said. "You wanted to kill her."

"It wasn't personal."

"Then, what? It got personal?" Hardin never understood why Kitty had just let the incident go. She hadn't wanted to press charges. And now they were what, best friends?

"Kitty has a way of growing on you."

Hardin smiled, just a little, because she knew what he was talking about. Kitty had a big mouth, and it made her charming rather than annoying. Most of the time.

She pulled a folder from her attaché case, drew out the eight-by-ten crime-scene photos, and held them up to the glass. "I have a body. Well, half a body. It's pretty spectacular and it's not in any of the books."

Bennett studied the photos a long time, and she waited, watching him carefully. He didn't seem shocked or disgusted. Of course he didn't. He was curious. Maybe even admiring? She tried not to judge. This was like Manuel's shed; she only saw Bennett as sinister because she knew what he was capable of.

"What the hell?" he said finally. "How are they even still standing? Are they attached to something?"

"No," she said. "I have a set of free-standing legs attached to a pelvis, detached cleanly above the fifth lumbar vertebra. The wound is covered with a layer of table salt that appears to have caused the flesh to scorch. Try explaining that one to my captain."

"No thanks," he said. "That's your job. I'm just the criminal reprobate."

"So you've never seen anything like this."

"Hell, no."

"Have you ever heard of anything like this?" She'd set the photos flat on the table. He was still studying them.

"No. You have any leads at all?"

"No. We've ID'd the body. She was Filipina, a recent immigrant. We're still trying to find the other half of the body. There has to be another half somewhere, right?"

He sat back, shaking his head. "I wouldn't bet on it."

"You're sure you don't know anything? You're not just yanking my chain out of spite?"

"I get nothing out of yanking your chain. Not here."

Scowling, she put the photos back in her case. "Well, this was worth a try. Sorry for wasting your time."

"I've got nothing but time."

He was yanking her chain, she was sure of it. "If you think of anything, if you get any bright ideas, call me." As the guard arrived to escort him back to his cell, she said, "And get some sleep. You look awful."

Hardin was at her desk, looking over the latest reports from the crime lab. Nothing. They hadn't had rain, the ground was hard, so no footprints. No blood. No fibers. No prints on the shed. Someone wearing gloves had cut off the lock in order to stuff half the body inside—then hadn't bothered to lock the shed again. The murderer had simply closed the door and vanished.

The phone rang, and she answered, frustrated and surly. "Detective Hardin."

"Will you accept the charges from Cormac Bennett at the Colorado Territorial Correctional Facility?"

It took her a moment to realize what that meant. She was shocked. "Yes, I will. Hello? Bennett?"

"*Manananggal*," he said. "Don't ask me how to spell it."

She wrote down the word, sounding it out as best she could. The Internet would help her find the correct spelling. "Okay, but what is it?"

"Filipino version of the vampire."

That made no sense. But really, did that matter? It made as much sense as anything else. It was a trail to follow. "Hot damn," she said, suddenly almost happy. "The victim was from the Philippines. It fits. So the suspect was Filipino, too? Do Filipino vampires eat entire torsos, or what?"

"No," he said. "That body *is* the vampire, the *manananggal*. You're looking for a vampire hunter."

Her brain stopped at that one. "Excuse me?"

"These creatures, these vampires—they detach the top halves of their bodies to hunt. They're killed when someone sprinkles salt on the bottom half. They can't return to reattach to their legs, and they die at sunrise. If they're anything like European vampires, the top half disintegrates. You're never going to find the rest of the body."

Well. She still wouldn't admit that any of this made sense, but the pieces fit. The bottom half, the salt burns. Never mind—she was still looking for a murderer here, right?

"Detective?" Cormac said.

"Yeah, I'm here," she said. "This fits all the pieces we have. Looks like I have some reading to do to figure out what really happened."

He managed to sound grim. "Detective, you might check to see if there've been a higher than usual number of miscarriages in the neighborhood."

"Why?"

"I used the term 'vampire' kind of loosely. This thing eats fetuses. Sucks them through the mother's navel while she sleeps."

She almost hung up on him because it was too much. What was it Kitty sometimes said? Just when you thought you were getting a handle on the supernatural, just when you thought you'd seen it all, something even more unbelievable came along.

"You're kidding." She sighed. "So, what—this may have been a revenge killing? Who's the victim here?"

"You'll have to figure that one out yourself."

"Isn't that always the way?" she muttered. "Hey—now that we know you really were holding out on me, what made you decide to remember?"

"Look, I got my own shit going on and I'm not going to try to explain it to you."

She was pretty sure she didn't really want to know. "Fine. Okay. But thanks for the tip, anyway."

"Maybe you could put in a good word for me," he said.

She supposed she owed him the favor. Maybe she would after she got the whole story of how he ended up in prison in the first place. Then again, she pretty much thought he belonged there. "I'll see what I can do."

She hung up, found a phone book, and started calling hospitals.

Hardin called every hospital in downtown Denver. Every emergency room, every ob-gyn, free clinic, and even Planned Parenthood. She had to do a lot of arguing.

"I'm not looking for names, I'm just looking for numbers. Rates. I want to know if there's been an increase in the number of miscarriages in the downtown Denver area over the last three years. No, I'm not from the EPA. Or from *60 Minutes*. This isn't an exposé, I'm Detective Hardin with Denver PD and I'm investigating a case. *Thank* you."

It took some of them a couple of days to get back to her. When they did, they seemed just as astonished as she was: Yes, miscarriage rates had tripled over the last three years. There had actually been a small decline in the local area's birth rate.

"Do I need to worry?" one doctor asked her. "Is there something in the water? What is this related to?"

She hesitated about what to tell him. She could tell the truth—and he would never believe her. It would take too long to explain, to try to persuade him. "I'm sorry, sir, I can't talk about it until the case is wrapped up. But there's nothing to worry about. Whatever was causing this has passed, I think."

He didn't sound particularly comforted, and neither was she. Because what else was out there? What other unbelievable crisis would strike next?

Hardin knocked on the Martinals' front door. Julia Martinal, the mother, answered again. On seeing the detective, her expression turned confused. "Yes?"

"I just have one more question for you, Mrs. Martinal. Are you pregnant?"

"No." She sounded offended, looking Hardin up and down as if to say, *how dare you?*

Hardin took a deep breath and carried on. "I'm sorry for prying into your personal business, but I have some new information. About Dora Manuel."

Julia Martinal's eyes grew wide, and her hand gripped the edge of the door. Hardin thought she was going to slam it closed.

Hardin said, "Have you had any miscarriages in the last couple of years?"

At that, the woman's lips pursed. She took a step back. "I know what you're talking about, and that's crazy. It's crazy! It's just old stories. Sure, nobody liked Dora Manuel, but that doesn't make her a—a—"

So Hardin didn't have to explain it.

The daughter, Teresa Martinal, appeared where she had before, lingering at the edge of the foyer, staring out with suspicion. Her hand rested on her stomach. That gesture was the answer.

Hardin bowed her head to hide a wry smile. "Teresa? Can you come out and answer a few questions?"

Julia moved to stand protectively in front of her daughter. "You don't have to say anything, Teresa. This woman's crazy."

"Teresa, are you pregnant?" Hardin asked, around Julia's defense.

Teresa didn't answer. The pause drew on, and on. Her mother stepped aside, astonished, studying her daughter. "Teresa? Are you? Teresa!"

The young woman's expression became hard, determined. "I'm not sorry."

"You spied on her," Hardin said, to Teresa, ignoring her mother. "You knew what she was, you knew what that meant, and you spied to find out where she left her legs. You waited for the opportunity, then you broke into the shed. You knew the stories. You knew what to do."

"Teresa?" Mrs. Martinal said, her disbelief growing.

The girl still wouldn't say anything.

Hardin continued. "We've only been at this a few days, but we'll find something. We'll find the bolt-cutters you used and match them to the cut marks on the padlock. We'll match the salt in your cupboard with the salt on the body. We'll make a case for murder. But if you cooperate, I can help you. I can make a pretty good argument that this was self-defense. What do you say?"

Hardin was making wild claims—the girl had been careful and the physical evidence was scant. They might not find the bolt-cutters, and the salt thing was pure television. And while Hardin might scrounge together the evidence and some witness testimony, she might never convince the DA's office that this had really happened.

Teresa looked stricken, like she was trying to decide if Hardin was right, and if they had the evidence. If a jury would believe that a meek, pregnant teenager like her could even murder another person.

It would be a hard sell—but Hardin was hoping this would never make it to court. She wasn't stretching the truth about the self-defense plea. By some accounts, Teresa probably deserved a medal. But Hardin wouldn't go that far.

In a perfect world, Hardin would be slapping cuffs on Dora Manuel, not Teresa. But until the legal world caught up with the shadow world, this would have to do.

Teresa finally spoke in a rush. "I had to do it. You know I had to do it. My mother's been pregnant twice since Ms. Manuel moved in. They died. I heard her talking. She knew what it was. She knew what was happening. I had to stop it." She had both hands laced in a protective barrier over her stomach now. She wasn't showing much yet. Just a swell she could hold in her hands.

Julia Martinal covered her mouth. Hardin couldn't imagine which part of this shocked her more—that her daughter was pregnant, or a murderer.

Hardin imagined trying to explain this to the captain. She'd managed to get the werewolves pushed through and on record, but this was so much weirder. At least, not having grown up with the stories, it was. But the case was solved. On the other hand, she could just walk away. Without Teresa's confession, they'd never be able to close the case. Hardin had a hard time thinking of Teresa as a murderer—she wasn't like Cormac Bennett. Hardin could just walk away. But not really.

In the end, Hardin called it in and arrested Teresa. But her next call was to the DA about what kind of deal they could work out. There had to be a way to work this out within the system. Get Teresa off on probation on a minor charge. There had to be a way to drag the shadow world, kicking and screaming, into the light.

Somehow, Hardin would figure it out.

BELLUM ROMANUM

GAIUS ALBINUS stood before the locked gates of Diocletian's Palace. Fifteen hundred years of planning, and he could not get to where he needed to go because of a chain and padlock, an electronic security system, and a modern sense of reasonable working hours, helpfully marked out on a placard bolted to the stone. What had once been a palace was now a museum, and it was closed.

So many obstacles in this modern era did not involve armies, weapons, or violence. No, they were barriers of bureaucracy and officious politeness. Venerable institutions of old Rome he ought to know well, passed down to successive civilizations.

He couldn't help but smile, amused. To come so far, and to be confronted now by a sign telling him the site had closed several hours before and that he could not enter until daylight. Impossible for him.

Well. He would simply have to find another way. There was *always* another way.

What most impressed Gaius Albinus wasn't how much the city of Split had changed, but how much remained the same and recognizable. Even now, the city felt Roman.

The central palace complex still stood, amidst the sprawl that had grown up around it. The temple walls were identifiable. Many pitted stone blocks had fallen long ago and were now arranged in artistic piles, in the interest of archeological curiosity. At some point, cast-off stones had become valuable, worthy of admiration. Entire towns had turned into relics, museum pieces. And the roads—the roads still marked out routes across the Empire. The great engineers of Rome remained triumphant.

These days the one-time retirement retreat of Emperor Diocletian was a university and tourist town, raucous with nightlife, young people crowding into cafés, spilling onto the beach, drinking hard under strings of electric lights. Not so different from youth cavorting under suspended oil lamps back in the day, letting clothing slip off shoulders while pretending not to notice, making eyes at each other, offering invitations. That hadn't changed either, not in all his years.

Now, as then, tourists were easy to spot by the way they wandered through it all with startled, awestruck expressions. Most likely not understanding the local language. Gaius remembered going to Palestine as a young soldier, expecting to hear a cacophony of languages, yet not being prepared for the sense of displacement, a kind of intellectual vertigo, that came from standing in the middle of a market and hearing people shout at one another using strange words, laughing at jokes he couldn't understand. The way people became subdued when he spoke his native Latin. More often than not they understood him, even when they pretended not to. They marked him as a foreigner, a conqueror.

Since then, he had learned not to particularly care what people thought of him.

Outside the old Roman center, the city was comprised of the blend of modernity and semi-modernity along narrow medieval streets that marked so many European cities. After traveling out by car, he stopped at a squat town house of middling modern construction: aluminum and plywood. Clearly a product of the time when this country had been part of Yugoslavia, communist and short on resources. That era had lasted less than a century. The blink of an eye. Hardly worth remembering.

The hour was late. Gaius knocked on the door anyway, and a mousy-looking man answered. In his thirties, he had tousled black hair, and wore dark-rimmed glasses and a plain T-shirt with sweats. An average man dressed for a night in. He blinked, uncertain and ready to close the door on the stranger.

"I need your help," Gaius said, in the local Croatian.

"What is it?" The guy looked over Gaius's shoulder as if searching for a broken-down car. There wasn't one.

"If you could just step out for a moment." The man did, coming out to the concrete stoop in front of the door. People were so trusting.

Gaius needed him outside his house, across the protection of his threshold. In the open, under a wide sky, the Roman could step in the man's line of sight and catch his gaze. Then draw that attention close, wrap his own will around the small mortal's mind, and pull. In the space of three of the man's own heartbeats, Gaius possessed him.

Gaius's heart hadn't beat once in two thousand years.

"Professor Dimic, I need to get inside the palace. You have access. You'll help me."

He didn't even question how Gaius knew his name. "Yes, of course."

Gaius drove the archaeologist back to the city center, navigated the crowds to the quiet alley where the gate to the lower level was located. Gaius could have broken in himself—picked the lock, disabled the security system. But this was simpler and would leave no evidence. No one must track him. No one must know what he did.

Dimic unlocked the gate, keyed in the security code, and they were inside.

"Anything else?" he asked, almost eagerly. His gaze was intent but vacant, focused on Gaius without really seeing anything.

"Show me how to reset all this when I leave."

"Certainly."

The archaeologist gave him the code, showed him the lock, and even left a key. He helpfully pointed out restrooms at the far end of the hallway.

"Go home now," Gaius instructed the man. "Go inside. Sit in the first chair you come to and close your eyes. When you open them again you won't remember any of this. Do you understand?"

"I do." He nodded firmly, as if he'd just been given a dangerous mission and was determined to see it through.

"Go."

The archaeologist, a man who had dedicated his life to studying the detritus Gaius's people had left behind, turned and walked away, without ever knowing he'd been in the presence of a one-time Roman centurion. He'd weep if he ever found out.

Gaius made sure the gates were closed behind him and went into the tunnels beneath the palace. The vaulted spaces were lit only by faint emergency lights at the intersections. Columns made forests of shadows.

He had to orient himself. The main gallery had been turned into some kind of gift shop or market. The eastern chambers had become an art gallery, scattered with unremarkable modern sculptures, indulgent satire. But along the western corridor, he found a familiar passageway, and from there was able to locate the series of chambers he needed. He reached the farthest, not taking time to glance at any of the exhibits—he knew it all already. Then, he counted seven stones along the floor to the right spot on the wall, two bricks up. Anyone who'd come along this passage and happened to knock on this row of stones would have noticed that one made a slightly different sound. A more hollow sound. But in all that time, it seemed that no one had ever done so.

He drew a crowbar from inside his jacket and used it to scrape out mortar and grime from around the brick, then worked to pry the brick free. He had to lean his body into it; the wall had settled over the centuries. Dust had sealed the cracks. But he was strong, very strong, and with a couple of great shoves and a grunt, the brick slipped and thudded to the ground at his feet.

Gaius reached inside the exposed alcove.

A thousand disasters could have befallen this site. A dozen wars had crossed this country since the last time he'd been here. But he'd chosen his hiding place well. The palace area had been continually lived in and not left for ruin. The town was off the main crossroads of Europe. Armies generally didn't have a reason to level a coastal village with no strategic value. The place was still mostly intact, mostly preserved. Even better, over the last couple of centuries it had been cleaned up and maintained.

And in all that time, no one had discovered what he'd left buried. He drew out his prize and held it up to check its condition.

The artifact was a clay lamp, terra-cotta orange, small enough to fit in the palm of his hand. A spout at one end would hold a wick; oil would be poured in through the top. It was a poor man's lamp, too plain and commonplace for wealth. The designs imprinted around the top were of fire. The thing was dusty, covered in grime, but otherwise in good shape. Just as he'd left it. A couple of swipes with his gloved hand cleared some of the dirt. There'd be plenty of time later to clean it more thoroughly. It didn't need to be clean, it needed to be intact, safe in hand. The Manus Herculei. The Hand of Hercules, which he would use to bring fire down upon the Earth.

If archaeologists had found it, they'd have tagged it, catalogued it. Stuck it behind glass or simply put it on a shelf in some climate-controlled archival storage. He might have had a harder time claiming it then, and some of the artifact's power might have diminished. But this . . . this was the best outcome he could have hoped for, and it made him wonder if there wasn't in fact some weight of destiny on his side. He was meant to do this, and he was being guided.

He had been on this path, unwavering, for two thousand years.

79 C.E.

When Gaius Albinus arrived in Pompeii, he had not aged in eighty years. He still looked like a hale man in his thirties. A bright centurion of Rome, though he'd left his armor behind decades before. Who needed armor when one was practically immortal?

He'd never wanted to be immortal. He'd wanted to die for Rome. That chance had been taken from him by a monster. Since then, he had looked for purpose. Some kind of revenge against the one who had done this. Unfortunately, Kumarbis was as indestructible as he was.

The force of Gaius's rage surprised him. He'd never had a reason to be angry before. When he looked for an outlet, something he could break or destroy to somehow quiet his fury, he found one worthy target: the world. If one was going to be immortal, one might as well use that time to attempt the impossible.

In Herculaneum, he rented a house. This was a port village up the coast from the more decadent, raucous Pompeii. Here, he'd have quiet and not have to answer so many questions. The place was small, just a couple of rooms on the outside of town, but it had a courtyard behind high walls. In privacy, he could burn herbs and write on the flagstones in charcoal, washing them off when he finished.

Then, he learned to make lamps.

He couldn't simply buy one in a market and have it be pure, so he went out one night to a pottery workshop and persuaded the master there to help him. The potter was skeptical, even with Gaius's particular brand of persuasion. Gaius was well dressed and held himself like a soldier—why would he need to learn to make lamps? "It's a hobby," Gaius said, and the man seemed to accept that. The potter taught him to fashion clay, bake it, fire it. His first few efforts were rough, lopsided. One shattered in the kiln.

"Practice," the potter said. "Even a simple thing takes practice. Keep trying."

Gaius understood that, and at the end of a week of working long nights he had a lamp, all of his own making. He paid the potter well, which seemed to confuse the man.

That was the first step. Next: the inscription.

He washed, wore a light, undyed tunic, and went barefoot. The summer air was thick, sticky, but his skin was cool, was always cool. He'd taken blood from his servant, who now slept in the house, out of the way. The borrowed strength buoyed him and would be enough to carry him through the night.

A full moon rose as dusk fell, and the smallest hint of sunset still touched the deep blue sky when Gaius arranged his tools in the courtyard. Charcoal, candles, string, braziers, and incense. His lamp. He had a hundred incantations to learn, a hundred symbols to memorize and write, then write again, until he had them perfect. Practice, as the potter had told him.

Such good advice.

He had a lamp to infuse with power.

Kneeling, tools in hand and bright moonlight silvering the courtyard, he hesitated. The hair on his arms stood up, and a sudden tension knotted his shoulders. It was the sensation of being stalked by a lion. He resisted the urge to look over his shoulder.

The danger was outside the courtyard, approaching. If he quieted himself, he could sense every beating heart in the town, he could follow the scent of warm blood and the sound of breathing to every hidden soul. But the thing approaching had no heartbeat, and its blood was cold. The hold it had on Gaius Albinus was difficult to define, but even after decades, the bond remained and called to him.

He set down his tools and marched to the courtyard door, wrenched it open, and looked.

An old man, his skin shriveled, his bones bent, pulled himself along the alley wall, creeping from one shadow to the next on crooked limbs. Hairless, joints bulging, he should not have been alive. His ragged linen tunic hung off him like a crucifixion. This was the source of nightmare tales that kept children awake, the stories of ghouls and demons that hid under beds and in wells.

Frozen, Gaius watched him approach. His teeth ground, his jaw clenched with rage, but he couldn't move, he couldn't flee. He ought to murder this monster. But he couldn't.

The shriveled old man heaved up against the wall and stared back at him. Laughing, he pointed a crooked finger. "*Salve*, Gaius Albinus, s*alve*! I found you. Given enough time, I knew I would find you. And my dear son, all I have is time."

"I am not your son," Gaius said reflexively, as he had done a hundred times before, uselessly. He glanced around the street; he didn't want anyone to witness this.

"Yes, you are. I made you. You are my son."

The old man, Kumarbis, looked desiccated, as if he had been wandering in a desert, baked by the sun. Which was impossible for one like him. This meant he had not been eating, going weeks between feeding on blood, instead of days. He was starved; he was weak. How was he still existing?

Something dug hooks into Gaius; a connection between them that he'd never be able to deny, however much he wanted to. A feeling: compassion; gratitude. A tangle emanating from this creature, binding them together. Gaius had tried to escape these lines of power, fed through blood and woven with terrible magic, created when Kumarbis had transformed him.

"No! I disavow you. I broke from you!"

"You are my son—"

"You are a mockery, you are not my father!" Gaius's father had died decades ago, never knowing what had become of his son, who'd vanished into the service of Rome.

The old man stepped forward, reaching an angular hand, and grinning, skull-like. "You owe me . . . hospitality. The tribute due to a master from his progeny. You owe me . . . sustenance." Horribly, he licked his peeling lips.

"You've fended for yourself for millennia before you ruined me. I will give you nothing."

Perversely, the old man chuckled, the sound of cracking papyrus. "I knew you were a strong man. Able to resist our bond? Very strong. I knew it. I chose you well."

"*Leave* here. Leave. I never want to see you again."

"Never? *Never?* Do you know what that means? You are only just beginning to realize what that means. We will always be here, we will always be bound."

"Come in, get off the street." Gaius grabbed the old man's tunic—he refused to touch that leathered skin—and pulled him into the courtyard, slamming the door behind. The ancient fabric of the tunic tore under the pressure, as if it rotted in place.

Kumarbis slumped against the wall and grinned again at Gaius as if he'd won a prize. "You have servants."

"They're mine, not yours."

"You are mine."

"I am not." He sounded like a mewling child.

What he ought to do was drink the old man dry. Suck whatever used-up blood was left in him, destroying him and taking all his power. But he would have to touch the monster for that. And . . . that pull. That bond. It made the very idea of harming the man repulsive. He couldn't even bear the thought of stabbing him through the heart with a length of wood, putting him out of his misery. It was the terrible magic of his curse that he could not bring himself to kill the one being in the universe that he most wanted to.

"I don't have time for this," Gaius said, turning back to his tools, the mission. He should just buy a slave for the old man to drain and be done with him.

Kumarbis pressed himself against the stone. "What are you doing here, Gaius?"

"Showing my strength. Proving a point."

Wincing, craning his neck forward, the old man studied what Gaius had prepared, the writing he had begun. "This magic . . . have I seen anything like it?"

Gaius spared a moment to glare. "I wouldn't know."

"Explain this to me." He seemed genuinely confused, his brow furrowed, a hand plucking at the hem of his garment. "You're working a spell . . . a spell made of fire?"

"No! I owe you nothing!" He stomped forward, raised his hand to the old man—and could not strike. Fist trembling, he snarled.

A knock came at the door. Both Gaius and Kumarbis froze, looking at each other as if to ask, *Were you expecting someone?* This night was cursed with interruptions. Gaius went to the door and cracked it open.

"What?"

"May I enter? Am I interrupting anything important?" He seemed like a young man, but Gaius had learned not to trust appearances of age. Bright eyes set in finely wrought features, the confident stance of a patrician, this man would be at home in the Forum at Rome. The kind of man who always had a curl at the corner of his lip, as if all he gazed on amused him. His tunic and wrap were expensive, trimmed with gold thread.

"Who are you?" Gaius demanded, and seemingly of its own will the door opened and the stranger stepped inside.

At the same time, Kumarbis dropped to his knees, which cracked on the flagstones.

"Hello, there," the stranger said amiably to him.

"You! It was always you!" the old man cried. "Your voice in the dark, drawing me forward. I tried! Don't you know I tried to build your army? I tried!"

The stranger's mouth cracked into a grin, and he turned to Gaius. "Is this man bothering you?"

Some sort of balance tipped in that moment. Gaius felt it in the prickling of skin on the back of his neck. In the way this stranger drew the eye, held the attention, though there seemed to be nothing noteworthy about him.

"Please! Why have you forsaken me?" Kumarbis had prostrated himself and was weeping. It was . . . almost sad.

The stranger said, "I found a stronger man. Or, you did. Thank you for that." He looked Gaius up and down, as if surveying livestock.

"For thousands of years I've—"

"And? Do you expect pity from me?"

"Perhaps . . . perhaps . . . mercy?"

The stranger laughed. "Oh, no, old man. No. Not from me."

"But—"

"Get out. Go." The stranger took Kumarbis by the arm, hauled him to his feet. He had no care for brittle bones or bent back. Why should he, when the old man didn't seem inclined to break? Only to weep.

He pushed the old man out and gently closed the door. Almost, Gaius worried. Where would Kumarbis go? Would he find shelter by daybreak? Would he find sustenance? But no, Kumarbis had survived this long, he didn't need help. He didn't need pity.

The stranger turned back to Gaius. "There. Where were we?"

Gaius stood, amazed. "Who *are* you?"

"Call me Lucien," the man said, smiling like he had something to sell.

"What do you want?"

The man paced around the courtyard, studying stone walls, looking over the charcoal and candles Gaius had laid out. "That's not the question. The question is this: What do *you* want?"

His words held a largeness, a vastness to them that expanded far beyond mere sound. They spoke to the depth of Gaius's anger, his urge to grab Kumarbis's skull and smash it against the wall. To break everything that would break, to shatter it all. But a dozen skulls would not satisfy. And rage was unbecoming to a soldier of Rome.

He said, "I want to see how much of the world I can change with my actions."

"Change?" Lucien said. "Or destroy? I see what you're doing here—this isn't change."

"Destruction is a kind of a change."

"So it is." His pacing brought him in a spiral to the middle of the courtyard. To the candles, the charcoal, the wax tablet with the symbols Gaius had copied for practice. The precious lamp. For a moment, he was afraid Lucien would break it. That he was some crusader who had somehow gotten wind of his plan.

Lucien had just tossed a two-thousand-year-old vampire out on the street. Gaius was fairly certain he wasn't powerful enough to stop this man—this whatever-he-was—from doing whatever he wanted.

Lucien turned to him and stopped smiling. "I know your plan. I support your plan. Be my general, Gaius Albinus. Gather my army for me. And you will have power."

"What . . . what army?" Gaius asked.

"Ones like you. There are more than you think, and by rights they should serve me. Also the werewolves, the demons, the succubi—"

"Werewolves?"

Lucien smiled. "You'll meet them soon enough. Use that army, destroy what you must. And hand it all over to me at the end of days. Agreed?"

A cause to march with. Gaius had missed the structure of direction, of order delivered for a righteous cause. And here this man appeared. This easy, smiling patrician with an answer and quip for everything. Gaius could see a moment, some years or decades—or even centuries—in the future, when Lucien would turn his back on him. Literally throw him on the street as he had done with Kumarbis. This man used and disposed of tools as needed.

But at least Gaius understood his role here.

Lucien offered his hand. "Come, my friend. I can make sure your talents don't go to waste."

Stepping forward, Gaius placed his hands between Lucien's and pledged his loyalty. He was surprised at how warm Lucien's skin was against his own chilled, bloodless hands. As if the man were made of fire.

And then he was at the door, a light of victory in his face. "Good journeys to you, until next we meet."

"When will that be?"

Lucien shrugged, his lips pursed. He might have known, he might not have. Maybe he wanted to keep secrets.

Gaius said, "Then I will simply go on as I see fit. Gather this army for you. Gather power."

"And this," Lucien said, "proves that I have chosen well this time. *Vale*, my Dux Bellorum."

"*Vale*," Gaius said softly, but the man was already gone.

Gaius had work to do.

He assumed that Kumarbis still rested in Herculaneum. That he had somehow found a safe place to sleep out the day, as he had every day for the last however many hundreds of years. Gaius couldn't confirm this, and he had no desire to waste time looking for the old man, however much a thread of worry tugged at him. That thread was false, and Gaius owed it nothing. But the suspicion determined the target of his strike. Of his masterpiece.

The next night, he woke at dusk and gathered his tools: flint and steel, chalk and charcoal and ash for making marks, candles for light, his own will for power. The lamp to ignite it all. He slung the bag containing everything over his shoulder, wrapped his cloak around himself, and took the road out of town.

Some half hour of walking brought him to a field where goats grazed in the day, at the foot of the great mountain Vesuvius. The eaten-down scrub gave him a surface on which to write, after he kicked away stones and goat droppings. The open space gave him a vista in almost every direction; the lamplight of the towns along the coast; the bulge of the mountain blocking out stars behind him. He had some six hours of night in which to work. He moved quickly but carefully—he had limited time but needed perfection.

Once he began he could not stop. No different than any other campaign march. He cleared a space some twenty cubits across. Marked the center with a stake. Then, he began writing in powdered charcoal carefully poured out from a funnel.

The first circle of characters was an anchoring to drive the spell deep underground, hundreds of feet, to the molten fissures that fueled the mountain. The next ring of symbols built potential, stoked fires that already existed within the mountain. The third ring directed those energies outward. Then the next, and the next. Thirteen layers of spells on top of the work he'd already sealed within the lamp. The casting took all night. He almost wouldn't have time before the sun rose and destroyed him. He didn't think so much of the time that passed, only of the work that needed to be done, methodically and precisely. The good work of a Roman engineer.

The thirteenth circle, the outermost ring, was for containment, protection. The power he raised here would not dissipate, but would instead burst out at once, and only at his signal. As great a show of power as any god could produce.

A deep irony: magic provided him with the knowledge that gods did not operate the Earth and Heavens. A volcano's fury was not the anger of Vulcan making itself known. No, it was a natural process, pieces of the world crashing together and breaking apart. The resulting energies caused disasters. Sparks from the striking of flint and steel, writ large. The fires of the Earth bursting forth under pressure.

Magic didn't create. It manipulated what was already there. Placed the power of the gods in human hands. Or vampire hands.

At last the text was done. The moon reached its apex; dawn approached. He had finished in time, but only just. He went to the center of his great canvas and placed the lamp.

The object served as a focus and a fuse. A battle of primal elements and energies, a physical poetry. Words only captured a shadow of the true forces. Many languages, symbolic conventions, all of them together were still an imperfect representation and only approached the sublime. Magic was the art of trying.

In the middle of it all remained a need for brute force. The inchoate power of the Earth itself. He lit the lamp and waited a moment. Another moment. The lamp burned with a single buttery flame. The terra-cotta orange of the clay seemed to glow, and he couldn't tell if this was the natural light or burgeoning magic. The slight, rounded shadow of the lamp on the ground shuddered. Then vanished, as a circle of illumination spread out, stretching along the pasture and up the side of Vesuvius. The scrub-covered ground seemed to glow with the same light. People in the town would think the hillside had caught on fire.

Gaius waited, the nails of his hands digging welts into his palms. He didn't know what would happen, what signal he should wait for. He only knew what he wanted to happen, and waiting for that was agonizing. To the east the sky faded with a hint of the gray of dawn. He had to get out of the open, but he wanted to see the spell ignite.

Then, the faint glow on the hillside disappeared. It didn't fade, didn't dissipate. Gaius swore he saw the light itself sink into the ground. Then, the Earth rumbled. Just an earthquake. Tiny, inconsequential. The kind anyone living near a volcano must sense from time to time.

But this—he had triggered it. He was sure of it. And he was sure this was just the start. He laughed. Put up his arms in triumph and brayed like a fool.

The lamp in the middle of his circle had burned out. The clay was cold. Its power had all gone into the mountain. It was *working*!

He scooped up the lamp, the charcoal, the candles, knife, wicks, and other tools and shoved them into the bag. Then, before the sun rose, he raced back to Herculaneum, and from there to safety.

He had arranged for a boat to wait for him. He gave careful instructions to the captain: However strange and chaotic the world became, they should not leave until Gaius Albinus was on board, or they would forfeit their very large fee. The galley had a cabin belowdecks, and a cupboard that Gaius sealed up with waxed leather and blankets until the place was perfectly dark. He paid enough that the captain asked no questions.

The middle of that day, Vesuvius exploded. While he was sorry he missed the main of the eruption, asleep in his sealed cabin, that night from the safety of the boat at sea he watched the fires light up the darkness. It was glorious.

In the centuries after, he collected eyewitness testimonies. Pliny the Younger and other historians gave a great accounting of the disaster that buried Pompeii and Herculaneum. Some eighteen hundred years later, the first excavations of the cities revealed grotesqueries, shapes of despair frozen in ash and preserved in plaster by archaeologists. Gray husks of mothers bent over children, of dogs chained helplessly to walls. They had known they were going to die. They'd had moments to prepare, to wait. Squeeze shut their eyes, hold their breath, and hope that they would survive the flood of ash. Seeing photographs of those cast figures so many years later, Gaius felt that stab of triumph all over again. That thrill of realization: he had done it, he had caused this terrible thing to happen, this explosion of the Earth.

And he could do it again.

Gaius Albinus emerged from the basement of Diocletian's Palace with the lamp, which he had named the Manus Herculei, safely in hand.

He had heard and read the speculation of philosophers on the topic of immortality. Did humankind need the challenge of mortality? A limited span of time in order to feel the drive of ambition? Would ambition even exist, without the need to leave one's mark on the world before one died? If granted immortality, would a person become bored? Would they long for death?

Would they cease to even remember all the time they had experienced? Would they become little more than ghosts?

Gaius held the two-thousand-year-old clay lamp in his hand and could declare that immortality did not cause forgetfulness, did not dampen ambition. He remembered everything. He could smell the musk of goat and the tang of dried grass of that field; he remembered the fires of Vesuvius lighting up the night, the last of the screams that came from the town as the ash flow settled. The satisfaction, knowing that hideous old vampire was likely burned to nothing and buried under a ton of ash. The touch of clay against his skin was like a spark that transported him through time.

The power of the lamp had not diminished. No, by hiding it he had allowed it to sleep until its power grew. The next disaster he triggered with this artifact would make Vesuvius seem like a candle.

He was securing the gates as the archaeologist had instructed when he sensed a presence, an eddy of power in the night. Several of them. Enemies.

A call echoed on stone and through shadow. "Dux Bellorum! Your time is done!" Arrogant laughter followed.

Gaius knew the voice, though he had not heard it in decades. Not every vampire chose to follow Gaius, to join his army. Some rebelled. This man was an upstart, Master of the city of Barcelona, with centuries of power pressing from him. Still a child, really. Nothing to worry about for Gaius Albinus, known as Dux Bellorum, also called Roman. Last of his people.

Gaius slapped the crowbar against his hand and waited, mindful of the precious artifact wrapped in cloth and tucked in his pocket.

Early on, there had been those who recognized what he was doing and opposed his quest. Even if they didn't entirely understand the nature of his quest and its origins. That he was merely a general, following orders from his Caesar. Everyone who had opposed him, mortal or monster, full of power or merely earnest and naive, had failed. They would fail now, and he would enjoy putting them down.

One more hurdle, then, before leaving Split. Then, he could begin his journey to the park called Yellowstone, in North America.

KITTY LEARNS THE ROPES

I HIT PLAY on the laptop DVD software and sat back to watch.
This was a recording of a boxing match in Las Vegas last year.
The Heavyweight World Championships, the caption read. I was
glad it did, because I knew nothing about boxing, nothing about
who these guys were. Two beefy, sweaty men—one white, with a
dark buzz cut and heavy brow, the other black, bald, snarling—were
pounding on each other in rage. I winced as their blows sent sweat
and spit flying. As sports went, this was more unappealing than
most, in my opinion.

Then the white boxer, Ian Jacobson, the defending champion,
laid one into his opponent, Jerome Macy. The punch came in like a
pile driver, snapped Macy's head around, and sent the big man spinning. He crashed into the mat headfirst. The crack of bone carried
over the roars and cheers of the crowd. I resisted an urge to look
away, sure I was witnessing the boxer's death.

The arena fell silent, watching Macy lie still. Jacobson had retreated to an empty corner of the ring, looking agitated, while the
referee counted down over Macy. Ringside officials leaned in, uncertain whether to rush in to help or wait for the count to end.
Macy lay with his head twisted, his body crumpled, clearly badly

injured. Blood leaked out his nose.

Then, he moved. First a hand, then an arm. He levered himself up, shaking his head, shaking it again, stretching his neck back into alignment. Slowly, he regained his feet.

He turned, looking for his opponent with fire blazing in his eyes. Jacobson stared back, eyes wide, fearful. Obviously, he hadn't wanted Macy to be seriously hurt. But this—rising from the dead almost—must have seemed worse.

The roar of the crowd at the apparent resurrection was visceral thunder.

They returned to the fight, and Macy knocked out Jacobson a minute later, winning the title.

A hand reached over me and hit the pause button on the laptop.

"That wasn't normal," said Jenna Larson, the woman who had brought me the recording of the match. She was a rarity, a female sports reporter with national standing, known for hunting down the big stories, breaking the big news, from drug scandals to criminal records. "Tell me that wasn't human. Jerome Macy isn't human."

Which was why Larson was here, showing me this video. She wanted to know if I could tell Macy was a werewolf or some other supernatural/superhuman creature with rapid healing, or the kind of invulnerability that would let him not only stand back up after a blow like that, but go on to beat up his opponent. I couldn't tell, not by just watching the clip. But it wouldn't be hard for me to find out, if I could get close enough to smell him. I'd know if he was a werewolf by his scent, because I was one.

She'd brought her laptop to my office. I sat at my desk, staring at the frozen image of Macy, shoulders slouched, looming over his fallen opponent. Larson stood over me—a position of dominance, my Wolf side noted testily—waiting for my reaction.

I pushed my chair away from the desk so I was out from under her, looking at her eye to eye without craning my neck. "I can't say one way or the other without meeting him."

"I can arrange that," she said. "His next bout is here in Denver this weekend. You come meet him, and if there is something going on, we share the scoop on the story."

This was making me nervous. "Jenna. Here's the thing: Even if he is a werewolf, he probably doesn't want to advertise the fact. He's kept it hidden for a reason."

"If he is a werewolf, do you think it's fair that he's competing against normal human beings in feats of strength and endurance?"

I shrugged, because she was right on some level. However talented a boxer he was, did Macy have an unfair advantage?

It also begged the question, in this modern age when werewolves, vampires, witches, and other things that went bump in the night were emerging from shadows and announcing themselves—like hosting talk radio shows that delved into this secret world—how many other people had hidden identities? How many actors, politicians, and athletes weren't entirely human?

Larson was in her thirties, her shoulder-length brown hair shining and perfectly arranged around her face, her makeup calculated to look stunning and natural, like she wasn't wearing any. She wore a pantsuit with high heels and never missed a step. She was a woman in a man's profession, driven to make a name for herself. I had to respect that. The territorial side of me couldn't help but see an alpha female on the prowl.

She was brusque, busy, and clearly didn't have time to hang around because she shut down the laptop and started packing it into her sleek black shoulder bag.

"I know you're interested in this," she said. "If you don't help me, I'll get someone else. One way or another, with or without your help, I'm going to break this story. How about it?"

There wasn't even a question. She called me pretty well: I wouldn't let a story like this get away from me.

"I'm in," I said.

I came within a hair of changing my mind outside the Pepsi Center the night of the bout. The crowd swarmed, jostling around me as they elbowed their way through the doors. This many people, all of them with an underlying aggression—they had paid a lot of money to watch two guys beat the crap out of each other—was making me want to growl. The Wolf side of my being didn't like crowds, didn't like aggression. I wanted to fight back, snarl, claw my way free to a place where I could run, where no one could touch me.

Concentrating, I worked to keep that part of me buried. I had to keep myself together to do my job.

I still wasn't sure I wanted to do this job. If Larson turned out to be right and Macy was a werewolf, what if he didn't want to be exposed? Should I step in and somehow talk her into keeping his secret? He had a right to the life he was carving out for himself. I'd been in his position, once. On the other hand, maybe Macy would be okay with exposing his werewolf identity. Then I could claim his first exclusive interview for my radio show. Larson could break the story in print, I'd get the first live interview—part of me really hoped Macy was okay with telling the world about this.

The other part hoped he wasn't a werewolf at all. Luck had saved him during that bout in Vegas.

Larson met me inside the doors with a press pass that got us close to ringside. I wasn't sure I wanted to be ringside. Flying sweat and spit would hit us at this range. The arena smelled of crowds, of old sweat and layers of energy. Basketball, hockey, arena football, concerts, and circuses had all played here. A little of each remained, along with the thousands of people who watched. Popcorn, soda, beer, hot dogs, semi-fresh, semi-stale, ground into the concrete floor, never to be erased. And the echoes of shouting.

The arena filled. Larson talked with her colleagues, talked on her cell phone, punched notes into her laptop. We waited for the gladiators to appear.

"You look nervous," she said to me, fifteen minutes into the waiting. I'd been hugging myself. "You ever been to a fight?"

I shook my head and unclenched my arms, trying to relax. "I'm not much into the whole sports thing. Crowds make me nervous." Made me want to howl and run, actually.

The announcer came on the booming PA system, his rich, modulated voice echoing through the whole place and rattling my bones. Lights on scoreboards flashed. The sensory input was overwhelming. I guessed we were starting.

The boxers—opponents, combatants, gladiators—appeared. A great cheer traveled through the crowd. Ironically, the people in the upper bleachers saw them before those of us with front row seats. We didn't see them until they climbed into the ring. The challenger, Ian Jacobson, looked even more fierce in person, muscles flexing, glaring. Already, sweat gleamed on his pale skin.

Then came Jerome Macy.

I smelled him before I saw him, a feral hint of musk and wild in this otherwise artificial environment. It was the smell of fur just under the skin, waiting to break free. Two werewolves could smell each other across the room, catching that distinctive mark.

No one who wasn't a werewolf would recognize it. He looked normal as he ducked between the ropes and entered the ring. Normal as any heavyweight boxer could look, that is. He seemed hard as stone, his body brown, huge, solid. Black hair was cropped close to his head. In his wolf form, he'd be a giant. He went through the same routine, his manager caring for him like he was a racehorse.

Just as I spotted him, he could sense me. He glanced over the ropes, scanning for the source of that lycanthropic odor. Then he spotted me sitting next to Jenna Larson, and his eyes narrowed. He must have known why I was here. He must have guessed.

My first instinct, wolf's instinct, was to cringe. He was bigger than I, meaner, he could destroy me, so I must show deference. But we weren't wolves here. The human side, the side that needed to get to the bottom of this story and negotiate with Larson, met Macy's gaze. I had my own strengths that made me his equal, and I wanted him to know that.

As soon as he entered the ring, Larson leaned over to me. "Well?" She didn't take her gaze off the boxer.

Macy kept glancing at us and his mouth turned in a scowl. He must have known who—and what—I was, and surely he knew about Larson. He noted the conspiracy between us, and must have known what it meant. Must have realized the implications.

"Yeah, he is," I said.

Larson pressed her lips together in an expression of subdued triumph.

"What are you going to do?" I said. "Jump in and announce it to the world?"

"No," she said. "I'll wait until the fight's over for that." She was already typing on her laptop, making notes for her big exposé. Almost, I wanted no part of this. It was like she held this man's life in her hands.

But more, I wanted to talk to Macy, to learn how he did this. I knew from experience—vivid, hard-fought experience—that aggression and danger brought the wolf side to the fore. If a lycanthrope felt threatened, the animal, monstrous side of him would rise to the surface to defend him, to use more powerful teeth and claws in the battle.

So how did Macy train, fight, and win as a boxer without losing control of his wolf? I never could have done it.

In the ring, the two fighters circled each other—like wolves, almost—separated only by the referee, who seemed small and weak next to them. Then, they fell together. Gloves smacked against skin. I winced at the pounding each delivered, jackhammer blows slamming over and over again.

Around me, the journalists in the press box regarded the scene with cool detachment, unemotional, watching the fight clinically, an attitude so at odds with the chaos of the crowd around us.

I flinched at the vehemence of the crowd, the shouts, fierce screams, the wall of emotion like a physical force pressing from all corners of the arena to the central ring. Wolf, the creature inside me, recognized the bloodlust. She—I—wanted to growl, feeling cornered. I hunched my back against the emotion and focused on being human.

The line between civilized and wild was so very thin, after all. No one watching this display could argue otherwise.

They pounded the crap out of each other and kept coming back for more. That was the only way to describe it. An enthusiast could probably talk about the skill of various punches and blocks, maybe even the graceful way they danced back and forth across the ring, giving and pressing in turn in some kind of strategy I couldn't discern. The strategy may have involved simply tiring each other out. I just waited for it to be over. I couldn't decide who I was rooting for.

Catching bits of conversation between rounds, I gathered that the previous fight between Macy and Jacobson had been considered inconclusive. The blow that had struck Macy down had been a fluke. That he had stood up without being knocked out—or killed—had been a fluke. No one could agree on which of the two had gotten lucky. The rematch had seemed inevitable.

This time, Macy clearly had the upper hand. His punches continued to be calculated and carefully placed, even in the later rounds. To my eyes, Macy looked like he was holding back. A werewolf should have been able to knock an enemy across the room. As a werewolf, I could have faced down Jacobson. But Macy couldn't do that. He had to make it look like a fair fight.

Jacobson started to sway. He shook his head, as if trying to wake himself up. Macy landed yet another solid punch that made Jacobson's entire body quiver for a moment. Then the big boxer went down, boneless, collapsing flat on his back and lying there, arms and legs splayed.

Chaos reigned after that. The crowd was screaming with one multi-layered voice; the referee knelt by Jacobson's head, counting; Jacobson's trainers hovered in the wings, waiting to spring forward. Around me, journalists and announcers were speaking a mile a minute into phones or mikes, describing the scene.

Macy retreated to a neutral corner, bouncing in place a little, arms hanging at his sides. He hunched his back and glared out with dark eyes that seemed fierce and animal. Maybe they only did to me.

The referee declared the fight over. Jacobson was knocked out, and only started climbing to his feet when his trainers helped him. Macy raised his arms, taking in the crowd's adulation.

That was it. The whole thing started to seem anticlimactic. There was some chaotic concluding business, strobe lights of a million cameras flashing. Then the journalists started packing up, the crowd dispersed, and the cleaning crew started coming through with garbage bags. A swarm of fans and reporters lurched toward Macy, but an equally enthusiastic swarm of guards and assistants kept them at bay while trainers guided Macy from the ring and down the aisle to the locker area, which was strictly off-limits.

Larson slung her laptop bag over her shoulder and tugged my sleeve. "Come on," she said.

Walking briskly, snaking through the mass of people, she led me to a different doorway, and from there to a tiled corridor. This was the behind-the-scenes area, leading to maintenance, storage—and locker rooms, from the other side. Larson knew where she was going. I followed, willing to let her lead the way, quietly hanging back, observing. Other reporters marched along with us, all jostling to get in front, but Larson led the way.

She stopped by a door where a hulking man in a security uniform stood guard. Other reporters pressed up behind us.

"Mr. Macy isn't giving interviews now." The bear of a man scowled at the crowd.

"I'm Jenna Larson," she said, flashing an ID badge at him. "Tell him I'm here with Kitty Norville. I think he'll talk to us."

"I *said*, Mr. Macy isn't giving interviews." The other reporters complained at that.

Larson pursed her lips, as if considering answers, then said, "I'll wait."

"You'll wait?" I said.

"He's got to come out sometime. Though if he gives an interview to one of the guys, I swear I'll . . ."

The door opened, and one of the trainers leaned out to speak a few words with the guard.

"Is who here? Her? Really?" the guard said, glancing at Larson. Grudgingly, he stood back from the open door. "He's asking for you. Come on in."

I stuck close to Larson as she slipped through the door, while the guard held back the rest of the reporters, most of whom were protesting loudly.

Male locker room. There's no other smell like it. Lots and lots of sweat, new and old, stale, baked into the flat carpet, into the paint on the walls. And adrenaline, like someone had aerosolized it. Like someone had lit a scented candle of it. Pure, concentrated, competitive maleness. Wolf didn't know whether to howl or whine.

"This way," the trainer said and guided us through the front, a brightly lit area filled with lockers, to a smaller, darker side room with only one light in the corner turned on.

The smell of alcohol almost overpowered the smell of maleness here. It looked like an infirmary. Cabinets with clear doors held gauze, cotton balls, bandages, and dozens of bottles. On a padded massage table in the middle of the room sat Jerome Macy.

A shadow in the dim light, he smelled of sweat, adrenaline, maleness—and wolf. His eyes were a deep, rich brown. I could almost see the wolf in them, sizing me up. Challenging me. I didn't meet his gaze, didn't give him any aggressive signals. This was his territory. I was the visitor here, and I didn't have anything to prove.

"It's okay, Frank," Macy said to the trainer, who lingered by the door. The man gave a curt nod, then left, closing the door behind him.

So not even Macy's trainers knew. The three of us were alone in the room, with the secret.

His hands were raw, chapped, swollen. Tape bound his wrists. He leaned on his knees and let the limbs dangle. Werewolves had rapid healing, but he'd still taken a beating. Macy kept his challenging stare focused on me. I started to bristle under the attention. I crossed my arms and lurked.

Larson drew a small digital recorder out of her pocket and made a show of turning it on. "Mr. Macy. Is it true that you're infected with the recently identified disease known as lycanthropy?"

His gaze shifted from me to her. After a moment, he chuckled. "It's not going to do me any good to say no, is it? You planned this out pretty good."

He was almost soft-spoken. His voice was hushed, belying the power of his body. It gave him a calculating air. Not all brute force, this guy. I wanted to warn Larson, *Don't underestimate him.*

"I think the public has a right to know," Larson said. "Don't you?"

He considered. Sizing her up, like a hunter deciding whether this prey would be worth the effort, gazing at her through half-lidded eyes. He was making a challenge. In wolf body language, the stare, the shoulders, the slight snarl to his open lips, showing teeth, all pointed to the aggressive stance. I recognized it. There was no way fully human Larson could. For all her journalist's instincts, she wouldn't recognize the body language.

He said, "What would I have to pay you to keep you quiet?"

I was betting he couldn't have said anything that would make her more angry. She said, "Bribery. Real nice. Be smarter about this, Macy: You can't suppress this. You can't keep this quiet forever. You might as well let me break the story. I'll give you a chance to have your say, tell your side of the story."

She approached this the way she would any other stubborn interview; she turned on her own aggression, glaring back, stepping forward into his space. Exactly the wrong response if she wanted him to open up.

The boxer didn't flinch. His expression never changed. He was still on the hunt. He said, "Then what would I have to *do* to keep you quiet?"

That threw Larson off her script. She blinked with some amount of astonishment. "Are you threatening me?"

I stepped between them, trying to forestall what the press would call an "unfortunate incident." Glancing between them, I tried to be chipper, happy, and tail-waggy.

"Jerome! May I call you Jerome?" I said, running my mouth like always. "I'm really glad Jenna asked me to come along for this. Normally I wouldn't give boxing a second thought. But this. I'd never have believed it if I hadn't seen it. How do you do it? Why don't you shapeshift when you're in the ring?" Larson still held her recorder out, and she let me keep talking.

I had seen animals in cages at the zoo look like this. Quiet, glaring. Simmering. Like a predator who was prepared to wait forever for that one day, that one minute you forgot to lock the cage. On that day, God help you.

"You're Kitty Norville, right? I've heard about you."

"Great!" I said, my bravado false. "Nothing bad, I hope. So are you going to answer my question?"

He straightened a little, rolled his shoulders, and the mood was broken, the predator image slipped away. His lip turned in a half-smile.

"I think about my hands," he said. Which seemed strange. I must have looked bemused, because he explained. "I have to punch. I can only do that with human hands. Fists and arms. Not claws, not teeth. So I think about my hands. But Kitty—just because I don't shift doesn't mean I don't change." Some of that animal side bled into his gaze. He must have carried all his animal fighting instinct into the ring.

That was creepy. I had an urge to slouch, grovel, stick an imaginary tail between my legs. *Please don't hurt me . . .*

"So you do have an unfair advantage?" Larson said.

"I use what I have," he said. "I use my talents, like anyone else out there."

"But it's not a level playing field," she said, pressing. "Tell me about the fight in Vegas. About taking the punch that would have killed a normal human being."

"That fight doesn't prove anything."

"But a lot of people are asking questions, aren't they?" Larson said.

"What exactly do you want from me?"

"Your participation."

"You want to ruin me, and you want me to *help*?" This sounded like a growl.

The trouble was, I sympathized with them both. Jenna Larson and I were both women working in the media, journalists of a sort, ambitious in a tough profession. She constantly needed to hustle, needed that leg-up. That was why she was here. I could understand that. But I'd also been in Jerome Macy's shoes, struggling to do my job while hiding my wolf nature. I'd been exposed in a situation like this one: forced, against my will.

I didn't know who to side with.

"Here's a question," I said, gathering my thoughts even as I talked. "Clearly you have a talent for boxing. But did you before the lycanthropy? Did you box before, and this gave you an edge? Or did you become a werewolf and decide a werewolf would make a good boxer? Are you here because you're a boxer, or because you're a werewolf?"

"Does it matter?"

Did it? The distinction, the value judgment I was applying here was subtle. Was Macy a boxer in spite of his lycanthropy—or because of it? Was I sure that the former was any better, more noble, than the latter?

"This isn't any different than steroids," Larson said before I could respond. "You're using something to create an unfair advantage."

"It's different," Macy said, frowning. "What I have isn't voluntary."

She continued, "But can't you see it? Kids going out and trying to get themselves bitten by werewolves so they can get ahead in boxing, or football, or anything?"

"Nobody's that stupid," he said. The curl in his lips was almost a snarl.

Larson frowned. "If it's not me who breaks the story, it'll be someone else, and the next person may not let you know about it first. In exchange for an exclusive, I can guarantee you'll get to tell your side of the story—"

I saw it coming, but I didn't have time to warn her, or stop him.

He sprang, a growl rumbling deep in his throat, arms outstretched and reaching for Larson. She dropped her recorder and screamed.

He was fast, planting his hands on her shoulders and shoving her to the wall. In response I shouldered him, pushing him off balance and away from the reporter. Normally, a five-six skinny blond like me wouldn't have been able to budge a heavyweight like Macy off his stride. But as a werewolf I had a little supernatural strength of my own, and he wasn't expecting it. No one ever expected much out of me at first glance.

He didn't stumble far, unfortunately. He shuffled sideways, while I kind of bounced off him. But at least he took his hands off Larson, and I ended up standing in between them. I glared, trying to look tough, but I was quivering inside. Macy could take me apart.

"You bastard, you're trying to kill me!" Larson yelled. She was wide eyed, breathing hard, panicked like a hunted rabbit.

Macy stepped back. His smile showed teeth. "If I wanted to kill you, you'd be dead."

"I'll charge you with assault," she said, almost snarling herself.

"Both of you shut up," I said, glaring, pulling out a bit of my own monster to quell them.

"You're not as tough as you think you are," he said, looking down at me, a growl in his voice, his fingers curling at his sides, like claws.

"Well I don't have to be, because we're going to sit down and discuss this like human beings, got it?" I said.

Never taking his eyes off Larson, he stepped back to the table and returned to sitting. He was breathing calmly, though his scent was musky, animal. He was a werewolf, but he was in complete control of himself. I'd never seen anything like it.

He was in enough control that Larson would never talk him into an exclusive interview.

She'd retrieved her recorder and was pushing buttons and holding it to her ear. By the annoyed look on her face, I was guessing it was damaged. "I don't need your permission," she muttered. "I've got Kitty to back me up. The truth will come out."

I frowned. "Jenna, I'm not sure this is the right way to go about this. This doesn't feel right."

"This isn't about right, it's about the truth."

Macy looked at me, and I almost flinched. His gaze was intent— he was thinking fast. "Kitty. Why did you go public?"

"I was forced into it," I said. "Kind of like this."

"So—has going public helped you? Hurt you? If you could change it, would you?"

I'd worked hard to keep my lycanthropy secret, until I'd been forced into announcing what I was on the air. It hadn't been my choice. I could have let it ruin me, but I made a decision to own that identity. To embrace it. It had made me notorious, and I had profited by it.

I had to admit it: "I don't think I'd be nearly as successful as I am if I hadn't gone public. I'd still be just another cult radio show."

He nodded, like I'd helped him make a decision.

"We're not here to talk about Kitty," Larson said. "Last chance, Macy. Are you in or out?" She was still treating this with aggression, like she was attacking. She was only offending him.

"Write your story," he said. "Say what you need to. But do it without me. I won't answer any questions. Now, get out." He hopped off his table, went to the door, and opened it.

"You can't do this. You'll have to talk to someone. Sooner or later."

I hooked my arm around hers and pulled her to the door, glancing at Macy over my shoulder one last time. I met his gaze. He seemed calm, determined, without an ounce of trepidation. Before I turned away, he smiled at me, gave a little nod. He was a wolf confident in his territory. I'd do best to slink away and avoid his wrath.

Larson and I left, and the door closed behind us.

Silent, we made our way back to the lobby of the arena. I said, "That went well."

She'd gone a bit glassy eyed and had lost the purposeful energy in her stride.

"Are you okay?" I said.

"I think I'm going to be sick," she murmured.

"You need to get to a bathroom? Go outside?" I started hurrying.

She shook her head, but leaned against the wall and covered her face. "This must be what the rabbit feels like, after it gets away from a fox."

Post-traumatic stress from a simple interview? Maybe. Most people considered themselves the top of the food chain. Few of them ever encountered something that trumped them.

"I don't know," I said. "I'm usually not on the rabbit side of things."

She stared at me and didn't have to say it: I wasn't helping.

"Is he going to come after me? Was he really threatening me? If I run this story, am I in danger?"

I urged her off the wall and toward the doors, so we could get outside and into the air. The closed space and pervasive odor of sweat was starting to get to me.

"No. It's intimidation." It was what people like him—boxer or werewolf—were good at. "He can't touch you without getting in trouble, even if he is a werewolf."

A few more steps brought us outside, into the night. I turned my face to the sky and took in a deep breath of fresh air, or as fresh as city air ever got.

"What are we going to do?" she said. "The story's going to look pretty half-assed without a statement from him."

The lack of an exclusive interview wasn't the end of the world. I'd dealt with worse. We could still break the story.

"You'll have a statement from me," I said. "And I'll have one from you. We'll do the best we can with what we have." What Larson had told Macy was true: the truth would come out eventually. Maybe by being part of the revelation I could mitigate the impact of it—mitigate Larson's ire over it.

"It's not fair," she grumbled. "It's just not fair."

I wondered if Macy was thinking the same thing.

As it turned out, Jerome Macy scooped us both. He held a press conference the next morning, revealed his werewolf identity to the world, and promptly announced his retirement from boxing, before anyone could kick him out. Jenna Larson's exposé and call to action, and my interview of her on my show, were lost in the uproar. Almost immediately, there was talk of stripping him of his heavyweight title. The debate was ongoing.

About a month later, I got a press kit from the WWE. For the new season of one of their pro-wrestling spectacle TV series, they were "unleashing"—they actually used the word *unleashing*—a new force: The Wolf. Aka Jerome Macy.

So. He was starting a new career. A whole new persona. He had chosen to embrace his werewolf identity and looked like he was going gangbusters with it. I had to admire that. And I could stop feeling guilty about him and his story.

This changed everything, of course. He was going to have to do a lot of publicity, wasn't he? A ton of promotion. Sometimes, patience was a virtue, and sometimes, what goes around comes around.

I picked up my phone and called the number listed in the press kit. I was betting I could get that interview with him now.

Kitty Busts the Feds

"I'M JUST SAYING if anybody should know about this, it oughta be you, right?"

Putting my elbows on the desk, I rubbed my scalp and winced at the microphone. "Yes, you're right, of course. If anyone ought to know the effects of recreational marijuana on lycanthropes it should be me, even though I've never actually tried the stuff, even though I live in Colorado. I'm so sorry to disappoint you."

I wasn't sorry, and I seemed to be completely unable to steer the show off this topic.

"All right, checking the monitor . . . and all the calls are about pot. Okay. Fine. Matt, are we violating any FCC regulations by talking about pot on the air this much?" Pot might have been legal in Colorado, but the show was syndicated all over the country and I didn't want to get any affiliate stations in trouble. On the other side of the booth window, Matt, my engineer, gave me a big shrug. I figured if I was in trouble, Ozzie, the station manager, would have called by now to ax this whole line of discussion. "What the hell, NPR has done a million news stories on pot, right? It's not like we're telling people how to get the stuff. Next caller, you're on the air."

"I mean, if you don't live in Colorado how *do* you get the stuff—"

"I cannot help you with this. Next call, please. Linda, what's your question?"

"Hi, Kitty, thanks so much for taking my call. There really are so many medical applications for cannabis, especially in terms of reducing anxiety and alleviating chronic pain, it seems that if we wanted to look anywhere for a cure for lycanthropy it would be with CBD oil."

I had voted in favor of legalized marijuana. It seemed like a good idea at the time.

"It's not magic, okay? It's not a cure-all. Alleviating symptoms and curing the underlying condition are two different things. Even medical marijuana advocates know that. And frankly, I can't get past the notion of a werewolf with the munchies. Can you imagine?"

"I suppose I didn't think of that . . ."

"The law of unintended consequences, people. Thanks for your call, Linda. Look, if any lycanthropes with any actual, real experience with pot want to chime in here, please call me." None had yet, according to the monitor. I hit the line for the next call at random because my carefully reasoned choices sure hadn't helped me tonight. "Hello, Ray from Seattle, what have you got for me?"

"Vampires actually can smoke pot," he said by way of introduction.

"Oh? Are you a vampire? How does that work?" Vampires technically didn't need to breathe to live. They drew air into their lungs in order to speak, laugh, whatever. But did pot actually work on them?

This guy had just been waiting for a chance to lecture. "I *am* a vampire, and I happen to have a long history of smoking, well, *lots* of things. As you know—at least I'm assuming you know—vampires can't ingest narcotics. We can't ingest anything but human blood. But smoking narcotics? That works." His accent was American, maybe someplace from the east coast. That didn't tell me anything about how old he was or where he came from.

"*Do* tell me more." The vampires I knew in real life never seemed to tell me *anything*.

"There's a catch. You have to be full up on blood. And I mean full. When you smoke pot, or tobacco, or opium, or"—he rattled off three more names of things I hadn't even heard of—"the active ingredients enter the bloodstream through the lungs. We vampires can take in air when we need to, but we don't need the oxygen because, well—"

"Because you're basically dead. In stasis. Whatever."

"That's a simplification—"

"I want to hear about vampires smoking pot."

"For drugs to work there has to be enough blood in our systems for anything in the lungs to transfer. Not enough blood, you're just inhaling smoke. Really, it's a lot faster to find someone who's already high and take theirs. Since you need the blood anyway. Cuts out a step, if you know what I mean."

"I have no idea what you mean," I said, fascinated. "But okay."

"Some vampires will tell you blood on its own is enough of a high, but sometimes you just want a little variety."

"I guess so," I said. "Thanks so much for calling in, Ray from Seattle."

"Happy to, love your show! We should hang out sometime! Because you know what I haven't done? Taken blood from a werewolf who's high on pot—"

"Moving on now, we're going to take a short break for messages, but I'll be right here waiting for you. This is Kitty and you're listening to *The Midnight Hour.*"

Meanwhile, something was happening in the booth. Three people had entered, two men and a woman. All three were white, wore dark suits, had subdued professional manners. They moved in behind Matt's chair and loomed. Matt looked around, his eyes wide, a little freaked. I caught his gaze through the window, and he shook his head, confused.

"Hey, what's going on?" I asked through the intercom. The public service announcements playing on the air filled the background. One of the men escorted Matt out of the booth. The remaining two looked out the window, at me.

"If you'll stay right there, ma'am," the woman said.

I didn't. I went straight for the door, which opened—and the pair of them stood blocking my way. Matt and the other agent were heading down the hall. What were they doing? They couldn't take away my sound guy in the middle of a show. I tried to push past, to go after him—they didn't even flinch.

Calming myself, I took a steadying breath. They smelled human, plain, ordinary. Nothing unusual to speak of. I wasn't sure why I expected them to smell ominous. Probably because everything else about them was ominous. They didn't even have guns, and somehow I had expected them to have guns.

I curled my lip, showing teeth, a challenge they would have recognized if they'd been werewolves.

"Ms. Norville? We'd like to talk to you for a few moments," the woman said.

"Then you should call and make an appointment." Their glares told me that no, they didn't do that sort of thing. "I'm in the middle of a show, I can't just leave dead air."

"Then do something about it."

"I don't suppose you'd be up for an interview? We could talk—"

"I don't think you want that," the man said darkly.

The monitor was filling up with incoming calls. I couldn't do anything about it. Alrighty, then. "Fine," I muttered, and went into the sound booth to plug in my phone. I couldn't leave the broadcast empty, and I didn't want to go hunting through the archives for past interviews I could re-run. So I pulled up a ten-hour loop of the sax riff in "Careless Whisper" and let it play.

The two agents in black were still blocking the hallway; I invited them into the studio.

"Have a seat, Ms. Norville," the man said.

I didn't. "Who are you? Can I see some badges or ID or something? I mean, obviously you're some kind of government agents."

"Are you sure?"

"Yeah. The last two Men in Black who came after me weren't from the government *at all*, and they were way scarier than you. You two are just . . . creepy."

The woman sighed and pulled a badge out of her inside jacket pocket. In movies and TV, agents flashed their badges and the people looking at them seemed to be able to take in all the information with a glance. That didn't work in real life. I had to lean in close to study the fine print.

"Agent Martin?" I said. "And you are?"

The man scowled like he was revealing something important. "Agent Ivers."

"And what exactly is the Paranatural Security Administration?" I asked.

"We're a division of the Department of Homeland Security," Martin said.

Well, that couldn't be good. "Why haven't I heard about you guys before now? Because I would have heard of you guys before now."

"We're still a provisional agency," Ivers said, walking around the studio, appearing to study equipment, frowning at the no-doubt subversive-looking concert flyers and new-age festival announcements pinned to the bulletin board. KNOB was public radio, what did he expect?

"What does that even mean?" I asked.

Martin peered at the monitor. "You get a lot of phone calls each week?"

"It depends on the topic, depends on the week. Things really ramp up right around Halloween. And Christmas, weirdly enough."

"Do you keep records of all the calls you receive?"

My hackles rose, a stiffening across my shoulders. If I could have growled, I would have. I steadied myself, remaining cautious. "Why do you want to know?"

"If you got a suspicious call from a stalker, someone making threats . . . we know you've received threats on the air. You keep some kind of record of that to pass to the police, don't you?"

I was afraid to say yes. I didn't want to say yes. That would open a door. "Look, it's literally the middle of the night. I think you should be having this conversation with the station manager."

Ivers said, "You meet a lot of people doing your show, don't you? You've met a lot of people—creatures—that don't necessarily go through the station's records. Is that right?"

"If you're asking if I have a life outside my job—"

"You know people, Ms. Norville," he continued. "People. Other things. That's what we're interested in."

I had one of them on each side of me now. They might not have had guns, but what else did they have stashed in their jackets? My phone was on the desk, plugged in, and not in my hand. I maybe hadn't thought this through.

"How many vampires do you personally know?" Martin asked.

"I don't know—"

"Just a guess. I imagine it's quite a lot."

Ivers, tag-teaming: "If I were to list cities, would you be able to tell me who the Masters of those cities are?"

"What a minute," I said. "You want me to name names. You're asking me to name names. Like some kind of HUAC shit?"

"We're just asking for your help on a matter of national security," Ivers said.

"*What* national security? What's the danger here?"

"This is just for informational purposes."

The saxophone riff was still going, over and over. "I think . . . I think I'm going to refer you to my attorney." My heart was racing. Claws pressed against the inside of my fingertips. Calm, calm. Slow breaths.

Martin tilted her head. "Ms. Norville, are you all right?"

"You do know that I'm a werewolf, right? You've seen the video. You know it's not a good idea to stress us out."

They exchanged a concerned glance, then both of them looked away from me. Turned aside, non-confrontational. Body language meant to de-escalate a confrontation. They'd had some training in dealing with stressed-out werewolves. Somehow that made me more worried, not less. Who else had they been harassing?

Martin sounded like she was trying to be soothing, but instead came across as condescending. "You're not under investigation here. You're under no suspicion yourself. We know that you'll be happy to help, should the need ever arise. I'm sure you have nothing to hide—"

"Then I have nothing to fear? Is that what you're about to say?"

Glancing down the barest little bit, Martin said, "It's hard to say that line without sounding just a little ironic."

"And they say satire is dead," I muttered. We could keep going in circles all night. "How about I pull the plug on George Michael over there and broadcast this conversation to everybody, hm?"

Martin said, "I don't recommend—"

Her partner jumped in. "The saxophonist on that track is Steve Gregory."

"Well. Score one for precision. But seriously, I need to get back to the show. I can't help you. Come back during office hours."

Ivers glanced out the door. "Your sound guy, Matt—he's been with you a long time, hasn't he?"

A chill passed over me. "Yeah, from the start. Where is he? Where did you take him?"

"Our colleague is just having a few words with him. Kind of like we're doing with you. Nothing to worry about."

I sank into the chair at my desk. I had tried to imagine this moment. Reading the history, I had to wonder if I would have named names in front of the HUAC during the Red Scare, or if I would have stood firm and suffered blacklisting. Of course I liked to think I would stand firm, but who could say? Who really knew, until the moment was upon you, what you would do? If I had a choice between collaboration or standing for actual principles despite the risk, what would I do?

Some people would blame me for this situation coming about in the first place. Before I started the show, werewolves, vampires, the whole supernatural world remained secret. Anyone trying to expose that world could be written off as a crackpot. Then came my show, the revelation from the NIH that this was all real—and then came the scrutiny. One of the issues the current administration campaigned on was the need for monitoring and controlling—read registering and incarcerating—vampires and werewolves, and regulating witchcraft and psychics, or even making them illegal. So far, none of this had happened, Constitutional protections had been upheld. But for how long?

I have here in my hand a list of known lycanthropes . . .

"I can't do it," I said. "There's been talk—I know you've heard the talk, you all are probably at the center of it—of registering vampires and werewolves, other supernatural beings. For safety reasons, you understand. It's simply tracking potential threats to the public. Nothing to worry about. Except the next step after registration is restriction. Travel bans, housing limitations. And the next step after that is confinement. You see where I'm going with this?"

"It will never—"

I held up a hand. "Say the rest of that line with a straight face. I dare you."

She couldn't. Neither of them could.

I sighed and tried to shake some of the stress out of my nerves. "If you're looking for a specific name for a specific investigation you can get a court order, but you'll still have to go through my lawyer—"

"We're not going to do that, Ms. Norville."

"But—" And it suddenly occurred to me: They didn't want to go through lawyers. This *was* a specific investigation, they *were* looking for a specific name—they just didn't want anyone to know who it was. "What is this *really* about?"

They exchanged a glance, and for the first time seemed not entirely sure of themselves. Maybe even just a little bit nervous.

"This is all back channel bullshit," I said. "On the one hand, I'm kind of relieved this isn't actually the start of some kind of round-up. But seriously—who is it among all my connections you're trying to track down?" It could have been anyone, I knew some pretty far-out people. People who knew where the bodies were buried, and where they should have been, but weren't.

The pair was playing an unspoken game of "No, you say something," and Martin appeared to lose. She said, "Ms. Norville, I'm really not at liberty to say—"

"Kitty? You there?" A voice echoed from down the hallway. And with that, my anxiety vanished.

Martin and Ivers reached into their jackets and drew out weapons. Not guns—when they took up defensive stances by the door, they each had a stake in one hand and knife in the other. I bet those knives had silver worked into the blades.

"Who's that?" Ivers demanded.

I smiled a wolfish, relieved smile. "My lawyer." My husband, Ben, actually. But I thought 'lawyer' would scare them more. "I'm here," I called out. "There's company, just to let you know."

A pause. "The good kind of company or the interesting kind?" That wasn't Ben answering—that was Cormac, his cousin. Hunter of supernatural creatures turned paranormal detective.

"Interesting. They're armed."

"And who is that? Another lawyer?" Ivers hissed at me.

"That's the muscle," I said, leering.

"What are they going to do?" Martin asked. She seemed the steadier of the two, gazing into the hallway outside with a look of determination.

"If you put your toys away and walk out—nothing." I called past them, "Hey, Ben, you see Matt on the way up?"

"Yeah, he and your security guy seemed to be having a tense conversation with a government suit."

"He's okay?"

"Worried, but yeah. Are *you* okay?"

I studied Martin and Ivers, waiting for them to answer the question. Was I okay? Martin pocketed her knife and stake first, and Ivers followed. "Come on in. Meet the rest of the government suits."

I checked the clock. We'd run a couple minutes over the end of the show. I was going to have to do a lot of explaining next week. Out of a sense of closure, though, I needed to unplug the music, get back on the mike, and wrap up. Maybe the affiliates would give me that extra minute.

"All right, sorry about that, folks. This is Kitty Norville and you're listening to *The Midnight Hour*. This musical interlude has been brought to you by two agents of the Paranatural Security Administration, which they tell me is a division of the Department of Homeland Security, and if you think that sounds ominous, well, you're not alone. They tell me this new agency hasn't been completely finalized yet and definitely hasn't been announced to the public. So just remember, you heard it here first. Agent Martin, Agent Ivers, either of you have anything to say to the fans out there?" No, they did not. "I for one will be calling my congresspeople in the morning to see if I can learn any more about how our tax dollars are supporting this exciting new enterprise."

To their credit, both agents looked chagrined.

"See you all next week," I said. "This is Kitty Norville, and I am still your voice of the night."

"I wish you hadn't said that," Martin said.

"If wishes were horses."

Ben and Cormac came into the studio then, side by side, scruffy and heroic, like they were starring in their own TV show or something. The two pairs looked each other up and down, scowling, appraising.

Agent Martin looked at me. "We'll be in touch, Ms. Norville."

"I'm sure you will," I said.

They gave one last look around the studio, like they were memorizing it, and strolled out, as if this had all gone exactly the way they'd planned. Yes, I expected I would be hearing from them again. I wondered how many watch lists I'd just been put on. I'd always trusted that my fame would protect me, but now I wondered if that would last. And if it would protect my family.

Matt, along with the late-shift DJ, pounded into the studio next, and another flustered round of questions and reassurances followed, until Ben and Cormac finally walked me out. I wanted to go home.

First thing first, though. "Where's the baby?" I asked Ben.

"Rachel's looking after him. What's the point of being part of a wolf pack if you can't call in babysitting favors?"

Rachel was the oldest member of our werewolf pack and something of an auntie to us all. The baby loved her. I was relieved. "How did you know something was wrong?" I asked.

"You put Wham! on loop. I figured it was an S.O.S."

"Honey. I love you."

"What're the Feds doing here?" Cormac said, hitching a thumb back to the hallway.

"They wanted phone records. Names," I said tiredly.

"Did they have a warrant?" Cormac asked.

"Never mind a warrant, it's unconstitutional," Ben said. "Violation of privacy, unreasonable search."

I got out my phone and made a call, right there in the KNOB parking lot, because I did know people and I did have numbers, and the fun thing about vampires is knowing if you call them in the middle of the night they'll be awake.

A calm female voice answered, "Who is this, please?" I didn't recognize her, so there must have been new staff at the house.

"This is Kitty Norville, can I speak to Alette please?"

"If you could just wait a moment, Ms. Norville."

Some vampires had secretaries. Alette was the Mistress of Washington, D.C. She was old, powerful, and had her fangs in everything. If anyone knew what was really going on with this Paranatural Security Administration bullshit, she would. Ben and Cormac drew close, listening, and I put the phone on speaker.

"Katherine, how lovely to hear from you, how are you?" Alette's crisp English voice came on the line, sounding as warm and welcoming as she ever did, but leaving no doubt who had the power here.

"I've just had a strange encounter, a couple of federal agents saying they're from the Paranatural Security Administration, which as far as I know hasn't existed until very recently. I wondered if you'd heard anything about this?"

She remained silent for a long moment, which wasn't like her. She was in control, she knew everything, that was why I called her. I met Ben's gaze. His lips were pursed, concerned.

"So they've been to see you already, have they?" she said finally, and wasn't that interesting? "What did you tell them?"

"Nothing. I told them to come back with a warrant and talk to the lawyers. What was I supposed to do? It felt like some kind of HUAC bullshit."

"How would you know what HUAC felt like?" she said, amused. Maybe just a little condescending.

"But you would, you were Mistress of D.C. during the McCarthy Era. So tell me, what did that feel like? Did it feel like this? With actual politicians talking about actual registration and camps—vampires would never put up with that, they'd never let it get so far, would they? You all have survived wars, inquisitions—"

"Katherine. Who do you think runs the inquisitions, when it suits them?"

I could feel my heartbeat. Wolf wanted to growl. "You would tell me, wouldn't you? If you knew something."

"You've had a trying evening. Why don't you get some rest? There's nothing to worry about."

"I don't believe you," I said starkly. "I mean, I appreciate the gesture. But I don't believe you. The Long Game isn't over, is it?"

"Katherine. It's so good to hear from you, as always. But I must be going, I have other matters to attend to."

"Like secret government agencies keeping tabs on supernatural beings?"

"Goodnight, Katherine." She clicked off.

The Long Game, the battle for power between vampires that had lasted for thousands of years. Why had I ever thought there would be an end to it?

"Well," Ben said. "I think I want to break something now." Cormac just stood there, looking out into the night as if he expected something to be watching us. Maybe something was.

I wanted to go home. "We saved the world. I thought we could relax. I thought everything would be fine, now. Sunshine and daffodils."

"These things never end," Cormac said. "Ten thousand years of human civilization and it just keeps going."

"We'll do what we always do," Ben said. "Only thing we can do, when you get right down to it."

I smiled, took his hand. "We look out for each other."

Story Notes and Playlist

A s I write this, I finished working on the last Kitty novel, *Kitty Saves the World*, five years ago. I've written a lot of other novels and stories since then, but I keep coming back to Kitty's world, as I knew I would. I still have questions to answer, and more corners to explore.

Two questions I get asked a lot: First, am I sad about finishing the series? This may come as a surprise but the answer is no, because writing a cohesive fourteen-book series, plus all the short stories, and wrapping it up exactly when and how and I wanted is a hell of an achievement. I don't feel sad, I feel triumphant. I'm really proud of what I accomplished, and I'm grateful for the readers who made the journey possible.

Second, will I ever write more novels about Kitty? Well. I know what happens next. I know how her story continues. I'm not ready to write it yet, though. I've still got other threads to follow before I return to the main one—as you'll see in these pages.

Many of these stories were responses to specific anthology invitations: write a story about your hero's antagonist, or about magicians, or about supernatural detectives. Some of these stories— "Sealskin," for example—are sequels to other stories. Because in the two decades I've been writing professionally, I've learned that almost every story can lead to another story. Stories are layers, and there's always more to discover.

I love having a pre-existing world already in place for whenever I want to write a story about werewolves, vampires, ghosts, monsters, and the magic that seems to follow them around. It will all end up right here. Stay tuned.

Carrie Vaughn
January 2020

A

1: "Don't You (Forget About Me)," Simple Minds
2: "As Time Goes By," Billie Holiday
3: "Hexhamshire Lass," Fairport Convention
4: "Farewell, Farewell," Fairport Convention
5: "Irgendwo auf der Welt," Palast Orchester
6: "Blue Moon," Billie Holiday
7: "Surrender," Cheap Trick

B

8: "Saucy Sailor," The Wailin' Jennys
9: "Abracadabra," The Steve Miller Band
10: "Ain't That a Kick in the Head," Dean Martin
11: "Elephants," Warpaint
12: "Kingdom," VNV Nation
13: "Ball of Confusion," The Temptations
14: "Antmusic," Adam Ant

THE KITTY PLAYLISTS

I listen to music when I write. It settles the type-A, anxiety-ridden, list-making part of my brain that is always sure I left the stove on, so that I can actually *write*. Frequently, I find music that fuels what I'm writing. Swing for a story set in World War II, a pavane for a Renaissance-flavored fantasy.

When I wrote the first Kitty novel, I collected a whole list of songs that embodied the story for me, and since Kitty started out as a radio DJ, bringing those songs together in a playlist felt thematically awesome and offered another way into her personality. And sharing music is always *a lot* of fun! So I kept doing it, for fourteen novels and now two collections. I've discovered a lot of great new music, searching for the perfect songs.

Thank you for reading—and listening!

"Kitty Walks on By, Calls Your Name"
"Don't You (Forget About Me)" by Simple Minds

I've been trying to write a high school class reunion story since my own ten-year class reunion in 2001. (I went with my good friend Andrea, who is a journalist, and on the drive there we both talked about writing stories about the experience. I said, "I've already started mine." She said, "But how . . . oh." One of the perks of fiction.) Ten years is the big one. The one where you all show up and realize you're grownups now and are shocked you survived. And shocked that some of you didn't survive. It's not like the movies at all, really. In the end, the story needed time to cook, and it needed Kitty's world to be fully developed before it could come to fruition.

"It's Still the Same Old Story"
"As Time Goes By" by Billie Holiday

This is the story that demonstrated to me how much my portrayal of vampires had been influenced by the character of Duncan McLeod in the *Highlander* TV series. It's the way those episodes jumped back and forth in time, to show the character how he was and how he is now, the way this story does. Explains so much, doesn't it? *Highlander* focuses on the bit about immortality I'm really interested in: How does it change one's relationships and perception of history? Much like Rick, I'm not interested in blood and power games. I really love writing about Rick throughout history. This appeared in *Down These Strange Streets*, edited by George R. R. Martin and the late, great Gardner Dozois.

"The Island of Beasts" and "The Beaux Wilde"
"Hexhamshire Lass" and "Farewell, Farewell"
by Fairport Convention

I really like Jane Austen. It took me a long time to warm up to her writing, but she's one of the sharpest, wittiest authors out there. And I really love movies based on Jane Austen's books. The clothes, the English countryside, the dancing! When you're writing a long-running werewolf series, and watching a lot of Jane Austen movies to unwind, the inevitable question presents itself: what would life be like for werewolves in Regency England? Not easy, for sure. Part of what I want to explore in these stories is why a stereotypical, rage-filled, uncontrollable monster would *want* to conform to the formality and severe societal constraints of this culture. These are beasts who consider themselves civilized. I want to do more with these characters and stories. "The Island of Beasts" originally appeared in *Nightmare Magazine*, and "The Beaux Wilde" appeared in *Urban Fantasy Magazine*.

"Unternehmen Werwolf"
"Irgendwo auf der Welt" by Palast Orchester

In *Kitty Goes to Washington* we meet Fritz, who as a young man fought for Germany in World War II, revealing that yes, the Nazis used werewolves. I definitely wanted to make sure I told his origin story, and this gave me an opportunity to do so. It appeared in *Halloween: Magic, Mystery, and the Macabre*, edited by Paula Guran.

"Kitty and the Full Super Bloodmoon Thing" and
"Kitty and the Super Blue Blood or Whatever Moon Thing"
"Blue Moon" by Billie Holiday

These are two flash pieces I wrote on social media and posted to my blog during two of the recent spates of "Oh my gosh, the moon is going to do something amazing and weird tonight!" The moon's behavior is predictable and has been having eclipses and going super and so on and so forth for a really long time. But for a while there, social media made it AN EVENT. And everyone asked me, "So what happens to werewolves during [specific lunar event]?" So I answered.

"Kitty and Cormac's Excellent Adventure"
"Surrender" by Cheap Trick

The world has so many stories about magic and mayhem to explore. So many potential characters and discoveries. I haven't even scratched the surface. There are more things in heaven and Earth, Horatio . . .

"Sealskin"
"Saucy Sailor" by The Wailin' Jennys

This is a sequel to the selkie story, "The Temptation of Robin Green" (in *Kitty's Greatest Hits*). It tells the story of Robin and the selkie's child, a son, who grows up to become a Navy SEAL because of course he does. But now his mother has passed away and he's looking for answers. I really ought to write more about selkies, shouldn't I? (You see how this whole sequel thing starts.) This appeared in *Operation Arcana*, edited by John Joseph Adams.

"The Arcane Art of Misdirection"
"Abracadabra" by The Steve Miller Band

One of the most popular characters in the series, probably right after Cormac, Rick, and Kitty herself, is Odysseus Grant, stage magician. So when I was invited to submit a story to P. N. Elrod's anthology *Hex Appeal*, my main character was obvious. I know a lot about Odysseus I haven't had a chance to write about yet. I haven't yet told his origin story, about growing up in Providence,

Rhode Island, next door to an old vaudeville stage magician who knew such incredible lore and such dark secrets . . . But never mind, I'll save that for another time.

"What Happened to Ben in Vegas"
"Ain't That a Kick in the Head" by Dean Martin

In *Kitty and the Dead Man's Hand*, Ben has an adventure, and Kitty spends a chunk of the book beside herself trying to figure out what happened to him. He shows up at the end, having rescued himself, with only a healed gunshot wound to show for it. We, the readers, never actually find out what happened to him. Well, now we do.

"Defining Shadows"
"Elephants" by Warpaint

I wrote this one for an anthology that wanted stories about supernatural detectives. I chose to write about Detective Jessi Harden, Kitty's sometime-friend and sometime-nemesis, the Denver cop who has inadvertently become an expert in supernatural criminals and crime. That's only half the story. The other half came from a story told by a Filipina friend about a strange and hideous form of vampire found in the Philippines: the manananggal. The manananggal isn't even really a vampire. It detaches from its torso and flies around seeking out pregnant women. Then it sucks their unborn fetuses out through their navels. Basically, when I can cross that thin, thin line between urban fantasy and horror I will do so with gusto. I think everyone needs to know about this creature. Also, if you want to read Cormac's side of his conversations with Detective Hardin, you can do so in "Long Time Waiting," in *Kitty's Greatest Hits*. This story appeared in *Those Who Hunt Monsters*, edited by Justin Gustainis.

"Bellum Romanum"
"Kingdom" by VNV Nation

I was invited to send a story to an anthology called *Urban Enemies*, edited by Joseph Nassise. The premise: stories about the villains of urban fantasy series. Our hero's rivals and enemies. Of course I only had one real option: Gaius Albinus, Dux Bellorum, Roman, the two-thousand-year-old former centurion who has used his immortal life to manipulate vampire kind into an army that can bring about the apocalypse. This isn't quite his origin story—this doesn't tell how he became a vampire. Rather, it tells how he became a magician with the power to destroy the world. Much of the background laid out here is referenced in *Kitty in the Underworld* and *Kitty Saves the World*. This is a good example of how not all the information I know about a story necessarily makes it into the story. Because the Kitty novels are written in first-person point of view, they can only tell you what Kitty knows. It turns out, there's a lot Kitty doesn't know.

"Kitty Learns the Ropes"
"Ball of Confusion" by The Temptations

Here, I explore one of my big questions about the supernatural in the "real world": what happens when supernatural creatures take part in professional sports? Of course a werewolf boxer is going to have significant advantages—as long as he can keep it a secret. The story happens when he can't keep it a secret anymore. It also features Kitty doing what she does best—getting people to talk. It originally appeared in the anthology *Full Moon City*, edited by Darrell Schweitzer and Martin H. Greenberg.

CARRIE VAUGHN

"Kitty Busts the Feds"
"Antmusic" by Adam Ant

It's probably just as well I wrapped up the series when I did, because I would be unable to continue writing stories featuring Kitty without also commenting on various current political issues.

CARRIE VAUGHN is the *New York Times* best-selling author best known for her Kitty Norville urban fantasy series. The series, about a werewolf who hosts a talk radio advice show for supernatural beings, includes fourteen novels and a collection of short stories.

Vaughn is also the author of the superhero novels in the Golden Age saga and has been a regular contributor to the Wild Cards shared-world novels edited by George R. R. Martin. In addition, Vaughn writes the Harry and Marlowe steampunk short stories featuring alien technology in an alternate nineteenth-century setting.

Vaughn received the 2018 Philip K. Dick Award for her novel *Bannerless*. She is also the winner of the RT Reviewer Choice Award for Best First Mystery for *Kitty and the Midnight Hour* and the WSFA Small Press Award for best short story for "Amaryllis." She has a master's degree in English literature, graduated from the Odyssey Fantasy Writing Workshop in 1998, and returned to the workshop as writer in residence in 2009. Her most recent books are *The Ghosts of Sherwood* and *The Immortal Conquistador*.

A bona fide Air-Force brat (her father served on a B-52 flight crew during the Vietnam War), Vaughn grew up all over the U.S. but managed to put down roots in the area of Boulder, Colorado, where she pursues an endlessly growing list of hobbies and enjoys the outdoors as much as she can. She is fiercely guarded by a miniature American Eskimo dog named Lily.

EMMA BULL (*War for the Oaks*), won the Locus Award for best first novel and has been a cult favorite ever since. She's gone on to publish fantasy and science fiction novels and short stories and a children's picture book. Her novel *Bone Dance* was a finalist for the Hugo, Nebula, and World Fantasy Awards, and received a Philip K. Dick Award Special Citation.

Bull teaches creative writing at Hamline University in Saint Paul, Minnesota. As of this writing, she's working on *Claim,* a sequel to her novel *Territory*, which is a historical fantasy set in Arizona in 1881.